DROWNING ARE THE DEAD

A MARK HAYES STORY

BRENT TOWNS

Drowning are the Dead
Paperback Edition
Copyright © 2022 Brent Towns

Rough Edges Press
An Imprint of Wolfpack Publishing
5130 S. Fort Apache Rd. 215-380
Las Vegas, NV 89148

roughedgespress.com

Paperback ISBN 978-1-68549-087-4
eBook ISBN 978-1-68549-086-7
LCCN 2022936950

DROWNING ARE
THE DEAD

CHAPTER ONE

In my years as a private investigator, I've never had to look for work. For some reason it seems to always find me, and I liken it to a wolf hunting its prey. To continue the analogy, as with the wolf it quite often brought danger with it. This time was no different but came in the guise of a thirty-four-year-old woman who'd lost a sister eighteen years earlier. Climbing from my battered Ford Festiva, I turned my head toward a voice that came from behind me, "Mister Hayes?"

Standing before me was a woman in a short floral dress. Her face was lined from years of worry, and I assumed that in the not-too-distant past she'd been quite pretty. I nodded. "Yes, that's me."

"Um, you're Mark Hayes the private investigator?"

"Last time I looked."

It could have been my attire that threw her. Denim jeans, short-sleeved shirt; or maybe it was my messed up dark hair. She was probably expecting a suit and tie akin to those worn by private investigators in old black and white movies of yesteryear. "I—I was told to get in contact with you by a friend. He said you did some work for him a while back. His name was Ray Burns."

I sifted through the overstuffed filing cabinet inside my head until I came up with the right one. Ray Burns, wife was having an affair. Hired me to get evidence for an upcoming court case. One of the easier jobs I'd done in fact. The bloke's wife hadn't been overly discreet about her extramarital activities. When I'd tracked her down, she and her partner were practically humping in the street, so a half day was all it had taken. Easiest five-hundred dollars I'd made for the year.

A gust of wind came off Port Philip Bay carrying on it the scent of salt and the sea. It whipped at the hem of the woman's dress, lifting it slightly and providing a glimpse of tanned and toned thighs. With a nod I said, "I remember him. He sent you my way?"

"Yes, he said you could be found here by the bay. That you'd be able to help me."

"I'll do what I can." I pointed towards the food van which had taken up residence in the carpark. "Do you mind if I get something to eat before we discuss business? I missed breakfast and I'm bloody starving."

She smiled sadly. "That's fine. My problem has been with me for eighteen years, a little longer won't hurt."

I walked over to the food van and ordered a pie with fries. Mort, the big guy behind the counter, said, "There were two Fijian blokes down here earlier looking for you."

I winced. "What did they want?"

"They said that if you didn't refund their money, they were going to take it out of your hide."

"What did you tell them?"

"That if they wanted to kick your butt all across Melbourne they should go right ahead."

"Thanks," I groaned.

"They said they'll be back tomorrow. How much do you owe them, anyway?"

Giving a derisive snort, I said, "According to them, five grand."

Which wasn't exactly true. They'd paid me for a service which I'd performed as directed. Them not liking the outcome isn't grounds for a refund. Mind you, the size of these two Fijians gave me pause. Hulking gorillas the pair of them. My solidly-built six-foot frame looked puny against them. Perhaps it was time to up my hospital cover.

"Who's the lady?" Mort asked, leaning on the counter and raising his eyebrows at my new client.

"Customer," I replied.

"She's a looker," he said with a smile. "You going to bang her?"

I frowned at him. "What?"

"Don't you PI dudes bang all your good-looking clients?"

"Where's the bloody food, Mort?" I growled, embarrassed at the possibility that she'd heard his question.

He held it up.

"Give it here," I snapped.

He held it out and I took it. I turned away and started to walk to the table where—shit, I didn't even know her name yet—she waited for me.

"What about some money, Hayes? Those blokes won't be the only ones after you for money," Mort called after me.

Without looking back, I flipped him the bird. He could wait.

———

"What's your name?" I asked her as I sat down.

"Marion Lawler."

"Miss or Mrs.?"

"Mrs. I'm divorced."

"All right. Before we get started let's get the bull—a few things out of the way. I charge five hundred a day plus expenses. I get three days paid up front because most cases I work usually only go that long. If you don't like the results, there is no refund. Understood?"

"What if it only takes you two?" Marion asked.

"Then I give you back five-hundred."

Marion nodded.

"Now, what is it you want me to do?"

She took a deep breath then began to tell her story hesitatingly. "Eighteen years ago...my sister and her friend...were murdered. Lucy and Ruby. They were... victims of a twisted killer everyone called...Ten Cent."

I recalled some of the stories although no real details of what had actually happened at the time. I was only fifteen and had more important things on my mind besides some deranged killer who was taking young women off the street. "I've heard of him."

"The police never caught him. Even though he killed five victims. The investigation remains open but kind of petered out. But two months ago, another body showed up and I think that it could be him."

"What makes you think that?" I asked curiously.

"A young woman was recently found near the town of Friar's Lake in western New South Wales. You must have seen it. It ran on the news cycle for days."

Did I mention that I don't own a television? "Sorry, Marion, I didn't."

"A friend in New South Wales police reached out and gave me some information. He's been a policeman for a long time, and we've known each other since my sister and her friend disappeared."

"Do the police have any suspects?"

"No."

"What did your friend say?"

"He said that the murder had all but two of the same markings of the previous ones."

I waited for Marion to continue. It felt like she had paused for effect, but I waited in silence.

She added, "The body wasn't buried, and the ten-cent piece was beside the body and not in the mouth."

"Other than that?"

"The rest hit the markers."

I was unsure and said, "Eighteen years is a long time for a serial killer to stop killing for."

"But what if he never stopped?" she replied. "What if the bodies just haven't been found yet?"

I nodded thoughtfully. "It's possible I suppose. What is it that you want me to do?"

"I want you to find the killer."

I took a bite of my pie and spoke around a mouthful of pastry and meat, "Let the police take care of it."

"They're doing nothing."

Swallowing what was in my mouth I said, "I'm not really one to investigate murders. It's a police thing."

"But you can look for missing persons though, can't you?"

All right, I'll bite. "Who is missing?"

"Do you know Trent Jacobs?"

"Yes," I replied. Jacobs was another PI working around Melbourne. Confident, smug prick who'd crossed paths with me on more than one occasion. Competent in his job, however. "I know him. We've tangled a time or two."

"I hired him three weeks ago to go to Friar's Lake and investigate. Now, he's disappeared."

I put the pie down, wiping my hands and mouth with the paper napkin. "How long since you've heard from him?"

"Two weeks."

"Did you not go to the police?"

"I did. To the ones here in Melbourne. They didn't seem too worried about him."

They wouldn't be. Jacobs had on more than one occasion rubbed the local constabulary the wrong way. "What did they say?"

"That they would pass my concerns on to the proper people and left it at that."

"Sounds about right," I sighed.

"Will you do it or not?" Marion asked.

I ran up a quick tab in my head. "I'll do it, but you should be aware that this might run up a penny or two. I will also need you to sign a contract engaging my services. I have one in my car."

"Money is no object." She actually seemed relieved that I agreed to take the job. "Come with me and I'll give you some money up front."

Now she was talking my language. I grabbed my pie and fries and followed her across the carpark to where a blue BMW X7 was parked. I was impressed. Marion opened the passenger door and took out a cheque book from the glove compartment. *Who has a cheque book these days* I thought to myself? Nearly everyone dealt in plastic. Normally I would have balked right away. I'd been burned in the past on more than one occasion by rubber cheques. However, I figured that if this one bounced, I'd come back and steal her Beamer. She passed it to me, and I looked at the number of zeros written on it. "Is that enough?" she asked.

Holy shit. There were four of them with a two at the front. "I think you might have added a zero too many, Marion."

She shook her head. "No, I calculated travelling and expenses into it as well. Looking at that sorrowful looking excuse of a car you drive I figured you might like to get another before you leave. Take the cheque into the bank and the funds should clear straight away. I'll call ahead so there shouldn't be any problem."

Wow. Money and influence. I was starting to like her. "Thank you. Just give me a moment to grab that contract."

I moved quickly across to my Ford, placing the remains of my breakfast on the roof before unlocking the door and reaching into my leather briefcase for a blank proforma contract I keep handy for just this reason. I backed out of the vehicle and crossed back to her, filled out some details before getting her to sign at the bottom.

"I would like to be kept updated daily once you leave," she said. "Are you good with that?"

I nodded. "I can do that."

"Please be careful, Mister Hayes. I have a bad feeling about this."

"Don't worry, Marion, careful is my middle name."

———

I watched her climb into the vehicle and drive off. Once she was gone, I walked back over to the food van where Mort was still waiting for his money. "Got a job?" he asked.

"Yes. I'm going away for a few days."

He suddenly looked agitated. "What about the Fijians? What do I tell them when they come back?"

"Tell them I've died."

Little did I know at the time that that little prophecy would almost come true.

Retrieving the pie and chips, I left the carpark on the bay and headed home via the local National Australia Bank. True to her word, the funds from the cheque were cleared immediately.

Arriving at home, I finished off the pie while my computer fired up, then began doing some homework around the case I had taken on. Marion Lawler, I found out she had spent most of her life in Sydney before moving to Melbourne after her sister had been murdered. She had been married to a real-estate tycoon who'd developed two large land packages on the outskirts of Melbourne's northern suburbs. The result of a ten-year marriage was a divorce settlement package which left her with quite a substantial sum.

Next, I looked into the Ten-Cent Killer. He'd surfaced eighteen years earlier, his first victim a young woman in her early twenties. Her body had been found north of Sydney, just south of Taree. She'd been strangled, the rope found still tied around her throat. Inside her mouth was a ten-cent piece. It was a warning that there were more to come. The killer had signed his kill.

Not long after that, another was found. Same MO, similar looks as the previous one. Long dark hair, around twentyish, athletic.

The second kill brought about the name The Ten-Cent Killer which seemed to embolden him. He struck next by taking two victims. Lucy Halder and Ruby Smith. The girls, both seventeen at the time, had lied about catching the bus to Byron Bay to spend a week with their friends. Instead, they'd got off at Taree with plans to meet boys.

It turned out that the boys had been unavoidably delayed and when they arrived at the pickup point it was dark and the girls were nowhere to be seen. Their bodies were discovered two weeks later by a bushwalker north of Taree. The Ten-Cent Killer had a hunting ground.

By this time the New South Wales Police had established a taskforce of twenty cops working day and night to track him down. Taskforce Ares.

Three months after the two girls were found, Jenny Gillam went missing one night after leaving the Taree Irish Club. She was found a week later, the bush north of Taree once more in the spotlight.

The taskforce fell upon the area searching for clues. But Ten-Cent was clever and seemed to be growing more so with each kill.

That was the last. It was as though someone had flicked a switch and Ten-Cent was no more.

I sighed, leaning back in my chair rubbing my hands through my hair. Why would a killer as proficient and as twisted as Ten-Cent just stop? There could have been any number of reasons I guessed. Got caught for something else and ended up in jail; the thrill of the kill was lost; maybe he had just died. Wouldn't that be something? But if what Marion Lawler was telling me was true, then Ten-Cent was still out there. And if he was, did he ever really stop killing?

I looked into the latest killing, the one at Friar's Lake. The victim a backpacker who'd been passing through. Her name was Inge Rasmussen. She was from one of those Nordic countries in Northern Europe. According to newspaper reports she'd been found beside the road in a dry creek bed. There had been a rope around her neck, and she was partially clothed. By partially I guessed that most of her garments were gone. According to the medical examiner she'd been there two days.

The detectives investigated until they ran out of leads.

Conclusions were drawn firstly by the media, when the coin was reportedly found beside the body, to Ten-Cent. Those suppositions were immediately dismissed by authorities.

I picked up my mobile phone and punched in a number I'd had cause to use on numerous occasions. That of Trent Jacobs. Just because I didn't like him didn't mean I wouldn't talk to him. His phone went straight to voicemail. Next, I tried his office which was located above a takeout shop in St. Kilda. It might be cliché, but I guess he wanted to model himself on some of the old PIs in the Gold Medal paperback books he used to read. No answer. All I got was the answering machine saying he was out of town.

My final act was to call my ex-wife. Yes, ex meaning ex. There were no fringe benefits to the separation. I'd read somewhere that after some people got divorced, they actually spent more time in each other's beds humping like rabbits. That wasn't Tia and me. Hell, the more time we spent in the same bed together the louder the screaming got. And not in a good way. However, whenever I headed out of town on a case, I always called her to let her know. That way I had backup if something happened. That and the fact she was a cop. Yes, sir, one of Victoria's finest. A detective too. And a great source if I needed information, even if it was unwilling.

"What do you want, Moron?"

She always treated me with the utmost of respect. I could picture her long golden tresses pulled back in a ponytail that hung past her shoulders. Her pale face and ice-blue eyes. Not to mention—

"Mark?"

"I'm here, Tia."

"I assume you called for a reason. I'm busy so make it fast."

"Another homicide in the city's seedy underbelly?" I asked her in my own special way.

"Some guy took to his flatmate with a kitchen knife. He—why the hell am I telling you this? It's got nothing to do with you."

"I'm going out of town on a job," I told her.

"How long for?" she asked.

"Could be a week."

"Where to?" she asked almost disinterestedly.

"A place called Friar's Lake," I replied.

Tia went silent for a while, and I could picture the look on her face. Her furrowed brow and the way her nose wrinkled when deep in thought trying to figure out what I was doing.

Five, four, three—

"Shit, Mark, what the hell?"

I could never get to zero. Maybe that was why she was a detective, and I was a PI. "Here we go."

"I hope you're not going up there to stick your nose into police business."

"How do you know what I'm doing, Tia?" I shot back at her feeling my temperature rise.

"I know there was a murder up there a couple of months back."

"How do you Melbourne detectives know what goes on in New South Wales?"

"Don't be a dick, Mark."

"If you must know, Tia, I'm looking for a missing person."

"Who?" she asked. Standard question for a detective, and Tia.

"Trent Jacobs." I winced.

"That bastard? Why does anyone want to find that leech?"

"It pays the bills, Babe."

"Don't babe me, Mark," Tia growled.

"I'll check in the same as usual."

Her voice softened. "Mark, be careful."

That was Tia. Couldn't be with me, couldn't stand to be without me. "I'll be fine, Tia. You take care. Love you."

"Bastard."

CHAPTER TWO

I was up early the next morning to a typical Melbourne summer day. It was pissing down rain. I decided to give it ten minutes. You know what they say about Melbourne? Four seasons in one day. I was hoping autumn or spring would be along soon. While I waited, I had a coffee, heavily sugared, and some toast, slick with Vegemite. True to form, spring arrived right on time as the sun burst through the grey overcast.

I tossed everything I needed into the back of the Festiva and reversed out of the garage, climbed out of the car to lower the roller door and true to form once more, was pissed on from a great height by a cantankerous grey cloud. "Shit." I need to invest in a remote-controlled garage door so I didn't have to get out of the car. Put it on my mental To-Do list.

I left my home in the suburbs and headed to a nearby car yard. Which happened to be the one from which I'd bought my ever-reliable Festiva. I say this with tongue in cheek for the car, I'm sure, was put on this earth to test me beyond all boundaries. I pulled up and climbed out into more glorious sunshine. The owner, a slippery Italian bloke with a large mustache similar to that of Lex Marinos from his Kingswood Country days, must have seen me coming. He came out of his office rubbing his hands together looking at me like he'd done to a hundred other suckers. "Mark, maate. How's it hanging, brother?"

"Straight up and down as always, Mario," I replied, already on edge.

He motioned to the dented Ford. "You've still got the Festiva, huh? I told you it was a great little car, didn't I?"

"It's a piece of shit, Mario," I said bluntly.

Keeping his composure, Mario said, "Easy, Mark. You might hurt its feelings."

"I want another car, Mario."

The car salesman's eyes lit up like a poker machine with a jackpot. "I'm sure we can find you something good. I think I know just the vehicle."

"I don't want your usual crap, Mario. Okay? I want something reliable."

He gave me an indignant look. "When was the last time I sold you something unreliable?"

I looked at the Festiva. "Yeah, I wonder when."

"Mark, maate—"

"Don't frigging mate me, Mario."

"All right, all right. Maybe we can do a little better than the Festiva this time around."

I grunted. "Yeah."

I followed him through the yard, and he stopped next to a silver Kia Rio. There was a scratch on the driver's door and what looked to be a bullet hole beside the number plate. "How about this?"

"You're kidding, aren't you?" I looked at him incredulously.

"What's wrong with it?"

"Piss off, Mario."

He pressed me. "It's cheap, Mark. Only seven grand."

I turned away from him and let my gaze roam over everything in the yard. A Nissan Pulsar, Toyota Corolla, Honda Civic, and—I stopped. Three rows away I saw a green 2007 SS Commodore. Ignoring Mario, I walked over to it. The price on the front windshield in a large yellow and orange banner had it at twenty thousand.

"It's a good deal," Mario said. "Low kilometres, worth every cent."

I opened the driver's door and was hit in the face by some foreign smell that threatened breakfast. "Who frigging died in here?"

"There is a bit of a smell—"

"A bit? Shit, Mario, the smell is bloody terrible."

"All right so I'll throw in some air freshener."

Trying not to breathe too deeply I climbed behind the wheel. Everything on the inside looked fine. I looked at the ignition. Surprisingly, there was a key in it. I turned it and the V8 engine thundered to life. The car rocked to the engine's thump-thump beat. I pumped the accelerator and the motor responded with a throaty roar. For a moment I was taken back to my youth.

Switching the engine off I climbed out. Before I did though, I pressed the button which popped the trunk.

"What do you think?" Mario asked eagerly.

I could see in his eyes the cheap bastard had an idea he was going to rip me off. The price on the window might have been fair but if he thought I was going to pay that amount for it, he had another think coming. I looked in the trunk. The smell was worse back there. I looked at Mario. "The body was in the boot, huh?"

A pained expression came over his face but finally a nod was elicited. "All right, Mark, there might have been an incident in Preston where this guy popped some bloke and put him in the boot."

"How long was he there before he was found?"

"A day."

"Mario."

"Two days."

I gave him a hard stare.

"All right, a week. That's it, honest."

I lifted the floor and checked for a spare in the well. It wasn't there. However, it did have a jack and handle. "Where's the spare?"

Mario shrugged. "It should have been there."

It was easy to tell he didn't know. "Uh, huh."

I looked over the roof of the car and saw a silver Audi pull up outside the yard. Two men climbed out of the passenger seats. They were dressed in suits and had slicked-back hair. The driver stayed with the vehicle. Immediately my senses screamed trouble. I didn't know them, so I knew they weren't there for me. Mario on the other hand, I was certain was the target. Then I saw one of them pull a handgun from under his suit jacket.

"Mario, who have you pissed off lately?"

Mario looked in the same direction I was, and his face suddenly turned white as though someone had doused it with a sack of flour. I heard him gasp, "Oh, no."

"Who are they?"

"Caputo," he managed to get out in a choked voice.

"The Caputo Brothers?" I asked.

His head bobbed up and down furiously. "Y-yes."

The Caputo Brothers were the local inner suburbs crime family. Big? No. Dangerous? Definitely. Especially since they looked as though they were both armed. I looked into the trunk and grabbed the jack handle. Not much of a weapon against guns but one does what they can when the chips are down. I looked at Mario who appeared as though he was about to run. I grabbed his collar and dragged him down behind me. "Stay there."

I looked through the gap between the trunk and the

open lid. I could see the two men walking towards the Commodore. Fantastic. I hadn't even got out of Melbourne and already there were people with guns coming at me.

The crunch of shoes on gravel became louder as they grew closer. I gripped the handle tightly, my knuckles turning white. I was about to see if I'd wasted my youth on the golf course as a kid.

With the appearance of the first brother past the rear quarter panel of the Commodore, Mario bolted. He just picked his skirts up and ran like his arse was on fire, leaving me there to deal with the brothers on my own. Maybe I should have let them shoot him. After all it wasn't my problem.

I wound up with the jack handle and swung hard. On the golf course I'd say the ball would have gone at least two-thirty. However, with the solid implement striking the would-be killer's forearm, sounded just as nice. Especially the part where it went crack.

The handgun dropped from nerveless fingers and the first Caputo brother let out a screech. I swung again. This time his screams stopped as he went down hard into the gravel. I whirled looking for his brother. He was behind me reaching for his own weapon, face curled up in a vicious snarl.

The jack handle whipped through the air again, the hard steel catching the second Caputo across the bridge of the nose. I winced even as the blow struck. This guy was definitely going to the emergency room. He joined his brother on the ground. I leaned down and picked up their handguns then looked around for Mario. "Hey, Mario, where'd you go?"

I saw a head pop up behind a Nissan Pulsar, the eyes wide with fear. "Is it safe?"

"Yeah."

I could hear the sirens in the distance. It didn't take anyone long to ring for police these days. "Mario, get over here."

He came across to where I stood, looking down at the two prone men as they squirmed on the ground. "What did they want?" I asked.

"I do not know."

"Mario?"

"I swear, Mark. I don't know."

I gave him my best stare and held up the jack handle which had a slight bend in it.

"All right, I owe them money," he blurted out.

"What for?"

He bowed his head. "Protection."

"They were shaking you down?" I asked, aware of the first police car skidding to a stop out on the street.

"Yes."

"Shit."

Two uniformed coppers walked towards us, hands on weapons, barking orders. Behind them a plain car stopped, and two detectives climbed out. One I recognised straight away. "Double-shit."

———

"I should have known you would be mixed up in this," Tia snarled at me. I felt like a school kid being reprimanded by the headmaster.

Mario and I were both handcuffed and leaning against the Commodore I'd decided by this time to buy, though not for the exorbitant price the slippery little salesman wanted for it. "Hello, my love," I greeted her in my best Ronnie Barker accent from the television show, Open All Hours.

"Don't you start that shit with me, Mark Hayes," she

snapped, fire burning in her eyes. "How is it when I get called to shit like this, it's always you who's drowning in it?"

"What can I say? I have enemies."

She gave an exasperated sigh. "What happened?"

I looked over at the first of the Caputo brothers being loaded carefully into the ambulance. "They interrupted my purchase."

Tia's eyes narrowed. "What purchase?"

"I was going to buy this car, here," I told her.

She glanced at the Commodore. "You can afford this? You can't even afford to pay me back what you owe."

I was hurt. "Sure. Only going to cost me five grand."

"It what?" Mario blurted out, eyes wide with surprise.

I looked at him. "After what I just did for you, Mario, it's bloody five grand."

"Come on, maate—"

"Don't fucking mate me, Mario. It's five grand and I'll throw the Festiva in."

His shoulders slumped and for a moment I thought he might actually cry. "All right. Five. Cash."

"Deal."

"Are you ladies done?" Tia asked. "I've got an investigation to conduct here."

I looked at her, my head cocked to the side. "Isn't this a little below you?"

"Shut up and listen," she growled at me. "What happened to Antonio Caputo?"

"Jack handle."

She stared at me. "His brother?"

I shrugged. "Jack handle."

"Why?"

"Reach into my coat pocket."

"If this is some kind of trick, Mark, I'll belt you with a phone book."

"I can't really do it, can I, Tia? My hands are tied."

She reached in and I saw her pretty blues widen. "Jesus Christ," she hissed as she took out the two hand-guns. "Didn't those dumb pricks search you when they put you in cuffs?"

"Now, does it really look like they did?"

"Shit. Are these yours?"

I rolled my eyes. "Don't be daft, Tia. You know the next time I get caught with a handgun I go before the magistrate. They belong to the Caputos. They were here to send Mario on the bullet express."

Tia glanced at Mario. "Why would they want to do that?"

"Can I go?" I asked her. "I have to get up to Friar's Lake."

"No. Mario?"

"I owe them money," Mario squeezed out.

"Why?"

Mario mumbled something inaudible. I rolled my eyes. "Oh, for crying out loud, Mario. Tia, they were putting the squeeze on him for protection. I reckon that if you ran through half the businesses around here, they're doing the same thing."

Mario stared at me in disbelief. I was starting to get really frustrated. "What, Mario? Did I leave something out?"

He shook his head.

"Now can I go, Tia?" I asked.

She glared at me. "No."

Cursing softly under my breath I watched her walk away. She went over to the ambulance and talked to one of the paramedics who'd just finished putting the last of the battered Caputos into the back. Then she went and spoke with her partner, Penis. His name was Dick and he actually was a dick; bald head with wrinkles at the back of his neck, so I decided to rename him. We had a mutual dislike for one another.

Tia came back towards me, walking with that sexy swagger she always had. It wasn't bad to watch coming at you, but even better when she was walking away. "How's Penis getting on?" I asked her.

"Christ, Mark, can't you be serious just for once? I'm trying to decide whether or not to charge you with assault. You're not doing yourself any favours."

I nodded. "All right Tia. Where do we go from here?"

She sighed. "I'm letting you go, all right?"

My smile answered her question. I had no complaints with that.

"You know once these guys get out of hospital, they're going to want a piece of you?"

"They can join the crew," I muttered.

She cocked one of her pencil thin eyebrows. I always thought it was kind of sexy the way she did that. "Who else is after you?"

"The Lenoa brothers."

She shook her head. "You don't believe in doing things by halves, do you?"

I gave her a mirthless grin. "It's a failing I have. Although if I was any other way, I doubt you would have been attracted to me like you were."

"One of *my* many failings," Tia replied and briefly I saw her smile.

"There she is," I said with a smile.

She frowned at me. "Who is?"

"The Tia I fell in love with. You know, if you play your cards right you could still win me back."

"From who?" she snorted.

"The multitudes of lovely ladies who are desperately throwing themselves at my feet."

"I think I'm going to be sick," she groaned. "Turn around."

I did as she asked, and she inserted the key to remove the handcuffs.

"You can go now," she said.

I crooked my head at Mario. "I need my man here so I can get the Commodore."

She looked at him. "I haven't finished with you, yet. Don't run off."

"I won't."

She undid his cuffs too before saying to me, "Get out of here. And be careful. By the way, who are you working for?"

"Marion Lawler."

She raised her eyebrows in a surprised expression. "Wow, I'm impressed. You going to bang her?"

"Damn it, Tia—"

Her lips split into a wide grin, and I felt a heart string go twang. "I'm just teasing, Mark. Get."

I left the yard twenty minutes later in my new, slightly ripe, green SS Commodore, leaving in my wake, a battered Ford Festiva and a sad looking Italian car salesman.

———

I drove up the Hume until I reached the Goulburn Valley Highway, taking the exit at the interchange, leaving the dual carriageway. From there I drove through Shepparton and on to Tocumwal where I decided to stop for the night. I figured I could make it the rest of the way tomorrow. It was there I found a motel for the night not far from the Murray River which formed a lazy flowing border between Victoria and New South Wales. The motel was small but clean; smelled overpoweringly like hospital strength disinfectant. What's more, it was cheap. The Commodore on the other hand, still smelled like death but drove like a dream compared to the Festiva.

Later that evening after I'd eaten a large meal of ribeye steak and chips smothered in pepper sauce at the motel's restaurant, I reached out to Marion Lawler to check in. I left out the bit about the trouble at the caryard.

Not long after I hung up from her, Tia called. "You're a bastard, you know that?"

"Great to hear from you too," I replied.

"Why is it that you always get under my skin?"

You mean apart from the fact that I always try? "It's not by choice."

"Damn you, Mark Hayes," she snarled and hung up.

That went well.

I had met Tia at the academy. I don't think I mentioned that at the start. But the fact is that yours truly at one point in his life was a police officer. Not a very good one. Young, gung ho, going to change the world by serving the thin blue line. I lasted two years, deciding it wasn't for me (with the help of a few good people higher up the ladder than me). But I digress, I was talking about Tia.

When I first met her, I fell head over heels in love. I did my best to win her over and after a couple of brilliant attempts, and more than a few dumb ones, Mark "The Romancer" Hayes struck gold. Life was good, we got married.

We got divorced.

I took out a note pad and made some notes while I thought of them. It was a good habit I picked up from my brief policing days. After that, I had a shower in a small cubicle with a water saving nozzle, one of those that dribble water at an annoying rate, which force you to dance around to get wet. I swear, I could have pissed on a fan and got wetter. Once clean I climbed between the crisp, twenty thread-count sheets on the nice hard bed. You had to love motels.

I was awake reasonably early the following morning after a not so good night sleep. I was woken by the delivery of my breakfast through the tray slot near the door and a call of "Breakfast!".

Rolling out of bed, I padded across the carpet like a zombie fresh from a grave to the bench where the tray was. On lifting the lid, I had to admit it looked pretty good. If I had ordered the bacon and eggs that is. I was hungry so I ate it anyway. I hoped whoever got my sausages enjoyed them. Before I left, I had another shower to wake me up some more.

When I walked outside to leave, it was already hot and was only going to get hotter. The cicadas were singing, and the air was almost suffocating.

It was around eight-thirty when the Commodore rolled out of the gravel motel driveway and onto the Newell Highway. To the west there was a slight smudge of dust in the air and the heat mirages had started to form.

I tracked the Newell to the small town of Finley where I left the highway and headed towards Deniliquin, home of the Deni Ute Muster. From there I headed in a northerly direction to Hay where I stopped for fuel.

While I was filling the thirsty beast, I noticed a young lass dressed in jeans and a T-shirt, carrying a red backpack, standing out the front of the servo, trying to thumb a ride. I shook my head. When would these people ever learn?

"Hey," I called out to her as I hung up the pump nozzle.

She turned and looked at me. She couldn't have been any more than twenty. Then something struck me. I'd seen her before—or girls very much like her before. The victims of the Ten-Cent killer. "Where you going?"

"Queensland," she replied.

"You're a little off the beaten track, aren't you?"

She walked towards me. "A little."

"I'm going as far as Friar's Lake if you want a ride?"

"You ain't some kind of serial killer, are you?"

I smiled unsure if she was being serious or not. Like I was going to admit it if I was. "Close, I'm a private investigator."

She nodded. "That's all right, I guess. Is that north?"

I nodded. "Just give me a chance to pay for the fuel and I'll be back."

"Sure."

I went inside and forked over the best part of a hundred dollars. The price of petrol just kept going up and up. Never was I so happy as I was then about claiming expenses. The beast was a good car, but it was bloody thirsty. When I returned to the heat outside, I found the girl already in the front passenger seat. Her backpack was in the back. I climbed in and she said, "I hope you don't mind?"

"All good," I replied. "My name is Mark."

"Tash," she said.

"Where you from, Tash?" I asked.

"Adelaide."

I nodded.

"Can I see your ID again?"

Shrugging my shoulders, I took it back out. Before I knew what was happening, she had taken a photo of it with her phone. I frowned at her and she said, "Every time I get a ride, I take a photo of the ID and send the picture to my friend in Adelaide. Kind of an insurance policy."

Sound in theory, I guessed, but in the real world things had a way of coming undone. I looked at my watch. It wasn't quite eleven, but I was hungry. "You feel like something to eat? My stomach is telling me it's hungry. I'll buy."

Tash shrugged. "Sure."

We found a small café in town which seemed to fit the brief of what we needed. By now the heat outside was scorching, and inside the café the little fans on the walls offered only minor relief. I ordered the usual pie and chips, while Tash chose some tofu burger monstrosity with a mountain of salad on it. I guessed it was a millennial thing. As I took a bite from my pie she said, "You should eat healthier, you know?"

I stared across the table at her. She had grey eyes and her skin was slightly marked with small blemishes. "I eat just fine."

"Pie, chips, and a Coke? Real healthy."

I smiled. "Where you headed to in Queensland?"

"Kingaroy," she replied. "Got a friend there."

"Bad time of the year to be hitching," I pointed out. "Especially dressed in jeans."

Tash shrugged. "It is what it is."

"You know that what you're doing isn't safe?"

"I can take care of myself." Her voice took on an edge of defiance.

I let it go and finished my food then looked on as Tash finished devouring hers. It was painful to watch. When she finished, she got up and said, "Have I got time to go to the toilet before we leave?"

"Go ahead."

While she was in the bathroom I paid for the food.

Outside the temperature had climbed to what felt like a hundred degrees. I was so glad I lived in Melbourne. A car drove past on the street and hit a patch of tar softened by the heat. The wheels made a sticking sound as they drove over it, the tread imprint left in its wake.

The cicadas were in full voice and their chirping seemed to get inside my head like I had a severe bout of tinnitus. While I waited for Tash, I couldn't help thinking about her, about what she was doing.

"You ready to go?" she asked as she reappeared. "It's bloody hot out here, isn't it?"

"Ain't that the truth," I replied and swatted at a fly. "The flies are almost as bad."

We climbed in the Commodore which by now was an oven on wheels. Tash wrinkled her nose, noticing the slight odour from before had grown into a foul stench which threatened to overwhelm the senses. "Man, what died in here?"

"Who?"

"Excuse me?"

"Not what, who," I said. "Who died in here?"

"You're not serious?"

"Afraid so. The salesman I bought it from told me there was a dead body in the boot for a while before it was found."

She screwed up her face in disgust. "Crap. Why would you buy it?"

"It was cheap."

I started the engine, rolled the windows down, and turned the air conditioning onto full power. After a minute or so I wound the windows back up and let the aircon take effect. At least that worked well.

"Tash," I said, "if I give you some money for a bus ticket, would you use it? After we get to Friar's Lake I mean?"

"Why would you do that?" she asked curiously.

"I'd just feel better if I did."

She shrugged. "Sure, why not?"

Satisfied with her answer, but unsure whether she would keep the money and continue to hitch, I put the beast in reverse and backed out of the carpark.

CHAPTER THREE

I swear to God Friar's Lake was thirty degrees hotter than Hay when we arrived that afternoon. I climbed out of the air-conditioned Commodore and felt like the skin was about to peel from my body. Tash followed my lead, and I could tell by the expression on her face that she felt the same way. "I'll ask someone about a bus for you."

She looked at me and shook her head. "I can do it. You've done enough."

Digging into my wallet I took out two-hundred dollars. "Here, I hope it's enough."

"That's way too much," she said trying to give a hundred back.

I pushed her hand away. "Just take it."

She smiled at me. A broad smile which showed her even white teeth. "Thanks, Mark, you're the best."

I said, "Give me your phone for a minute."

Tash handed it over and watched as I put my number into it. "Text me when you get there."

She rolled her eyes. "Yes, dad."

Tash then did something unexpected. She hugged me. I was surprised at first but overcame it and returned the embrace. She stepped back and said, "I wish I had a big brother like you."

"Just text me."

She picked up her backpack and started to walk along the main street of Friar's Lake.

The town itself wasn't overly big. I think I remembered the worn sign depicting a lake on the way in saying it had something in the vicinity of 1,200 people. Depending on how old the sign was, it could have been less or more.

Every second movement was an outback salute as I swiped at the flies. Maybe because I hadn't moved for a few heartbeats they were starting to think I might be roadkill or something similar. Towards the end of the street, I saw the police station sign and started walking in that direction.

The main street itself was coated in a fine red dust which no doubt had blown in on a dust storm at some point. I walked past a café and a large supermarket store which I assumed the locals all used for their shopping. I made a note to come back to it later to ask questions. On the opposite side of the street was a large pub. Two floors with a balcony running around it. *Friar's Pub* painted in large red letters ran along its front. The front doors and the windows on either side were wide open. For a moment I could hear the noise from within filter out before it was drowned out by a passing battered Land Cruiser tray-back.

I kept walking past a few smaller shops and a real estate office until I reached the police station. It looked as though it had once been a brown brick house and had been converted to its current use.

I walked through the open gate which separated two spans of Cyclone fence. To the right of the station were three police vehicles. Two Nissan four-wheel drives and a

Commodore. I made my way along the uneven footpath and up a single step onto a stoop to the front door. I noted that there was a doorbell buzzer to the left for after hours. On the door itself was a large poster with a uniformed cop pointing a finger at me. The words underneath him read: Policing Starts with You!

I opened the door and a gust of cold air reached out to embrace me. I liked this place already. Closing the door behind me I walked up to the counter which had a large Perspex or glass barrier. The main office I could see had three desks and two officers. One male, one female. Both with their head down doing paperwork. Neither of them looked up. Maybe they thought if they ignored me, I would go away.

Not today.

To my right on the counter was a small silver bell, the little button sitting proudly on top. I'd given them plenty of time to acknowledge my presence. I reached over and brought the flat of my palm down upon it.

Five times.

One of the officers looked up. He was a young constable with red hair. "You right, mate?" He looked irritable.

"I'd like to speak to the officer in charge, if that's all right with you? I'd hate to interrupt your colouring in."

"Who are you?"

I shrugged and retrieved my ID, holding it up against the barrier. "Mark Hayes. I'm a private investigator."

The policewoman turned her head to look up, seeing me for the first time. She put her pen down onto the desk and stood up with a sigh. "Another one?"

It was a rhetorical question, but I answered it anyway. "Yes, another one."

She walked across to the counter. Even though she had a disinterested expression on her face she looked to be quite pretty. I guessed she was about my age, in her early thirties. Her dark hair was tied up in a bun, and she wore no makeup. I made a point of staring at her name tag. "Senior Constable Nicole Berger?"

She gave me a mirthless grin. "You can read, I see. What can I do for you, Mister Hayes?"

Being a private investigator can be such a joy at times. Especially dealing with law enforcement. "I'm searching for a missing person."

"Really? What would the name of this person be?"

"Trent Jacobs."

Nicole stared at me for a long moment before saying, "Wait here."

She turned away and walked between the desks towards the back of the room where a large window sat to the left of an office door. She knocked on the door and went inside. I looked at Red. "I wouldn't have thought a town this small warranted three cops?"

He looked up at me. "Big area to cover. Thirteen thousand square kilometres and two other small towns."

"Oh. Keeps you busy?"

"Sometimes."

The door opened again, and Nicole motioned to me. "Come through, Mister Hayes. The boss will see you."

The Boss? Here I was imagining I was about to meet Tom Croydon of Blue Heelers fame, instead I was greeted by a female sergeant. However, she *was* named Tom. Tomika Rains, pushing forty, light hair cut into a bob, but no Croydon bulge. Actually, she didn't look too bad from where I was standing.

"Have a seat, Mister Hayes," she said to me and pointed at a chair. Nicole stayed in the room by the door.

"The senior constable tells me you're a private investigator."

The chair made a scraping sound as I dragged it out and creaked when I sat. "Yes, ma'am."

"I'm not a ma'am, Mister Hayes. Sergeant will be fine."

"Yes, ma'am." Sometimes I can't help myself.

Tom ignored the blatant attempt at poor humour and said, "Who is it that has gone missing?"

"Trent Jacobs."

Her head bobbed slowly. "The first PI who was here in town?"

"Supposedly. At least that's what I was told when I was hired to find him."

"By whom?"

"A woman."

Tom let it go for the moment. "We were under the impression that Trent Jacobs had shot through a day after he arrived."

"My client hasn't heard from him for two weeks and the last she knew he was here in Friar's Lake."

"I'm sorry but there's nothing I can tell you," Tom said to me.

"Did he come to see you?" I asked.

Tom nodded. "He did and asked a few questions which I didn't answer."

Which meant that he would have had to rely upon the good folks of Friar's Lake for his answers. It also meant that if Ten-Cent were in town, he would have known Jacobs was here asking questions.

"Sergeant, let's be straight up," I said. "You and I both know my main goal here isn't to find Jacobs. I mean it is, but it isn't."

She nodded slowly. "I'm not a detective, Mister Hayes—"

"Call me Mark. Mister makes me sound old."

"Mark. Like I was saying, I'm not a detective but I gathered that."

"What did Jacobs ask you about?"

Tom sighed. "The murder a couple of months back."

"What did you tell him?"

"Very little. Just where she was found. It was something that he would have found out on his own eventually anyway."

"Yes. Did he tell you why he was interested in the murdered girl?"

Tom rolled her eyes. "Here we go again. Listen, Mark, I'm not going to waste my time on theories. The Ten-Cent killer is long gone. He wasn't even anywhere near here."

"But what if he's not gone?"

"Well, he's bloody not here. If you want to know about the death of the young lady, talk to the detectives."

"Which will be a waste of time," I replied.

"Not my problem," Tom said abruptly.

"Do you mind if I hang around for a couple of days to inquire about Jacobs?"

With a sigh, Tom said, "That's fine. But if you start causing trouble about the other thing, I'm going to run you out of town myself. I tell you what, I'll have Senior Constable Berger here ask around for you too. All right? She might have more luck than you."

I stood up. "You won't even know I'm here."

———

I figured if I found out what happened to Jacobs then I would eventually work out the answer to the other. That was the theory, anyway, so I would work both angles. I found a room at a motel and dumped my stuff. It was late in the afternoon, and I was hungry so I decided to head to the pub, and maybe I could kill two birds with one stone. Eat and ask questions.

There are some smells in the world that make you feel great. Cooking food wafting from a pub kitchen is one of them.

I walked into the bar and ordered a beer from a tall thin guy with a beard. While he poured it, I looked around. There were a few people in. The usual suspects who held up the bar most afternoons while they reminisced about old times. Also, the few who came down to play Keno or punt on the horses. Then there were those who just came in for other reasons. They were easy to pick out.

The guy put my beer on the bar next to the ten-dollar bill I left for him. He took it away and brought back my change. Before he moved away, I said, "You got a minute, mate?"

"What's up?"

I reached into my pocket and took out a picture I had of Jacobs. "You seen this guy before?"

He frowned, then nodded slowly as recognition came slowly. "Yeah, I remember him. He was in here a couple of weeks ago. Bastard he was."

"What do you mean?"

"He was staying here. Left without paying. Funny though, he left his stuff behind. It's all still in the room."

I raised my eyebrows. It was odd that Jacobs would just leave and not take anything. "Really? What was he doing here, do you know?"

"He was asking questions about the girl they found out the road," he replied.

"What kind of questions?"

"Mate, are you a cop? Detective or something?"

"What's your name?"

"Paul."

I took out my ID. "Paul, I'm a private investigator. My name is Mark. The guy I'm asking about is missing. Never came home."

"No shit?"

Nodding, I said, "No shit. What can you tell me?"

He looked nervously along the bar. "I get a break in an hour or so. Could we talk then? My boss is really funny about talking too much while we're working."

"Yeah, sure. Would it be possible to look at the guy's room?"

Paul looked a little uncertain and then nodded. He hurried off and came back with a key. "Up the stairs, turn left, and along the hallway until you come to room four."

I took the key and said, "Thanks, Paul."

"Listen, you didn't get the key from me, okay?"

"Mum's the word. Keep an eye on my beer."

Following his directions, I went up the creaky wooden stairs, the worn carpet runner was clean as though it had not long been vacuumed. I admired the hand carved balustrade as I climbed, and when I hit the landing at the top I turned left and found room four a couple of doors down the hallway. I tried the key which slipped into the lock. Opening the door, I stepped inside, closing it behind me.

The room was dark and stuffy which accentuated the smell of the old carpet. I turned on the light. It was a dangling globe coming from the centre of a decorative plaster rose. I looked around. There was a gym bag in the corner. Us PIs travel light. A pair of pants thrown over the back of a chair and a half-empty bottle of Sprite on the dresser next to a small toiletry bag.

I wondered to myself why his stuff was still here in the room, why it wouldn't have been put in a shed or something to free up the room? I shook my head. It was beyond me. I grabbed the pants from the back of the chair and went through the pockets. A few coins and a half-eaten pack of gum. Jacobs was always chewing. It made him look like a cow chewing cud.

I crossed to his gym bag and picked it up. Undoing the zipper, I emptied it out on the bed. My eyebrows shot up. The guy certainly came prepared. I tossed the packet of condoms to one side and sifted through the clothes. Nothing there.

Surely, he would have had a file for the case. I looked at the dresser. Maybe in the drawers. I found it in the top left. Placing it on top of the dresser I opened it and flicked through the contents. I found a map, some notes, and a few other bits of paper. I checked the map first. It was one of the local areas and had a single cross on a location between Friar's Lake and a smaller town to the northeast. In small scrawl under it were the words: *Body Here*.

He'd marked where Inge Rasmussen was found.

Folding the map, I put it in my back pocket. Next came the notes. Reading through them I could see that most were groundwork Jacobs had done before coming to town. It made me wonder how long he was actually here before he disappeared. According to Tom they were under the impression he left the next day.

Digging into my pocket I took out my mobile. I punched in Marion Lawler's number and on the second ring she answered. "Marion Lawler."

"Marion, Mark Hayes."

"Yes, Mark."

"I'm in Friar's Lake. I have a couple of things I need cleared up. How long was Jacobs here?"

After a slight pause she said, "Three days."

"Was he in contact with you all that time?"

"Yes, he was."

"How did you communicate? Did you talk on the phone or some other way?"

"We talked on the phone the first time and he texted me each time after that," she told me.

"Was that what you had organized?" I asked.

"Not really. He just said he would keep me informed. I assumed he would just ring. Why?"

"No reason. I'm just trying to get a feel for where we're at. Thought I'd do that and check in at the same time."

"All right. Thank you."

I hung up.

I kept the notes and put the rest back in the drawer. I was about to leave when I realised, I hadn't checked the toiletry bag. I did the same with it as I did the gym bag. Sifting through the detritus I found nothing, then began replacing it. Brut stick, shaving cream, aftershave, toothbrush, toothpaste. I picked up a green plastic soap container with a broken lid. The damn thing fell apart as soon as I lifted it. The soap fell out onto the comforter along with two little plastic bags of Crystal Meth.

"Holy crap," I muttered. "What the fu—"

"Are you all right in here?"

Shit! I felt my butthole pucker at the sound of the familiar voice. My first reaction was to scoop up the meth bags. Even before I turned around. Clenching them tight in my fist I turned to Senior Constable Berger standing in the doorway. I hadn't even heard her come in. "Senior Constable."

"Nicole will do," she said curiously. "Did you find anything?"

My hand slipped into my pocket, and I hoped like shit she wouldn't notice. "Not really," I said. "Are you keeping an eye on me?"

She feigned innocence. "Me?"

"Your sergeant said earlier that she figured Trent left

the next day, right?" I asked trying to have her focus on something other than me.

"That's it. He came into the station, asked questions, and we never saw him again."

"Thanks."

Sometimes I have trouble disguising my tells. This happened to be one of them. "What is it?" Nicole asked me.

"Trent checked in with the woman who hired him the first night he was here," I explained. "He talked to her on the phone. After that, for the next couple of days when he checked in, he did it by text."

"What's your point?" she asked.

I shrugged. "No point. I just think it's odd."

"Why? Everybody texts these days."

"Maybe," I said. "One more thing. Do you have a drug problem in town?"

"No more than usual, I guess. Why?"

"Just curious."

"Have you finished here?" she asked.

I gave her a look of indifference. "Sure. Tell you what. Since your boss has you keeping an eye on me, how about you join me for a meal?"

Nicole eyed me suspiciously. "Maybe not."

"You have a senior constable at home?"

"No."

"Then there's no harm. I'll buy."

"Are you trying to bribe me, Mark?"

"I wouldn't dare," I replied. "The last copper I tried to bribe divorced me."

"Really?"

"Uh, huh. What do you say?"

"All right, I'll join you."

———

During the meal, the drugs in my pocket felt as though they weighed a ton. I cursed myself for asking her to join me. They were distracting and I was sure Nicole noticed. However, if she did, she never said anything.

"What's your theory on what happened to your friend?" she asked me as we ate.

"He's not my friend," I corrected her. "More like an acquaintance."

"Well?"

"I don't know."

"Why was he here looking for the Ten-Cent killer?"

I saw no harm in telling her, so I said, "Our client lost a sister to the first round of killings when Ten-Cent came on the scene."

"What made her think that this one was the same?"

I slopped a chip in the gravy left over from the roast meat I'd been eating. I held it up and the brown liquid dripped onto the plate. "The rope around the neck, the— who was the first on the scene, by the way?"

"I was."

"Okay. The rope. All of Ten-Cent's victims had ropes around their necks. They were female, between seventeen and twenty-three with long dark hair. And he always left the coin in their mouth."

"But this one didn't," Nicole pointed out.

"It wasn't buried either," I reminded her.

"And yet?"

"And yet my client believes it was the same killer. Eighteen years on. So does someone in the New South Wales Police Force."

"Really?" she seemed surprised.

"Yes."

"And now the private investigator has disappeared."

"Yes."

"Why did you ask if we had a drug problem?"

I was about to answer truthfully when raised voices sounded from the main bar. It was followed by the sound of glass breaking and a high-pitched scream.

We came to our feet at the same time and pushed through the door between the two rooms. Standing in the middle of the bar area were two men both dressed in jeans and shirts. A torn sleeve exposed an arm covered with tattoos. He was the one bleeding from a wound to his head while the other had a broken bottle grasped in his right hand. "I'm going to fucking kill you," snarled the man with the bottle.

"Come on then," the other shot back at him. "Give it your best shot, pussy."

"Hold it!" Nicole shouted above the noise. "Macca, put the bottle down."

Nothing like a good old family fight. Besides, statistics showed that if you weren't killed by a stranger, family was always a good bet.

The one called Macca looked at Nicole and his top lip curled into a sneer. "Piss off, bitch. This is between me and my brother."

I could see the resemblance between the two. Both were wiry, hollow-cheeked. The same dark hair and the same dark rings around their eyes.

"Don't make me pull my gun, Macca," Nicole warned him.

"You ain't got the balls, Senior Constable." Macca chuckled almost maniacally.

"Hey, mate," I said. "Why do you want to cut your brother?"

He looked at me disdainfully. "Who are you?"

"No one. But you don't want to do that to your brother."

"Who the hell are you to be telling me what I do or don't want to do?"

"I'm the bloke who's going to kick your arse if you don't put the bottle down."

With a snarl of rage, he focussed everything on me. I was expecting what came next when Macca lunged at me. The guy had a gut full of grog and it was an easy disarm. I stepped to one side and brought the side of my hand down in a chopping motion. The blow caught him just behind the hand holding the broken bottle. Instantly numb, the hand opened, and the broken bottle fell to the floor. Within moments I had him face down on the carpeted floor with an arm almost up between his shoulder blades.

"Let me go, you bastard," he shouted at me as he squirmed to get free.

"Just keep still or I'll pop your shoulder."

"You bloody mongrel," Macca's brother snarled at me and tried to come to his brother's aid. He only took one step before Nicole cracked him across the shins with her baton. He crumpled to the ground holding his leg. "Shit, you frigging broke it."

I looked up at Nicole who, instead of a look of gratitude on her face, wore one of irritation. "Don't you ever do that again."

CHAPTER FOUR

Sergeant Tom soon came along, and with Nicole, took the brothers away, leaving me to finish my now cold dinner. As I shovelled the last of it into my mouth, Paul appeared. "That was some fancy work out there, dude. Wish you could be here Friday and Saturday night."

"Who are they, anyway?" I asked.

"Macca and Johnno Pearce. They work on a station outside of town for old Ken Murphy. About ten kilometres west of here."

"Are they in here often?" I asked him.

"Every weekend without fail."

"That must cause a few headaches."

Paul nodded. "Isn't that the truth. Did you find anything of use in that guy's room?"

I shook my head. "Not really. Say, I heard there was a girl murdered here a while back."

Paul shook his head. "Not in town. Out on the Hampton Road."

I could see there was some pain in his eyes, so I pressed him. "Did you know her?"

Surprisingly, he nodded. "Yes. She did a few shifts here at the pub."

"How long for?"

"You sure ask a lot of questions," Paul protested.

"Sorry. Habit I guess."

He said, "Long enough. They found her two days after she left."

"After she left?"

"Yeah. She was headed north," he explained. "Hitching, like most of them who come through here."

"Couldn't she have taken the bus?" I asked.

"The bus only comes through once a week," he informed me.

"What day is that?"

"On Tuesday."

I thought of Tash. It was Thursday which meant as sure as shit she would be hitching. Damn it.

"She'd still be alive but for Macca Pearce," Paul growled.

Now I was more than a little curious. "What makes you say that?"

"The night before she left, he tried it on with her. Wouldn't take no for an answer if you know what I mean. Luckily, I came along when I did. Who knows what might have happened?"

"Was that a common thing with Macca?" I asked.

"He fancies himself a bit of a ladies' man."

"Did the police have any suspects?" I asked Paul.

"Yeah, Macca. After I told them what he did. They questioned him then cut him loose. No evidence. Even though I made a statement."

The conversation dried up for a moment then Paul said, "You should ask at the roadhouse. Most of the hitchers go there to get rides."

"Why would you say that?" I asked him.

"Because you're interested like the last guy before he shot through. I told him the same thing."

"Did he go there?"

Paul shrugged his shoulders. "I don't know. I never saw him again."

I thanked Paul and as he got to his feet I said, "What do you know about the drugs being sold in town?"

He hesitated before he shook his head and said, "Nothing."

After he'd gone, I went into the main bar and bought myself another beer. More people had come in since I'd last looked. A couple of cow cockies sat at the bar, deep in conversation. Two women, jillaroos by the looks of them, played pool over at a table in the corner. I took my beer, found a seat at a nice quiet table, and did what I do best. Observe.

———

I emerged from the motel the next morning to a beautiful clear blue sky and the lovely stern face of Nicole whose first question to me was, "Are you leaving today?"

Tired after an interrupted sleep on a hard mattress I was in a bit of a mood. "What? And miss your lovely face here to greet me first thing of a morning. I don't think so." There was more than a hint of sarcasm to my voice and as was meant, it didn't go unnoticed.

"Someone got out on the wrong side this morning," she replied with about the same amount of sarcasm as I let her have.

She looked bright and fresh while I on the other hand felt as though I'd been run over by a road train. I was about to say more when my phone rang. I took it out and saw the name on the screen. "Shit."

"Trouble?" Nicole asked smiling at the bastard ringtone I had.

"In the worst damned way," I replied before reluctantly hitting the answer button. I put it to me ear. "I'm sorry."

"Sorry don't cut it, motherfu—"

"Tia—"

"You missed your check-in," she snapped at me. "What frigging good is an agreement if you don't follow it."

She kept on berating me for a good minute and in the end, I held the phone away from my ear. I looked at Nicole who had a broad smirk on her face. "What are you laughing at?"

"I'm sorry, but this is funny."

The voice snarling at me from the phone stopped. I stared at it for a moment before, *"Mark!"*

I put it back to my ear. "I'm still here, my love."

"Who was that?"

"Nobody." I lied hoping it would end there.

"Don't you bullshit to me, Mark Hayes," Tia growled. "Is she why you missed your check-in? You were playing hide the sausage with some skank and didn't—"

I moved the phone away again. Sometimes a little bit of Tia goes a long way.

Looking at Nicole I saw she had her hand out. I gave her a WTF look and she said in a low voice, "Give it here."

Why not? What could it hurt? "It's your ear."

I handed it over and Nicole said, "Senior Constable Nicole Gerber speaking."

There was a back and forth for a moment before Nicole said, "I know." Then there was some more back and forth between them before she handed me back my phone and said, "You're an arsehole."

I rolled my eyes. "What now?"

I put the phone back up to my ear and found that Tia was gone. I looked at Nicole again who said, "She seems nice."

I thought of a snide reply but let it go. "If we're done here, I have things to do."

Nicole shook her head. "The boss wants me to babysit you today, so you're all mine."

"Wonderful," I replied sarcastically. "Are you going to ride me hard?"

She gave me a look. I didn't care, I was beyond it. The last thing I needed was for Tia to have an ally in this damn town.

"Where are we going?" she asked.

"The roadhouse."

———

"How does a woman like you, get to be cop in a shit hole like this?" I asked as we drove along the street in the police 4X4.

Nicole looked at me. "Really?"

"What?" I asked innocently.

"You're going to try a line like that?"

"That wasn't a line," I said.

"You might as well have said let's go back to your place and screw," she said. "It would have been more original."

"It wasn't what I meant," I told her. "I was asking a genuine question. But since you brought the other thing up—"

"Don't even go there," she warned.

"And you shouldn't make assumptions that all men are the same."

"Touché."

"Shall we start again?" I asked.

"Why not?"

"Hi, my name is Mark. How about a screw?"

Nicole chuckled. "You're an arsehole."

"Now you're getting to know me," I said with a grin.

"I've been here three years," Nicole told me. "It's mostly quiet and in spite of what people think, it's not a bad place to live."

"It's bloody hot," I pointed out.

"There is that."

The 4X4 bumped over a pothole. "Rough too," I said.

Nicole glanced at me with a smirk. "That too."

The roadhouse was at the edge of town on the highway. It had four pumps out the front and another two pumps around the side for the large trucks and semi-trailers which came through. The temperature was already climbing for the day and the landscape across the road shimmered with the heatwaves. Along the road, crows picked at what had once been a kangaroo, now a lump of red mince with a hint of reddish-grey fur mixed through. The roadhouse looked like it had once been a Golden Fleece in a previous life, now a privately owned business. I went inside followed by my new friend. We walked up to the counter, and I introduced myself.

The guy behind the counter was called Bruce. He nodded at Nicole and said, "Morning, Nicole."

"Bruce."

"What can I help you with this morning?"

I took out the photo of Jacobs. "You seen him before?"

Bruce leaned forward, squinting. He rubbed at his thinning hair and said, "Yeah, I remember him. He was in here asking about Inge."

"When was that?" I asked.

He stared thoughtfully at the wall behind us as though it would give him all the answers he needed. It must have worked because he said, "This time of the morning about two weeks ago."

I looked around the room and saw surveillance cameras. "You got cameras outside?"

"Sure."

"You mind if I have a look?"

"You can say, no, Bruce," Nicole said. "This isn't police business."

I took out my ID. "I'm a private investigator. My name is Mark Hayes, and I'm looking for the guy who came in here. He's disappeared."

He thought long about his response and said, "Sure. You only want that footage?"

I wanted a whole lot more but with Nicole looking over my shoulder I said, "Yeah, that'll be fine."

"Come into the office."

His office felt like a bloody pie warmer. Small, hot, and uncomfortable, especially with three people squeezed in there. As Bruce searched through the footage I asked, "Do you get hitchers through here often?"

"Sure."

"Did you have one yesterday? A girl." I went on to describe Tash.

"Yeah, I think so."

"Can you find that feed too?"

"Sure."

Nicole said, "What's with the interest in the girl?"

"She came to town with me yesterday," I explained. "I gave her money for a bus."

"The bus only comes through on a Tuesday," Nicole said.

"Yeah, I found that out."

Nicole gave me a curious stare. "You're worried about her."

"Yeah, I am, actually. There's a killer here somewhere and she's on her own." My voice held an edge to it.

"There," said Bruce as the fast-forwarding picture slowed and came into focus.

Jacobs had just entered the roadhouse and walked towards the counter. At the bottom of the picture, I could see Bruce. "What was he doing here?" I asked.

"He introduced himself and asked about Inge."

"What did you tell him?"

"The same as I told the detectives. That she was here the day she left."

"Did you have footage of that?"

"Yeah," he replied. "The detectives took it."

The video rolled on and Jacobs walked back outside. I asked, "Can we look at the outside cameras?"

"Sure."

He changed the feed and did the same as before. A buzzer sounded indicating someone had entered the roadhouse. Bruce looked up. "I have to go—"

"That's okay," I told him. "Do you mind if I keep looking?"

The roadhouse owner glanced at Nicole then said, "I guess it'll be all right."

He went to serve the customer and I sat down on the seat. It was hard and had an imprint of the man's butt cheeks in it. "He needs to get a new chair," I breathed.

"What are you looking for?" Nicole asked.

"I'm not sure."

Finding the footage of the outside cameras, I slowed the feed. Jacobs appeared and as Nicole and I watched, he walked over to a truck driver, and I presume asked questions. According to the tape as I fast-forwarded it intermittently, he talked to another three.

"Why is he talking to truck drivers?" Nicole pondered.

"Did the detectives follow any leads to do with a truck driver?" I asked her.

"I don't know. Tom would, she was the only one they dealt with. The Dubbo detectives treated the rest of us like second-class citizens."

While we watched I saw Jacobs take something out of his pocket and show it to a driver. "What is that?" Nicole asked.

I knew exactly what it was. "It's a small packet of Meth."

Bruce came back before the conversation could go any further. I climbed from the chair, and he sat down. I said, "Find me the footage of the girl from yesterday."

"Give me a minute."

Once more the footage sped up and after a few minutes it slowed, and I saw her. Tash with her backpack. I muttered a curse under my breath. "Is that her?" Nicole asked.

"Yes."

"You know," said Bruce. "Your man wasn't the only one to have come here asking about missing hitchers."

I glanced at Nicole then back to Bruce. "What do you mean? There have been others? How many?"

"Two others in the past ten years."

"Only two?"

"Yeah. I talked to both of them. One was a guy from Port Augusta in South Australia looking for his daughter and the other was a German bloke looking for his niece."

"When was this, Bruce?" Nicole asked.

"I'd have to find it for you. I write everything in my journals. It might take me a time to find them."

"Could you look and let me know when you find them?"

"Sure, Nicole. Should be by the end of the day."

"Thanks, Bruce."

We were attacked by a swarm of ravenous flies as soon as we stepped out the door. Waves of heat radiated up from the roadhouse's cracked concrete drive. We walked over to Nicole's police vehicle and climbed inside. She started the engine and we sat there as the aircon kicked in. I took a notebook from my pocket and started writing.

"You want to tell me about the drugs?" Nicole asked.

———

"I found two baggies in his stuff."

"Why the hell didn't you tell me?" Nicole snapped.

"I don't know. They're not his."

"How do you know?"

"Years ago, his younger brother died of a drug overdose. That's how I know."

"Then what was he doing with them? Just because of something which happened in his past doesn't mean he can't change."

"He must have got them from somewhere," I replied. "Maybe he was asking the truck drivers about them instead of the girl."

"Shit, Mark, you should have told me. Where are they?"

"Back at my room. Do you lot have any idea who is selling them?"

"We've been trying to work that out for a while now."

"You've got no idea?"

She shook her head. "No."

We sat there in silence for a good while. I could sense what little trust I'd earned from her was slowly ebbing away.

"Are we going?" I asked.

"Uh huh, back to your motel to get the damned drugs."

She slammed the vehicle into gear, and we sped off back along the street into town. I glanced at her. "I'm sorry," I said, trying to get some miniscule amount of her trust back.

"Good try but it's a bit late."

We went the rest of the distance back to the motel in silence and I gave Nicole the two baggies. Then she left me there while she went to the station.

I looked at my watch. It was creeping up towards eleven o'clock. Still a lot of the day left. Taking the map which Jacobs had been using, I got in the Commodore and drove out of town.

———

I slowed the V8 and pulled off the side of the road, stopping before a sign that told me I was at Snake Creek. I turned the motor off and climbed out. Cicadas welcomed me with a loud buzz. A couple of galahs called to me from a tall gum, making me look up. Already sweat was coating my brow. I opened the back door and took out a baseball cap which I had thrown in, placing it on my head. A broad-brimmed hat would have been better, but this would suffice.

The bridge looked reasonably new, perhaps a couple of years old and the road that ran across it was about the best I'd encountered so far. About a kilometre long, it was flat and smooth.

I walked past the sign and stopped, looking down into the gully. The hot breeze whipped up, carrying with it the smell of decay, strong, putrid. I looked up and saw the dead kangaroo on the other side of the bridge.

The creek bed was bone dry and had been for some

time. Further along the creekbanks were lined with stunted gums spread out sparsely along the water course. The banks themselves were steep, and the bottom dusty with rocks, sticks, and dead leaves spread throughout.

I climbed down and started to look around. I walked along the creek bed for a good distance, discovering that people like to use it as a rubbish tip. Cans, bottles, papers of all kinds littered the sandy bed.

I kept walking along its winding course, accompanied by the distant cawing of crows, until I figured I was a hundred and fifty metres from the bridge. Turning to start my way back, something caught my eye. I walked towards the far bank where in the shade of a gum I saw a small bag. I bent down and picked it up. Two months. After all this time it was still intact, and it still had the Meth inside.

CHAPTER FIVE

I placed the small drug bag on the counter in front of Nicole. She studied it for a moment and looked up. "Where did you find it?"

"In the creek bed where they found Inge—"

"What were you doing out there?" she asked cutting me off.

"Just looking. As I was saying, it was about a hundred and fifty metres from the bridge in the creek bed. Outside the search perimeter, I guess. Either that or someone missed it. My guess is that it was blown down there by the wind."

"I'll get the boss."

I stood there on the public side of the counter. While I waited, I looked at the missing person's signs on the wall. So many.

"You are just in everything at the moment, aren't you Mister Hayes?" Tom said to me as she poked at the bag of drugs with a pen. "I gather your prints will be on this?"

"About the only ones you'll find."

"Put it in the evidence lockup, Nicole," Tom said.

"You'd better come through, Mister Hayes and make a statement."

I followed Tom through and sat down at a desk. She said, "Nicole will be with you in a moment."

"Sergeant?"

"What?"

"Was Inge on drugs in any way?" I asked.

She stared at me for a moment. "I'm not sure."

"Can you find out?"

Maybe she could see what I was getting at. "I'll make a call."

Nicole came back and took a statement from me. By the time we were finished Sergeant Tom came back too. I could see there was some inner turmoil going on. I said, "There was none, was there?"

"No. No sign at all."

"Have we finished here?" I asked.

"Sure."

I stood up and walked towards the door. Tom called after me, "How long have you been a PI?"

"Seven or so years."

"What's your gut feeling about it?"

"I'm not sure. But if I get one, I'll let you know."

"You do that."

Nicole walked me outside. Once out in the stifling heat I asked her if there was anyone in town I could ask about the missing girls that Bruce mentioned?

"Mark—"

"I won't cause trouble. But if this is the reason that Jacobs disappeared, I need to know."

"There is someone who might know. His name is Jeff Andrews. He used to be the Senior Sergeant here until he took early retirement."

I raised my eyebrows. "That'll work."

"I'll give you his address on one condition," Nicole said sternly.

"Which is?"

"You say nothing about me giving it to you."

"Cross my heart."

———

The address Nicole gave me led me to a small, well-tended house on the edge of town. When I pulled up out front that afternoon, I found a grey-bearded man out in his garden working amongst the roses, chopping dead heads off. He looked up as I walked in through his front gate and said, "Who are you, Slick?"

"Mark Hayes," I replied. "I'm a private investigator."

He stared at me disdainfully. "A pretend detective, huh?"

I let the barb go and said, "I'm trying to find a missing man. He was last seen here a couple of weeks ago."

"Whoever told you that, Slick, lied. I never laid eyes on him."

I looked around the front yard. Everything seemed to be meticulously looked after. Quite a chore considering the climate of the outback. "I mean the town."

"Uh, huh," he grunted. "I figured that was what you meant. What do you think I can help you with?"

"The man I'm looking for was up here looking at the case of the young lass who was murdered a couple of months back. The backpacker. Now he's missing. I was talking to the owner of the roadhouse, and he mentioned that over the years there had been a couple more go missing."

Andrews sighed and took off his gardening gloves. "Let's get inside out of this heat, Slick. Follow me."

We went inside the house. It might have been small,

but it was air-conditioned, and the temperature felt like it dropped about twenty degrees in there. The house was clean and tidy. "You here on your own?"

"Yes, sir. Never married. I saw other officers go through all kinds of hell with their marriages and decided that it wasn't for me."

"I can understand that."

The tone in my voice must have triggered something. "You were a cop?"

"Not for long."

"And you married one?"

"Guilty."

He chuckled. "Slick, don't take this the wrong way, but you must be some kind of galah."

"Can't you see the tail feathers?" I asked, joking.

"Would you like a beer?"

"Sure, why not?"

He went to the fridge and took out two bottles of beer, handing one to me before he sat down. Almost immediately the condensation formed on the outside of the dark glass, and I twisted the top off before taking a pull from the frosty bottle. It tasted good.

"All right, Slick, where were we?"

"You were going to tell me about some missing girls."

He raised his eyebrows as though he thought me presumptuous. "Was I? Let's see. What do you want to know?"

"Bruce said there were two that he knew of. One from Adelaide and another from Germany. They had relatives come through looking for them."

Andrews nodded. "I think I know the ones he means. Was a long time back now. And the one from Adelaide was actually Port Augusta."

I was impressed. "How long have you been here?"

"Fifteen years. I retired two years ago. Tom got promoted and took over from me."

"You said you remember them?"

Andrews took a drink and said, "Vaguely. Like with most backpackers they were just passing through. We used to get a lot back then. Still do get them, although not as many."

"Anyone else ever gone missing while you were in charge?"

"You mean backpackers? People like that?"

I nodded. "Yeah."

He shrugged. "If there was, they weren't reported."

"You're bleeding," I said pointing at the back of his hand.

He looked at the back of his right hand. "Huh, damn roses."

"What about drugs?"

Andrews's face hardened. It was like he became someone else. "That is a whole other problem. Scum of the damn earth those bastards."

"So, there's a drug problem here? I was told no more than usual."

"Even that is too much," he growled.

"You have an idea who is behind it?"

"You could start looking at the Pearce brothers. Or maybe the pub. I heard a rumour the stuff was being sold out of there."

The Pearce brothers I could understand; the pub would also see a rolling business through the doors of the weekend. "You have anyone in mind from the pub?"

"Why don't you start with the stupid barman, Paul?"

"I asked him, and he said he didn't know anything."

Andrews snorted derisively. "He's been busted for drugs more than once, Slick. Go and question him again."

"I will, thanks. You wouldn't have an idea on how they're getting into town?"

"Trucks would be my guess."

I finished my beer. "Thanks again."

When I left Andrews's place, I had more questions than answers.

Who killed Inge Rasmussen?

Were the drugs in any way connected?

Did Jacobs's disappearance have anything to do with the drugs or the investigation into the dead girl?

Were the Pearces mixed up in it somehow?

What was Paul hiding?

And were there more bodies out there?

———

Dinner that evening consisted of steak and vegetables drowned in gravy and washed down with ice-cold tap beer. When I got back to the motel, I made sure that I called Marion Lawler to give her the little which I had and then I rang Tia who I wanted to run something by.

"You remembered," she said answering her phone. Her voice was laced with sarcasm. "How considerate."

"Ha, ha, very funny," I said in a droll voice. "Do you have time for a chat?"

"Sure, what's up?"

I told her what I'd found out so far and how I thought that the body and Jacobs might be linked. Once I'd finished, I asked her, "What do you think?"

"Finding drugs in the creek near where the body was dumped is weird that it wasn't found during the search."

"It is possible it was missed though, right?" I asked.

"Sure. Look what happened to you the other day."

"The time period worries me a little," I said.

"There is that."

"What about Jacobs?" I asked.

"It looks to me he's gone off on a bit of a tangent there," Tia replied. "What is your theory, Sherlock?"

"I think the girl and the drugs are connected somehow."

"I'd believe that."

"And I also think Trent's disappearance is connected there too."

"Follow the drugs," she told me.

"There is something else, Tia."

I heard her sigh. "There always is. Shoot."

"The two girls that have gone missing that I mentioned."

"Yes."

I gave a reluctant pause. "When you get to work tomorrow, could you check the missing person's database and see how many are missing in this area? I reckon there are more."

"I'll see what I can do, Mark."

"Thanks, Tia. You're the best."

"Whatever."

After I'd hung up, I made some more notes in my notebook. After that I had a shower and watched some television before turning in. Tomorrow was another day.

———

I was rudely awoken about five the next morning. Some idiot had forgotten to draw the block out curtain and now the sun streamed in as it tried to incinerate my eyes with its brightness. Then I remembered that I dressed beside the bed the previous night after my shower. I climbed out of bed and ripped the curtains across before returning to the covers.

Two hours later I was woken again. This time to a

knock and someone saying, "Breakfast!"

I groaned and rolled onto my back, trying to get rid of the gravel in my eyes before eventually getting up. I retrieved the tray and sat it on the small bench near the microwave. I lifted the cover from the plate and the smell of fresh bacon and eggs filled the room. I was about to start eating when I noticed the note under the knife and fork. I opened it and read the handwriting.

"Thanks for the show last night. I've got a bun for that sausage if you need it."

Double-shit!

I finished the meal and stealthily put the tray outside the door. I thought it was anyway. But as I straightened up, I looked across the carpark and saw two of the cleaners and the manager's wife looking at me. All three smiled and waved. I found myself wondering which one had sent the note and then dismissed it. This was a work venture. There was no time for any shenanigans.

My first mission for the day was a visit to the library. I figured that if there was anything about missing people over the past years, the town newspaper, or some other newspaper might have caught the story.

I arrived there at nine-thirty, right on opening time. I went up to the counter and asked the librarian if I might be able to use one of their computers. You might inquire why I had to go to the library to use the computer and not do a search on my wonderful technologically challenged mobile phone. Keywords, technologically challenged.

She looked at me and said, "Do you have a booking?"

"Ah, no."

"You need a booking to use them, sorry."

The librarian was probably in her mid-fifties and wore wire-framed glasses which sat atop a pointy nose. She reminded me of a school mistress from back in the day.

Her name badge said her name was Melody. "Miss Melody," I said, "I'm trying to solve a crime which is most urgent. A man is missing and if he's not found quickly, it might be too late when he is."

I showed her my ID. Her eyes widened with concern. "Oh, dear. I'll show you which one you can use."

Five minutes later, I was trolling through everything I could find about missing persons in Western New South Wales.

———

Have you ever set a ringtone on your phone that makes you cringe every time it goes off in public? Mine was a rooster. Not bad, you'd think. Try it going off in a silent library with Miss Marple staring daggers at you for making a noise. I made a mental note to have someone shoot it the next opportunity, and the bloody person who put it on there.

"Hey, Tia," I whispered.

"Are you okay?" she asked. "I can hardly hear you."

"I'm in a library."

"You in the kids' picture book section?" she chuckled.

"Shut—"

"Ahem?"

I looked around to see Judge Judy looking daggers at me. "Shit. What have you got?"

"Not a lot. There were two reported missing girls in that region over the past ten years."

"Is that it?"

"I'm not saying there are some that aren't in the database. Maybe they just haven't been reported. Some runaways often go missing in other places and hitch rides. If they were passing through there and something happened, no one would ever know."

My mind went to Tash. "Thanks, Tia."

"Are you okay?" she asked. "You sound different."

"I'm fine," I lied.

"What did you do?"

She could always tell. I quickly told her about Tash and what happened. Tia said, "You tried your best, Mark. There wasn't any more you could have done."

"Maybe I should have walked her to the bus."

"Uh, huh."

"Anyway—"

I stopped talking and stared at the computer screen.

"Mark, are you still there?" I heard Tia say.

Meanwhile I kept staring at the screen, silent.

"Mark?"

I reached into my pocket and took out the map that I'd found in Jacobs's folder.

"Mark?"

"I'm here, hang on," I said finally.

I ran my finger over the map until it came to rest on the town of Porter Creek, sixty-seven kilometres from where I now sat. "Tia, I have to go. I'll call you tonight."

"Is everything all right, Mark?"

"I think I've just found another one."

I hung up and looked over at Miss Prissy who was still scowling at me. "Could I get something printed off, please?"

She nodded grudgingly and a few minutes later I had the sheet of paper in my hand. It was a picture of a poster of a runaway girl called Eliza Carter who'd left Porter Creek in 2007. She was sixteen, had long black hair, and was just outside of Ten-Cent's age range. But to look at her, you'd have thought her to be twenty.

It was time to go for a drive.

———

Porter Creek was smaller than Friar's Lake. The road to it wasn't much wider than a single lane blacktop which when meeting a vehicle coming the other way, one needed to "go bush" to get by.

From a kilometre away the town seemed to rise out of a semi-treeless plain where it was camouflaged by the shimmering heat waves. The closer I drove the more distinct it became. At first, I saw the large concrete grain silos, giant and silent, standing sentinel over the minions in their shadow, then the smaller houses. An old rail line came out of the haze and joined alongside the road running parallel until it reached the edge of town then cut across in front of me.

As I drove along the main street, I saw that every second building was closed or boarded up. Not surprising considering there were about five cars parked in that part of the town. When I reached the main crossroads, I had to navigate a small roundabout. Centred inside was a small war memorial, evidence that the great conflicts of the world reached even the smallest corners.

I indicated and pulled into a parking bay out front of a small, one-person supermarket. More like your corner store, actually; not far from a tired-looking service station. According to my odometer I'd travelled sixty-five kilometres since I'd left Friar's Lake. I knew one thing for certain, Porter Creek was just as bloody hot.

As I climbed out of the Commodore, a crow cawed, and I looked up to see the black bird circling overhead as though waiting for the town to finally die so it could feast upon the carcass. I shut the door and stepped onto the cracked footpath. Ankle high weeds grew through the cracks. As I walked along, the dust and grit beneath my shoes crackled loudly.

I walked into the supermarket. Passing through the door an audible chirp from a hidden beam announced my arrival. A plump woman in her sixties emerged from the rear of the shop, passing through one of those old ribbon curtains designed to keep flies out. She gave me a warm smile and said, "Hello, there."

I nodded and gave her my best smile. "Hello."

"What can I do you for?"

Good old country greeting. I said, "Do you have pies?"

"Sure. The pie warmer is further along the counter there."

She pointed a crooked finger to my left. "So it is."

I walked over to it and looked inside. Two pies and two sausage rolls. I imagined that was probably all she put out at any one time. "I'll take them both, if that's all right."

It seemed that I'd made her day. She smiled broadly and said, "Not a problem at all. I'll just put them in a packet for you."

"You got dead horse?"

"One or two sachets?"

"One each, please."

I watched her put the pies into two small white paper bags followed by the tomato sauce. She walked back along the counter and sat them next to the register. "Is that all, sir?"

I held up a finger. "One moment."

I crossed to a drinks' refrigerator, studying the small selection before I grabbed a can of Coke. Then as I passed the magazine rack, I picked up a fishing magazine. Once at the counter, the lady punched the numbers and said, "That will be twenty-five dollars, please."

I almost fell over. However, I remained composed and took out my wallet. She said happily, "You wouldn't like a KitKat for an extra three dollars, would you?"

Oh crap. "Why not?"

I paid for the goods and before I left, I said, "Maybe you can help me with something."

Wanting to be helpful after I'd just about paid her wages for the week she smiled and said, "If I can."

I took out the picture of the girl and showed it to her. "Were you in town around this time?"

She looked at me confused for a moment. I reached into my pocket and took out my ID. "It's all right. My name is Mark Hayes, I'm a private investigator."

"Really? How exciting."

"It can be."

"My name is Mildred. Mildred Brown."

"Pleased to meet you, Mildred. Do you recognise the girl?"

She squinted at the picture. "Sorry, I don't have my glasses."

"It's okay. Take all the time you need."

After a moment she said, "Can you tell me her name?"

"The picture is of a poster that was run in the Friar's Lake paper years ago," I told her. "The print is small, but the name is Eliza Carter."

"Oh. Ooh, I remember now. Little Liza. She run off. I'm not surprised at all."

"Why is that?"

"Her father used to give her a hard time. After his wife died, he took to drinking. It used to get the better of him. He used to beat her. Then one day she'd had enough and cleared out."

"You don't know where she went?"

She shook her head. "Good Lord no. I haven't seen her since I gave her the money."

My eyebrows shot up. "Wait. You gave her money?"

Her head bobbed up and down. "I did. Three-hundred dollars."

"Which way did she go?"

"Headed down the road towards Friar's Lake where she could get the bus."

"Was that the last time you ever saw her?"

"Yes."

"How come the posters then?" I asked.

"That was her father. He reported her missing, got the paper involved. Jeff Andrews came out here, he had only just taken over the station at the time. I told him what had happened and that I gave Liza the money to leave."

"What did he say?"

"Just that he'd tell her father he'd look into it. He never took it any further because she was better off."

"Did he hear from her at all?" I asked.

"Ian Carter?"

"Was that his name?"

"Yes, and no he never as far as I know."

"Does he still live in town?"

Mildred shook her head. "He died maybe five years ago. Heart attack."

I nodded. "Okay, thanks, for that."

"Any time."

I picked up all my items and went outside. Climbing into the Commodore, I started the car and set the air conditioning running before taking out my phone. I punched in Tia's number and waited for her to pick up. "Talking twice in one day. That's something special."

"I have a favour to ask," I said.

"Gee, Mark, get to the point. Where's that famous foreplay you always come out with?"

"You know me, Tia. Once I get excited, I have a tendency to go off half-cocked."

"Isn't that the truth. What is it?"

"A girl. Well, she was at the time. Her name was Eliza

Carter. She was sixteen when she cleared out. I think she would have been born in eighty-nine."

"What do you want me to do about it?"

"See if you can find her name anywhere, match it all up. She originally came from a town called Porter Creek."

"Is that the one you had to get off the phone for?" Tia asked.

"Yes."

"Mark, I—"

"Please, Tia. Just put my mind at rest."

"All right, I'll see what I can do."

"Thanks, babe."

———

I went to the pub for dinner. Again. What the heck, I just can't pass up good food. Sausages and chips with onion gravy. Thick sausages, nothing like them. I sat away from everyone in the lounge, just me, a corner table, and my thoughts. I checked in as usual with Marion Lawler before I started.

I'd just finished my feed when Paul appeared. He came across to my table to collect my plate. "How was the meal?" he asked.

"Fine," I replied. I looked up at his face and noticed he had a bruise on his right cheek. "You walk into a door?"

He chuckled and said, "Forgot to duck."

"I hope you got one back on the other bloke?"

"Something like that. You want dessert?"

I shook my head. "I'm good, thanks, mate." Then remembered what Andrews had said. "You got time for a beer after? I'll buy."

"I can't. Things to do."

"You sure I can't twist your arm?"

"Nope."

"Another time, maybe?"

He nodded. "Yeah, another time."

He took the plate and left me there to finish my beer.

My phone rang. Bastard rooster again.

I looked around the lounge and noticed that most diners had left since I'd finished eating. Apart from me, there were only two other couples left. And Jeff Andrews the former senior sergeant.

"Tia?"

"Hey. I did a search on that name for you and came up empty. It's like she doesn't exist."

"Okay, thanks."

"It could mean she's changed her name," Tia pointed out.

"Yeah, sure. Thanks for your help."

"All right, talk tomorrow."

I disconnected, grabbed my beer and got up. Walking across to Andrews's table, I asked if I could join him. He motioned with his knife to the chair opposite him. "You know the one good thing about not being married and living on your own, Slick?"

"No," I said, "but I have a feeling you're going to tell me."

"I get to eat at the pub and not cook whenever I bloody want to. It's the best meal in town."

"I can't complain," I said agreeing with him.

"I hear you were out at Porter Creek today."

"Following something," I replied.

Andrews forked some more of his food into his mouth and fixed his gaze on me while he chewed. He said nothing for a minute until he finished chewing that mouthful. I tried to read his expression, but he was a closed book.

"Is there something you want to ask?" he said, breaking the silence.

"Why didn't you file a missing person's report on Eliza Carter?"

"Sounds like you're questioning my judgement, Slick," he said in a menacing voice. "Spent over forty years on the force, did you?"

"You know I never."

"Then what gives you the right to question my judgement, Slick?" Andrews asked quietly. I could see the fire in his eyes, but I wasn't done.

"You still could have done something," I said and put the printout on the table. "There's no record of her after she left here."

Andrews's eyes narrowed. "What's going on, Slick? Are you here looking for a missing person or trying to find fuckups in my career? Because if you are, I'm the first one to admit that it was far from perfect."

I shook my head. "Just trying to find out answers to a few questions."

He stood up. "And I was just trying to have a peaceful meal. Looks like we were both shit out of luck."

I watched him leave and then picked the picture back up. Once again, I had more questions than answers.

A thin, blonde waitress appeared and started to clear away Andrews's leftovers. I smiled at her and said, "At least you look in better shape than the last waitress."

She gave me a confused look. Sometimes my humour is wasted.

I pointed at my cheek. "Paul."

"Oh, yes, right. Him and Bruce from the roadhouse got into it in the carpark last night. Stupid if you ask me."

"Really? What was that about?"

She shrugged. "I wouldn't know."

CHAPTER SIX

The next day was Sunday. A day for family, a day for gatherings, a day for worship.

I started it off in the usual way. Out of bed early, had breakfast, and went over my notes. However, being a Sunday I wasn't sure what I was going to do. Everything would be shut. I thought about going out to where Inge Rasmussen's body was dumped but dismissed it. The fight between Paul and Bruce the roadhouse owner was interesting and had piqued my curiosity. Especially with Paul's drug background.

I took out the map that had been Trent's. I looked it over. I looked at Porter Creek. Another road cut across to Hampton around forty kilometres from there, and another travelled just over fifty back to Friar's Lake. It was a rough triangle with the lake and a large chunk of bushland at its centre. If I were a serial killer and I wanted a place to bury bodies, that wouldn't be a bad place.

But first, I decided I wanted to talk to Paul.

I looked at my watch. The pub probably wouldn't be

open until ten so I decided that I might as well take a walk around town until it opened.

Outside, the morning was definitely cooler than the day before. The flies hadn't diminished any, but I'd take small mercies. Then I saw Sergeant Tom and I knew the good start to the day was about to get worse.

"What did I tell you, Mister Hayes?" she asked me in a terse voice. "I think I can remember mentioning something about not causing trouble. Do you remember something like that?"

"Yes, ma'am, I think you said something like that."

Her butt came away from the bull bar where she'd been leaning against it. "Yet here I am because I get a complaint about you harassing the locals."

She was dressed in jeans and a white singlet top. She obviously worked out on a regular basis, and as a person of the opposite sex I could appreciate such things. "You look lovely this morning, Tomika. Not on duty?"

She scowled at me. I shrugged. I guess I have that effect on some women. They just can't handle my wit. She said, "I'm always on duty."

"All right, I'm guessing that it was Andrews who made the complaint. Yes?"

"No."

That was a surprise. Upon hearing about it I was certain it would be him. A cicada buzzed by as I waited for Tom to continue. When she said nothing, I took the lead. "I assume you're going to tell me who it was. Give me a right of reply?"

"You don't need to know. However, I'll let you go with a warning. If you cause any more trouble, I *will* run you out of town. Understood?"

"How long have you been here, Tom?" I asked.

"Ten years."

"Have you ever wanted to get out?"

She shook her head. "I fought three transfers to stay here. I like being a country copper."

"So, you know Jeff Andrews well then?"

"As well as anybody I guess."

"In all your time here did you hear anything about Eliza Carter?" As I spoke, I took out the paper and passed it over.

Tom looked at it and handed it back. "From what I've heard she was a runaway getting away from her abusive father. Nothing more."

"Would it surprise you to know that there is no record of Eliza Carter anywhere?"

"How would you know that?"

"Because I had my ex-wife do a search on her."

Tom frowned. "Ex-wife?"

Obviously, Nicole had failed to mention that part. "She's a Melbourne homicide detective."

"I see. Anyway, that doesn't mean much. She could have changed her name to keep away from her father."

"That's true," I allowed. "But look at it from my point of view. Since I've been here, I've found out about two missing girls, one other that's possible, add to that an unsolved murder, and there's a PI missing too, and the town has a drug problem."

She snorted derisively. "The town does not have a drug problem."

"According to Senior Sergeant Jeff Andrews it does."

She walked towards me. For a moment I felt nervous but then she stopped. Admittedly she was within arm's length but at least she never hit me.

She said, "No more trouble."

I raised my right hand. "I'll try."

Tom turned and walked back to the vehicle. I cocked my head to one side and watched her go. Yep, you've got to love a woman out of uniform.

"You're not staring at my arse, are you, Mister Hayes?"

"No, ma'am. I blinked at least twice."

Tom opened the door and stopped. "Tell me something. How is it that your wife never shot you?"

I smiled. "Would you believe my unbelievable charm?"

I got a smile. It wasn't much but it was there. Tom shook her head and climbed in. She started the Nissan, put it in gear and backed out of the park. Then she surprised me again. Before she drove away, she gave me a wave.

———

I walked into the pub a little after ten. It smelled of stale beer and carpet deodorizer. Apart from myself and the grey-haired guy behind the bar, there was no one else. I walked up to the bar. The man straightened up from placing something on a shelf under the counter. He looked at me and said, "You'd be the PI that's looking for the guy who shot through."

"And you'd be right."

He put out a hand across the bar. "Bluey Edwards. I own the pub."

I took his hand in mine. His was a firm grip, not limp like half the limp dick ones you get from disinterested parties you meet these days. I liked him straight away. "Mark Hayes. Pleased to meet you."

"You want a beer?"

I shook my head. "I was actually looking for Paul."

"That dickhead? He's on his day off."

"You don't have a high opinion of him?" I asked.

"Aw, he's all right. Turns up to work when I need him. Just does the odd dumb thing every now and then."

"Are you talking about the fight?" I asked curiously.

"Yeah. Sometimes I wonder what goes through his brain. Are you sure you don't want that beer? I'll buy."

"How long have you lived here in Friar's Lake?"

"Best part of fifteen years. Came in from the east coast and never went back."

"You know what, Bluey? I will take that beer."

He poured me a mid-strength beer and one for himself. I pulled up a seat to the bar and sat down.

"What are you going to do now for the day?" he asked.

"I thought I might go and have a look at the lake."

"The dry hole, you mean. The lake is dry this time of year. Be a few weeks before water starts coming back into it. When the storms come."

"Does it do that every year?"

"Yes. As regular as clockwork."

I thought and said, "I still might go anyway. What is the best way?"

"Doesn't matter. You can get in from either road. The one to Hampton is probably the best."

With a nod I thanked him and then said, "Can I ask you a couple of questions about Inge Rasmussen?"

An uncertain look crossed his face, but he nodded anyway. "Sure."

"Paul said she worked here. Did a few shifts, I believe his words were."

"Yeah. Although it was more than a few shifts," Bluey explained. "She worked here for almost two months. Bloody good worker, too."

"Did she have any trouble with anyone?"

Bluey shook his head. "Inge? No. She was liked by everyone."

"Paul said she had some trouble with Macca Pearce."

"Who doesn't?" he growled. "That drongo is a waste

of space. His mother should have dropped both of them on their heads at birth. Why all the questions about Inge, Mark? I thought you was looking for that other bloke."

"I am, but I can't help but think the two are tied together."

He nodded slowly. Thoughtfully. "I see."

"One other thing, before I go. You ever hear of any backpackers or hitchers disappearing around here?"

"All the bloody time," he growled.

For a moment I wondered if he was actually serious. "What do you mean?"

"I hire back packers all the time and they always shoot through on me. It's like they've had enough, and they get up one morning and see you later, I'm out of here."

"They all do that?"

He shook his head. "Not all of them. Some hang around and say goodbye. Others will wave on their way out the door."

"But some just left?"

"I exaggerate a lot, Mark, it comes from running a pub," Bluey said. "Probably only a couple did that."

"Were they women? Girls? Long dark hair, aged between say seventeen and twenty-three?"

"What are you saying?"

"I don't know." But I had the answer I needed.

————

I went out the Hampton road, over the bridge at Snake Creek where Inge Rasmussen was found and then on further until I reached the turnoff for the lake. The sign indicating the turn had the obligatory shotgun pellet holes that were prevalent right across the outback, although not as bad as it once was. At one-point signs like that seemed to have an open season on them.

The Commodore crunched down off the bitumen and onto the gravel road. It had patches which were rutted and others that held large potholes. It snaked through the trees, some of which were large gums, making it a slow drive in.

Eventually it opened up and I came to a stop. The outline of the lake was easy to see. It was marked by tufts of reeds and grasses. Every so often a large gum stood guard over the bank.

I climbed out of the Commodore to a chorus of galahs in the trees behind me. I could hear other parrots as well, talking, screeching. I closed the door and walked to the edge of where the water would come to when the lake was full.

From the bank drop off, I judged that the lake, when full, would be no more than four feet deep. Which was probably why it dried out each year. There were gouged out pieces around to my left where it looked as though vehicles had accessed it over the years.

I turned and looked back past the Commodore at the trees. It wasn't like I was pressed for time. I took one step, and then another. It wasn't long before I was amongst the gum trees looking for signs.

———————

Three long, hot, dusty hours later I finished having found the sum total of nothing. Nothing substantial anyway. I found plenty of rubbish. Empty bottles and cans, some lolly and chocolate wrappers. I even found the shell of an old Holden HQ. But that was it.

I had a water bottle in the car and when I emerged from the trees, I walked the short distance across the clearing to where it was parked. I leaned in and grabbed the bottle, releasing it immediately. The damn thing was hot. Some idiot had left it in the sun.

I heard the vehicle before I saw it. From the sound it was making it was moving fast along the road in. When I finally laid eyes on it there was a great cloud of dust following closely behind.

A brown Land Cruiser skidded to a stop no more than ten feet from where I stood. A familiar face leaned out the passenger window. "Well, well, well."

Three holes in the ground. "I see you're free of the lockup," I said to Macca Pearce.

"No thanks to you," he growled.

He opened the door and stepped out of the still running vehicle. I tensed just in case he was going to start trouble. He said, "What are you doing out here, Mister Nosey?"

"Bird watching."

"Smart arse, hey?"

"I'm just minding my own business. Now that I've done it, I'm going back to Friar's Lake."

"Are you now?"

I ignored his comment and climbed into the Commodore. I started the engine and put it into reverse, backing the car up and performing a three-point turn before driving out the way I'd come.

I must admit I felt relieved to get out of there and away from Macca Pearce and his brother. For a few moments there I had visions of getting the tar walloped out of me.

Once I reached the road I indicated to turn left then paused. I was almost halfway to Hampton and with a shrug turned the car in its general direction. Might as well go and have a look for myself, I thought as I put the pedal down and the power from the motor pressed me back into the seat.

————

If I thought Porter Creek was about dead, Hampton was a rotting carcass. Most of the shops in the main street were closed except for the obligatory one-stop supermarket and a servo-cum-garage. Only some of the houses were occupied, while the ones that were vacant were overgrown and had holes punched through the old fibro walls.

As the saying goes with small towns, 'if you blink, you miss it'. That was Hampton. I reached the edge of the dying community and turned around. I pulled up in the main street outside what had once been the post office. Now it had paint peeling off the exterior and the front window was smashed.

I climbed out of the Commodore and closed the door behind me. In the silence of the main street, it sounded as though I'd shoved the thing through to the other side. I turned almost a full circle before looking at the one-stop supermarket and wondering if my expense account could take the hit.

I began walking across the street towards it, not bothering to lock the car. Besides, who would steal the beast? Maybe someone desperate to escape the town's mortality but that was about all.

The floor of the shop was wood and was spongy under foot just inside the entrance. The place itself smelled like an old house that had been closed up for ten years. The magazine racks were all but empty as were the food shelves. I looked at the one and only newspaper dated six months earlier.

"Can I help you with anything, Mister?" a voice said.

I looked towards the old wooden counter where a young girl, maybe fourteen, long red hair, freckles, stood expecting a reply. I was about to say something when I saw the noticeboard. "I'm fine for the moment, thanks."

"Suit yourself."

I stepped closer to the noticeboard and looked at the picture on it. It was a poster of an Aboriginal girl, asking anyone who had seen her to contact the number below. According to the faded scrawl at the bottom her name was Lisa, and she was seventeen.

Turning to face the counter I asked the redheaded girl, "Has this girl been found?"

"Her? No."

"Now long has it been there?"

"Like forever."

"Can I take it?"

"Sure."

"Take what?" a voice demanded from somewhere out in a back room.

I saw the girl cringe and mouth the word, "Shit."

A man appeared, and like the girl, had red hair. He pushed her aside as he breasted the counter. "Get out of the way, girl."

She backed away not taking her eyes off the bastard. From where I stood, I could smell his body odour. He was unshaven and had dark circles around his eyes, scabs on his arms. It was hard to determine his age. Something nagged at me saying drug user.

His eyes narrowed at me as though he suspected I was up to something. "What do you want?"

"I asked the young lady if I might take the poster that was on the noticeboard," I explained.

He looked at it then gave me another suspicious expression. "Why?"

"I'd like to have it?"

"I told him it was all right, Dad," the girl said.

Without looking, his hand shot out and shoved her in the chest. The girl staggered back and hit the counter. "Shut your mouth, girl," he snarled.

That got me mad. "Your girl don't know her place, huh?"

"She's learning," he growled.

I walked over to the counter. "You'll teach her, huh?"

"Every day. Ever since her mother left, she's been getting teached what for."

I glanced at the girl who had shrunk back even further. I said in a whisper, "Come here."

The man frowned. My voice was so low that he didn't hear me. I said it again.

"What?" he asked confused and leaned in closer so that his top half was over the counter.

Reaching out, I grabbed a handful of greasy hair and pulled down as hard as I could. His face slammed into the countertop with a loud bang. His daughter gasped audibly as he reeled back, blood already flowing from his broken nose. He slumped to the floor holding his face.

"What the fuck, man? You broke my nose."

I walked around the counter, squeezed past the girl, and grabbed him by the shirt collar. Using all my strength I dragged him out from behind the counter and into the open, leaving a thin trail of blood.

"What are you doing, man?"

I dropped him and said, "You're an arsehole, you know that. You ever lay your hand on your daughter again and I hear about it, I'll be back for you."

"Screw you," he blurted out defiantly.

My right foot lashed out and the toe of my boot caught him in the ribs. It wasn't hard enough to break anything, but it did hurt. "I'm not sure I heard you right."

"All right! All right!"

I walked over to the noticeboard and took the poster off. It left a defined rectangle in its place from having been there so long that the board around it had discoloured. I looked around for the girl and couldn't see her. On the floor the man let out a moan. "Where do you get your drugs?"

"What?"

"Your drugs? What are you on? Ice."

"Go and fu—"

I stepped forward.

"The pub, the pub."

"In Friar's Lake?"

"Yes," he gasped.

"Who from?"

"I don't know," he replied.

Another step.

"I don't! I swear. I get them delivered. I leave money in a certain place, and they leave the Ice."

"You don't think I'm that dumb, do you?" I sneered.

"It's true," the girl said as she reappeared carrying a backpack. "They drop them off and take the money."

I gave him a disdainful look and walked out the door. As I crossed the street, I could hear shouts coming from the shop. I turned to go back but then I saw the girl emerge. "Can you give me a ride to the Lake?"

I stared at her. "You don't even know who I am."

She shrugged. "You kicked his arse so you can't be that bad."

"You got someone to stay with?"

"Yeah."

"All right then."

We got in the beast and started back to Friar's Lake. As we hit the outskirts of Hampton I glanced at her and said, "What's your name?"

"Helen. What's yours?"

"Mark Hayes. What's your dad's name?"

"Henry Miller. Why did you want the poster?" Helen asked.

"I'm a private investigator," I explained. "I'm up here looking for a missing person."

"Is she the one you're looking for?"

"No. I'm looking for a man."

"Oh."

"Has your father always been like that?" I asked her.

"No, only since mum died a few years back."

"I thought he told me she left."

"That's the drugs talking," she said. "She died from an aneurism."

"Sorry."

"It's all right."

"Not for you," I pointed out referring to her situation.

"Maybe you doing that to him will make him see sense," Helen said.

"Do you believe that?"

"No. I'm done," her voice cracked as she tried to keep her composure. "I—I'm not going back this time."

———

The white 4X4 came out of nowhere. One moment we were driving along the narrow strip of blacktop, the next we'd been crunched, and the Commodore was upside down. I would find out a few things later on, one of those being that the police knew stuff all.

They had no suspects. The vehicle involved disappeared. The accident investigation concluded that we were hit by a white 4X4 with a bulbar on the front. Which narrowed down the field no end because every second damn station in western New South Wales had a white 4X4.

The only good news was that Helen wasn't too badly injured seeing as it was the driver's side which took the brunt of the impact.

Someone had been keen to put me out of action. And for the time being, they'd done just that.

CHAPTER SEVEN

I had bruised ribs and a concussion. A couple of cuts and scrapes but other than that I was fine. Except that some doctor in his early thirties from Ireland decided that it would be best that I stay in hospital where they could keep an eye on the head injury. It wasn't pub food but when you're hungry you take what you can get.

Nicole came to see me on the day after the accident. The accident investigation guys were done. She stood at the foot of the rock-hard bed and actually looked concerned. "How are you feeling?" she asked.

"I wish I was back in my motel bed."

"That bad, huh?"

The sickly smell of hospital disinfectant was a constant reminder of why I hated them so much. I nodded. "Worse."

"What did the accident guys tell you?"

"Bugger all. Four-wheel drive, bull bar, no idea who."

"Do you have any idea who it could have been?" Nicole asked.

"I know who it wasn't," I replied to her question.

"Who's that?"

"The Pearce brothers."

"How do you know that?"

"I saw them out at the lake when I was there," I explained.

Nicole took her notebook out and started taking some notes. "What were you doing out at the lake?" she asked me.

"Looking around."

"What happened?"

I told her about the brothers turning up and the few words.

"So, they had a reason to do something like this?"

"I guess, but you're overlooking one thing," I told her.

"Which is?"

"They had a brown vehicle, not a white one."

"All right, tell me about what happened at Hampton."

"Helen, shit, where is she?" I blurted out.

"She's been taken back to her father," Nicole said.

Pain shot through my head as I tried to process what Nicole had just told me. "When?"

"This morning, Jace took her home. She's a minor, Mark. The law states that she should be with her parents. Or in her case, parent."

I could only imagine what would happen to her once she got home. Her old man was a nut. Worse, he was an Ice addict, and he was almost certain to belt the shit out of her. I swung my legs over the side of the bed and started to get up.

"Whoa there, Mark. What are you doing?"

"I'm going to get that kid back."

Nicole came around to the side of the bed just as I was about to rip the IV line from my arm. She placed a hand on my chest and said, "Get back in the bed, Mark."

"He's going to belt hell out of her, Nicole," I said. "Someone needs to stop him before he does it."

"Mark—"

"Tell me this," I demanded cutting her off. "Did she go home willingly?"

Her silence said everything.

"I didn't think so. The guy is an Ice addict. He started to shove her around while I was in the shop. I gave him a reminder while I was there how he should treat his daughter. She was coming to Friar's Lake to stay with someone."

"Who?" Nicole asked.

"I don't know."

"Anything else?"

"I asked him where he got his drugs from. They are delivered out there like by special courier. Can you believe that? He calls a number, and they deliver."

"He said that?"

"Yes. And it was confirmed by his daughter. Now, get out of my way, Nicole. I have somewhere to be."

She never moved and it pissed me off even further. "Damn it—"

"How are you going to get there, Mark? Your car is a bloody write-off."

"Is there a problem here?" Tom asked as she entered the room.

Nicole told her what I'd just relayed, and the sergeant pointed at the bed. "Get back in there. Nicole is right, we are bound by the law. However, we can look into it."

Relief at last. "All right."

I got back in and covered myself up. Tom made the call while Nicole took some more notes. I stared at her and she must have sensed it. She looked up. "What?"

I shook my head and shrugged. She went back to what she was doing while I looked on. When she was finished, she said, "Your ex-wife reached out last night."

I rolled my eyes. "Great."

"Don't be like that. I actually think she genuinely cares that you're still alive."

"What did she want?"

"Just to ask about the investigation," she explained.

A food trolley rattled along the hallway. I wrinkled my nose. Nothing like rock-hard roast and sloppy mash for lunch. Nicole said, "Would you like me to see if I can get you a burger?"

"You get me a pie and chips and I'll marry you, no questions asked," I replied.

She grinned. "Is that a proposal, Mister Hayes?"

"It's anything you want it to be. Just get the food."

Nicole chuckled and I saw how her eyes sparkled and her face seemed to light up when she did. "You should do that more often. It suits you."

She turned red and shuffled uncomfortably. "I'll go and see what I can find you, okay?"

"It doesn't appear that I'm going anywhere."

"I should think not," Tom said. "There is a case of assault you need to answer a few questions about."

"Shit."

———

Nicole came through, and just in time because when she walked into room 6, I was about to chew through something inedible that looked a cross between roadkill and by-products of a slaughterhouse.

My smile must have looked like the Grand Canyon when she re-entered the room because it sure felt like it. "You're a lifesaver."

"Don't eat it all at once."

Ripping open the packet I found the pie already had sauce on it. "You beauty," I whispered and took a bite. "Just right."

Nicole frowned. "What's just right?"

"The way you can hook in and devour it without burning your tongue."

A knowing look came to her face. "You too, huh?"

"Is there any other way?"

My doctor came into the room and stared at me demolishing the pie. Then he saw my chips and said, "I'll give you fifty dollars for them."

"Ha ha, piss off. Sorry, Doc, but you don't have enough money to buy these from me."

"Are you sure?"

An idea came into my head. "I tell you what. You let me out of here and I'll give them to you."

He licked his lips, brain cycling at a million miles a minute. I could see the uncertainty in his eyes and then his better judgement overcame his want for the food. "No, I can't. You need someone to keep an eye on you. You should be in here for five days."

"They look really good, Doc."

"Mark," Nicole said, "you heard the man."

I reached over, picked up a well-salted hot chip and put it in my mouth. The doctor said, "Do you have somewhere to go where someone can keep an eye on you?"

I looked at Nicole.

"No!" she said with a shake of her head.

"Think of it as community policing," I said to her with my best grin.

"No."

"Nicole, please?"

"No. I mean it, Mark. No."

———

"You have a really nice place," I said to Nicole as I looked around.

"Shut up," she said, glaring at me. "I have no idea how this happened."

"I do. You said yes."

"Don't look so happy about it," she growled. "I didn't agree to marry you."

It really was a nice place. The yard was neat and tidy, inside looked as though it had been freshly painted and the furniture added a personal touch. I sat on the lounge and leaned back. My body ached almost as much as my head. Nicole passed me the television remote and said, "There is food in the fridge, water in the tap, coffee and sugar in the pantry."

"Thank you."

"I should be home by six. Are you going to be all right until then?"

With a groan I said, "I'll be fine."

"One more thing. If you leave the toilet seat up, I'll shoot you. Understood?"

"Loud and clear." I had a thought. "If it's all right with you, could you swing by the motel and get my bag and notes, please?"

Nicole put her hands on her hips. "Do I look like your personal courier service?"

I could see she was still getting over the series of events that had led me to becoming her new house guest. "That's all right. If I feel okay, I'll go for a walk later and get them."

"You'll do no such thing. I'll get it after work."

"Thanks, Nic."

She shook her head and gave me a stern look. "Uh, uh. No way. You do not get that personal with me, Mark Hayes. Not after what you did."

"What did I do?" I asked innocently, unable to think of anything I might have done to get her offside.

"You lied to me about the drugs."

"I didn't lie," I pointed out. "I just didn't tell you about them."

"Don't split hairs. I'll see you when I get home."

Nicole left, and I took my shoes off and stretched out on the lounge. It felt like I'd gone from a backpacker's hostel to a 5-star resort. It took a whole two minutes before I'd closed my eyes and fallen asleep.

————

When Nicole arrived home, she brought with her, just not my things, but a better mood and a meat tray from the local supermarket. "You feel like a steak?"

"How is it that you aren't married yet?" I asked her.

"Are you offering?" she said holding up a sixpack of beers.

"I'm there."

"Do you think you can cook the meat while I do some vegies?"

I got off the lounge and said, "Let me at it."

Nicole started preparing the vegetables and I got the meat ready. I turned to her and said, "What happened with Helen?"

She said, "The matter is still under investigation, Mark. Tom informed Child Services and they will take it from here."

"Hopefully they'll figure something out and get her away."

While the dinner cooked, we talked and drank beer. It was actually nice to have some good adult conversation rather than talking to myself.

Eventually the discussion came around to chosen careers. "Why did you become a PI?" Nicole asked me.

"I got pushed out of the force," I told her honestly.

"Why would they do that?"

"I had an issue with authority," I answered truthfully.

"And that was it?" she asked.

"I found a young mother bludgeoned to death in her own home after I was asked to do a welfare check. Her little girl was hiding under the bed in another room. When I found her, she was utterly petrified. She'd wet herself she was that scared."

"How terrible."

"It really cut me when I saw how it had affected her. The detectives had a suspect but no evidence. The little girl was left so traumatised she turned into a mute. So, the case was left to run into a dead end."

Nicole eyed me for a moment before she said, "But you weren't willing to let it go, were you?"

"No. I started watching him. Tia warned me to let it go and I did. While she was home. The days we worked different shifts I did some extra. I didn't know what I was going to do I just knew I had to do something for that little girl."

"What happened then?" Nicole asked me.

"I became obsessed. I guess it's why I am taking more than a passing interest with this case."

Nicole drank some more of her beer. "I guess I can understand that. But it's not healthy."

"You can say that again. At the same time, I began to change, and my marriage went downhill. Eventually, I snapped and I beat the crap out of him. Ergo, end of career. I was lucky I didn't end up in front of a judge. That was the trade off."

"What happened to the suspect you assaulted?"

"He was nailed two months later," I explained. "And the kicker was that Tia was part of the team that got him."

"Ouch."

I took a pull of my beer. "Now you know my dark secret, what about yours?"

"There's nothing bad about mine. I'm your cliché. Grandfather was a cop, Father still is a cop. Just. Now I'm a cop."

"Aren't you boring?" I commented.

"I'm as boring as I want to be."

"What about Mister Boring?"

"Why do you think I'm here?" Nicole asked.

"I see."

She shook her head. "No, I don't think so. Something happened to him. He lost his job and started going to these self-help groups. I don't know what they were meant to do, but all they did was screw him up. He even stopped showering. Said it was all part of some screwed-up ideology. After a while he started to smell worse than a week-old corpse in the sun."

I screwed my nose up.

"Yes, it was that bad. Have you ever smelled one like that?"

"No."

"It's a sickly-sweet odour—" she stopped and shivered. "I think the steaks are ready."

"You're still hungry after that?"

"I spent almost thirty bucks on the bloody things. I'm eating them."

———

I stuffed one of Nicole's firm breasts into my mouth and bit the erect nipple. She cried out in ecstasy and grabbed fistfuls of my hair to pull me closer. I switched to the other one and elicited the same response. She ripped off her open shirt and then went the bra which I had pulled down under her breasts.

She reached down and fumbled with my belt, the rattle of the buckle telling me she had it undone. Next came the button as she tried to get it back through the hole. It was tight and she cursed at it. I leaned forward and kissed her passionately. "Wait," she said breathlessly. "It's almost there."

The button sprang free, and her hand dived inside my pants. I was already hard. Nicole leaned forward and whispered into my ear, "Have you ever smelled a week-old corpse?"

I pulled back. "What?"

Her eyes went dark. "It's sickly-sweet."

She leaned forward and licked my neck and repeated her words. "It's sickly-sweet."

"Are you all right?" I asked her suddenly losing interest in what we were doing.

She pulled back from my throat. She nodded and then smiled showing me two rows of pointed teeth. "Yesss!"

I shot up in bed, sweat pouring from my brow. The sun was blazing in through the window and brightly filled the room. I looked beside me. There was no one there. What a bloody relief that was.

I slumped back, my head on the pillow. The words from the dream replayed over and over in my mind. "It's sickly-sweet. It's sickly-sweet."

Suddenly I bolted upright again in the bed. "Holy double-shit!" I exclaimed.

I knew where Trent Jacobs was.

CHAPTER EIGHT

I waited for Nicole to go to work before I left the house. How hard is it to find a hire car in a small town like Friar's Lake? Bloody hard when they don't have a hire-car place. So, I went along to the local car yard and bought one. A thousand dollars and I had a Ford Falcon which looked as though it had hit more trees than lightning. I swear nearly every quarter panel had a dent in it, even if they were small. But I was assured that the motor would run fine. And I needed wheels.

The bloke who sold it to me was named Cyril. He had a bushy beard and wore an unironed suit. When I told him I wanted a car he almost fell over. When I chose the Ford Falcon, he threw in a month's rego and a tank of fuel. It kind of made me wonder which might run out first. The rego, the fuel, or the car itself.

I climbed into it and turned the engine over. With a cough and a roar, it blew a cloud of blue smoke from its exhaust. The accelerator stuck and I stomped on it a couple of times. Cyril gave a chuckle and said, "You might want to watch that."

"Thanks."

"I couldn't interest you in some work to get the panels done?" he asked me. "My brother has a panel-beating business."

"No, I'm fine."

I pulled out onto the street and turned right. To get to where I wanted to go, I needed to traverse the main street. I just hoped the Falcon made it. I came to a cross street with a give way sign and slowed to turn left. I eased the brakes on and with a shriek and a shudder the bloody things grabbed and almost put me through the windshield.

"Note to self, watch the brakes," I muttered.

Maybe the Festiva wasn't as bad as I thought. I indicated and turned left, depressed the accelerator and felt the Falcon shudder before the automatic gearbox kicked in. In the rear-view mirror I saw another cloud of blue smoke rise into the air. So much for going through the main street unnoticed.

I passed the pub and was approaching the police station when the nightmare I'd been trying to avoid came true. One of the police vehicles was backing out of the driveway. I wrenched hard on the wheel and the Falcon turned left. I parked it against the gutter and hoped like anything that my presence had gone unnoticed.

The police vehicle pulled in beside me. I slunk down lower in the seat hoping the driver would just move on. I heard the door open and close.

Nope.

The crunch of boots on gravel grew louder and a shadow fell across the window. Then came the tap on the window and I knew I was screwed. Without looking up I wound down the window.

"Step out of the car, sir."

It was Jace. I looked up and I saw a broad smile split his face. "Hello there, Mister Hayes. Are you trying to abscond?"

I shook my head. "No, no. Just out for a drive."

"Does Senior-Constable Berger know you're out and about?"

"Sure does."

He reached for his portable radio mic. "Let's find out."

"No, wait."

"Is there something wrong?"

I tried to think of an excuse but between the pain in my head and the damn cicadas I could come up with nothing. "You don't like hot chips, do you?"

———

"What the hell were you thinking?" Nicole asked through clenched teeth. I could virtually see the flames in her eyes and the smoke coming out of her ears. Her face was red, and a small vein seemed to be popping in her throat as her muscles tensed. She had just closed the door behind her to the tearoom, I guessed so she could yell at me.

I held a hand up in protest. "Wait. I—"

"Wait my arse," she barked. "You're going back to the hospital this afternoon. End of discussion."

"Nic—"

"Don't bloody Nic me. From now on it's Senior Constable Berger. Understand?"

"Just listen, please."

"Why?"

"Because I have something important to say. I wanted to check it for myself before getting you all involved," I explained. "But I guess it's too late now."

Nicole folded her arms. "I'm listening."

"Take me for a drive and I'll show you."

"Show me what?" she asked.

"I'm not sure."

She shook her head in disbelief. "Then you're off to hospital."

"Please, Nicole. Just trust me. If it doesn't work out, you'll only have lost a bit of time. And then I'll go back to the hospital."

A pained expression crossed her face. She shook her head and said, "This had better be something, Mark. For your sake."

———

We drove along the Hampton Road in silence. The Nissan 4X4 bounced every time it hit a rough patch which didn't do much for my headache that had come back with a vengeance. Inside felt like little men were banging away with picks trying hard to make my life a misery. We hit another and I let out a groan.

Nicole glanced at me from behind aviator sunglasses. "Are you all right?"

"I'll live."

"That wasn't what I asked."

"I'm fine."

Another kilometre of silence was followed by five more before Nicole said, "Are you going to tell me what this is all about?"

After a moment of thinking I said, "I was dreaming about you last night."

"Good grief."

"Not like that," I lied. "About what you said about the smell of a week-old dead person."

"Uh, huh. And?"

"I think I know where Trent is."

Nicole stabbed at the brake with her foot. The Nissan shuddered as the brakes tried hard not to lock and it came to a halt in the middle of the road. "You are un-bloody-believable," she fumed in exasperation. "You couldn't have said something before we left?"

"I didn't want to just in case I was wrong, and your boss called out the army for no reason."

"Where do you think it is?"

"Where you found Inge Rasmussen. I think he was there when I found the drugs."

"What makes you say that?" Nicole asked.

A car drove around us, and the driver beeped its horn. "You want to keep driving?"

She pressed the accelerator and the 4X4 moved off. I said, "I could smell him. I thought it was some roadkill, but when I woke up it hit me that the wind was coming from the wrong direction."

"I hope you're wrong," she said in a sullen voice.

"So do I. But I'm not."

We kept driving until we reached the bridge and Nicole pulled the Nissan off the road where I had parked the Commodore on my first visit. We got out and walked towards the gully. I looked back down into the dry wash. To the west a storm was brewing, and thunder rumbled. The sky above the horizon had taken on a hammerhead gray colour and the air was smelling damp. The tempera-ture was starting to drop in a hurry which meant the storm wasn't far off. Our arrival caught the attention of a couple of sheep in the paddock opposite the gully and they stopped eating to see what we were up to.

"Where do you think it is?" Nicole asked me.

I sniffed the air as a gust came through. This time the

wind was coming up the gully from the direction I had found the small bag of Ice. "In the culvert."

We climbed down into the creek bed and Nicole took her small torch off her equipment belt. "Wait here."

I did as I was told and watched her disappear into the gaping concrete tunnel before us. I could see the light flashing around and then heard Nicole say, "You were right."

I wished I hadn't been.

Nicole emerged from the concrete culvert and straightened up. I winced. "Bad?"

"He's been there for a while. The animals have been at him. We won't get a firm ID until everything has been run."

"I was hoping I was wrong."

"Well, you weren't. I'll call it in."

I stood there staring at the gaping concrete maw. Thunder crashed overhead and the wind picked up even more, whipping fine grit from the bottom of the creek bed through the air. I wondered how long he'd been in there. How he'd died? What had led him to this end? I knew one thing almost for certain; it wasn't Ten-Cent. This had something to do with the drugs. And the body being dumped in the same place as the last one, gave me reason to believe they were both connected.

I dug out my phone and called Marion Lawler.

"Hello?"

"Marion, it's Mark."

"Oh, Mark," she said in a caring voice. "Are you all right? Feeling better?"

"I'm fine. I just wanted to call you with an update. Keep it to yourself for the time being but I think we just found Trent's body."

"Oh, no," she gasped. "Was—was it him?"

I thought about my response for a moment and eventually said, "No."

Then it started to rain.

I stood with my back against the Nissan. There were small puddles on the ground and the air seemed to be crisper, washed clean by the fast-moving storm. Tom had arrived and was talking to Nicole. While waiting, Nicole had taped off a large section of the gully and shut down the road. After which she took a camera from her Nissan and began taking pictures.

I kept out of the way while all this went on. Now they had to wait for the circus to begin.

Nicole came over to me. "We got a wallet off the body. It's his."

"I don't think there was any doubt, was there?"

She shook her head. "Not really."

"Do you know how he died?"

"No, the body is too messed up."

The sound of an approaching car drew our attention back along the road towards Friar's Lake. It was coming fast, and I heard Nicole say, "It didn't take long for the scavengers to gather."

"You know the car?" I asked.

"George Timmins. He's a reporter for the paper."

As the car neared, I could see that it was an early model Mercedes Benz. It came to a hurried stop at the roadblock and the driver's door flew open. A tall, thin man climbed out bringing with him a camera.

Nicole walked towards the reporter, stopping him before he could get any closer. "Who is it, Nicole?" he blurted out. "Is it someone we know?"

"No comment, George."

"Come on, Nicole. You must know something," he said as he tried to coax something out of her.

"I know nothing."

"What?" he asked incredulously.

"It's the body of a female," I told him.

"Really?" he said digging into his pocket for a notepad.

Out of the corner of my eye I caught the glare Nicole gave me. I nodded. "Yes. She's about four-feet high—"

"Good grief," he said writing furiously. "A kid?"

"She's got grey hair and a long tail."

He stopped and gaped at me. "What was that?"

"Piss off and annoy someone else," I growled at him. "Let the dead lie in peace."

"It's my job."

"It's a prick of a job."

————

I caught a ride back to town with a pimply-faced young bloke who was going to have to take the long way around to reach his destination. The road was still damp from the storm, but it was quickly drying from the renewed heat. He dropped me in the main street, and I went to the pub instead of back to Nicole's. I bought myself a beer. The young barmaid who served me spoke with an accent and I figured her to be another backpacker.

I found a stool at the end of the counter and sat quietly, watching television. Even though the volume was turned down, I could get the gist of what was going on in the world. Murder and mayhem along with people holding up traffic on the Sydney Harbour bridge in some climate change protest. Every now and then I glanced around the bar looking for signs of anything suspicious.

I finished my beer and bought another. I was halfway through it when Bluey appeared. "Hey, Mark, how's it hanging?"

"A little to the left, today, Bluey," I replied.

"Too bad, huh."

"Yeah."

"Say, I heard on the grapevine about something going on out along the Hampton Road. You hear anything?"

I nodded. "Body."

His eyebrows shot up. "Shit. Really?"

"Yeah."

"Fuck. I wonder who it is?" he said out loud. "You know?"

"Nope," I lied and took another sip of my beer.

"You dining in tonight?"

"Nope, I'm dining with company, I think."

He nodded. "I heard you were over at Nicole's. How are you doing after your misadventure?"

Misadventure my arse. Someone had tried to kill me. "A little sore but I'm getting there."

"I got just what you need," Bluey said with a wink. "Be right back."

I watched him hurry away and grab a bottle from a high-up shelf. On his way back he grabbed a glass.

"This is the good stuff," he said to me with a smile. He poured it and sat the full glass in front of me. "On the house. Put hairs on your chest that will."

I took a sip and felt the burn. I gave a little cough and Bluey nudged my arm. "What did I tell you?"

"It's—it's something, that's for sure."

He chuckled. "I keep the bottle for special occasions."

"I see you've got a new girl on tonight," I said nodding towards the barmaid.

"That, my friend, is Helga. From Sweden."

"You're yanking my middle leg, aren't you?" I asked him suspiciously.

"I shit you not, Mark. That's her name."

"All right, I believe you."

"Shame I needed her though. I had to fire Paul."

I stared at him. "Why?"

"He was becoming too unreliable."

The front door opened, and two men walked in. They were smartly dressed and were of solid build with dark hair. They looked around the room before walking towards the bar. Bluey said, "Customers, got to go."

"Catch you later."

"Yeah, mate."

"Thanks for the whiskey."

He smiled and winked at me. "That isn't whiskey."

When I got back to Nicole's around six, she still wasn't home. I got dinner started and had it ready by seven. Sausages and mash. Simple but tasty fare. I was about to eat when she walked through the door, looking about done in.

"You look like shit," I said.

"Charming, thanks," she replied. Then said, "I feel like it."

"Any news?" I asked.

"I can't tell you much, Mark," she said. "It's an ongoing investigation. The detectives have arrived and I'm here for a shower and then I have to go back into work."

"Bugger."

"Yeah."

"I cooked your dinner so at least that's something."

I little brightness came into her eyes. "Wonderful. What is it?"

"Bangers and mash."

"I might have to marry you, you know," she said with a tired grin.

"Go and have that shower. I'll keep it hot for you."

Nicole disappeared and a few minutes later I heard the water go on. I left my own meal to wait so we could eat together. When she reappeared, she had on a pair of loose shorts and a white singlet top.

"You'll look good going to work in that," I said jokingly.

Nicole smiled at me. That same tired smile she had before. "One thing I learned long ago. If you're eating before you go to work, don't put on a clean uniform."

"Fair enough."

We ate in silence. The only sounds being the clink of cutlery on the plates. I was chewing my last mouthful when a thought came to me. Possibly something I should have thought of long before that moment. I'd been so wrapped up in the whole missing girl thing that I couldn't see the forest for the trees. "Nic, has anyone looked for Trent's car?"

She stared at me. "Why do you ask?"

I shrugged. "I only just thought of it."

"I don't think so. Now that the detectives are here and it's a murder investigation, I would expect they'd look into it."

"Ok."

"Stay away from it, Mark. It's a murder investigation."

I held up both hands. "I will not upset the detectives."

She eyed me suspiciously. "What does that mean?"

Nicole's mobile rang before I could answer. She sighed and picked it up from the table. "Berger."

The voice on the other end was audible, but not clear enough to understand what they were saying. After a few moments, Nicole said, "I'll be there directly."

She hung up and pushed her plate away from herself. "I have to go. I'm sorry to leave you the mess. It was nice, by the way."

"Go," I said. "I'll take care of it."

"Thanks, Mark. Don't wait up."

"Just take care, Nic."

CHAPTER NINE

Nicole still wasn't home by the following morning. I guessed the detectives had her doing scut work, or at least something they felt was below them. After finishing breakfast, I figured I might go and see a couple of blokes about a car getting run off the road.

I went to retrieve my car from where I'd left it near the police station. As luck would have it—even if it was bad—it was still there. I opened the door; keys were still in the ignition. I was beginning to feel like even the thieves knew something I didn't.

I climbed into the driver's seat and after putting the belt on I wound the motor over. It fired right away. Well, at least it was reliable. I put it into reverse and started to back out. I don't know what it was, but I'd say some kind of sixth sense because I suddenly stomped on the brake and the Falcon stopped dead.

Looking in the mirror I saw the black Audi. It had stopped almost behind me, the driver figuring I was going to back out must have done the same as me. Slowly it moved forward and continued past. Inside I caught a glimpse of the two men I'd seen in the pub the night before. I reached out through the side air-conditioning hole and gave them a wave. They drove on.

I cruised along the main street until I reached the newspaper shop and parked parallel to the kerb. Opening the Falcon's door, I looked around before going inside to pick up the local paper. On the front cover was a big headline regarding the body that was found. I read a few lines and then folded it. I'd read it all later.

At the counter I found a plump woman with glasses and iron-grey hair. She had a lined face, but her smile was warm. "Good morning, sir."

"Morning. How are you today?"

"I'm well, yourself?"

"I'm getting there," I replied, paying her for the paper.

"Terrible thing, isn't it?" she said in a troubled voice. "I wonder who the poor soul was."

"I'm sure we'll find out eventually," I told her. Then I asked, "Could you tell me where I can find Ken Murphy's place?"

She smiled. "Yes, love. It's ten kilometres out the old Moonee Road. It starts out as a narrow strip of bitumen and then turns to gravel, so don't be worried about going too far when you get to it. Then after that another three Ks and you'll see a large sign near a gate. The place is called Darling Station."

"Thank you."

I walked outside into the bright sunshine and… "Oh, crap."

"Aren't you meant to be home resting?" Nicole asked me. She was seated on the bonnet of the Falcon.

"Mind you don't scratch the duco," I cautioned her.

"Answer the question."

"I'm fine, the headaches have gone."

"Uh, huh."

"Are you going home?"

She nodded. "Yes. I'm going to crawl into bed for a week."

"Then it's a good thing I won't be there then," I told her. "You'll have peace and quiet."

"Where are you going?"

"Out to the Murphy place."

"Why?" Nicole asked tentatively.

"I wanted to talk to the Pearce brothers," I replied.

"You'd do well to stay away from them," she said.

"Has Trent's car turned up?" I asked, changing the direction of the conversation.

Nicole picked up on it I could tell. "Mark—"

"I'll be fine, promise."

She sighed. "I'm too tired to argue, Mark. Just be careful. Those pair are trouble."

Looking at the Falcon, Nicole winced. "You're not taking this shit heap, are you?"

"It's all I have."

"Take my car," she said.

I frowned. I didn't even know she had one. "You sure?"

"Yes. Leave that there and I'll have it towed."

I looked at it and shrugged. "Have at it."

———

Hidden away in the garage Nicole had a blue Isuzu D-Max turbo diesel 4X4. It drove like a dream and when I hit the corrugations on the gravel road it rode just as well. The surrounding countryside was flat sheep grazing land. The paddocks were almost bare but with the storms new growth would come. Still, whether it would be enough to stave off a new drought was anyone's guess.

The lady at the paper shop had been right. The

bitumen road was narrow, and at one point I had to go 'bush' to avoid a truck carrying a load of sheep coming the other way.

Once I hit the gravel I drove across a couple of flood-ways, indicators standing two metres tall. The creeks they crossed were bone dry, one even having the carcass of a sheep in it. Emus strutted along the side of the road looking for the feed which grew alongside. Of a night they would be replaced by kangaroos.

I found the sign that the woman mentioned. Big, bold letters telling me I'd reached Darling Station. What she'd failed to tell me, however, was that the homestead was a further ten kilometres from the gate.

By the time I reached the house I was glad that I didn't have the Falcon. I had serious doubts whether it would have made the journey. I pulled up in a large turn-around. To my right was the homestead, ahead of me, a large machinery shed, and to my left, a shearing shed and yards.

A young bloke no older than nineteen came out to meet me from the machinery shed. His clothes were covered in dirt and grease, much the same as his hands which he was wiping on a stained rag. "Can I help you, mate?"

"I'm looking for Macca Pearce and his brother," I said.

He gave me a surprised look and scratched his head. "Really?"

"Yes, why?"

"No one comes looking for those two unless they're dressed in a cop uniform."

"Makes for a pleasant change then, doesn't it?" I replied.

"It makes for something different, that's for sure."

"I'll take it from here, Reese," a gravelly voice said.

The young man looked at the man approaching us

and raised the rag in his hand. "Righto, Happy. Catch you later, chief."

"Yeah, see you later." I turned to meet the man who stopped in front of me. "Mark Hayes," I said.

"Happy Morris. Well, that's what the guys call me. I'm foreman for Ken Murphy. What can I do you for?"

"I was looking for Macca Pearce and his brother."

His eyes narrowed suspiciously. "You got a badge?"

I shook my head and took out my ID. "No, I don't have a badge. I'm a private investigator. And before you ask, they're not in any trouble that I'm aware of."

"That would be something different," he growled. "Good workers the both of them, just have to keep them off the piss."

"I saw that first-hand the other night."

"Hmm. I think they're out cleaning troughs. Come with me and we'll go have a look. Leave your four-wheel drive there."

I followed him over by the machinery shed where we climbed into an old Land Cruiser with a tray back. He started it and then we took off along a dusty track. "The boss is in Sydney for a week," Happy told me above the roar of the vehicle. "That leaves me in charge."

"How big is the station?"

"Fifty-thousand hectares. Twenty-thousand sheep."

"That's a fair size. What do you do for water?"

"We've got a river and bigger than average dams. We purchase water and when the river is running, we're able to fill the dams to get us through."

"What if it doesn't rain one year?" I asked curiously.

"The dams can hold enough for three years providing we don't overuse them. When drought hits, we've got another station in Queensland that can take the extra sheep. We just truck them up there and bring them back when it's possible."

"Ever had to do that?"

"A few times."

We continued along the track following a fence line until we reached a steel gate. I climbed out, opened it, and then closed it after Happy had driven through. From there he pointed the Land Cruiser in a northerly direction until we reached the trough the brothers were cleaning.

Climbing out of the battered Land Cruiser, we walked towards them. When the brothers saw who it was, Macca took a step towards me, his upper lip curled in anger. "What the hell do you want?"

"Back off, Macca," Happy warned him. "He wants to ask you two clowns a couple of questions."

"Like what?"

"Did you guys see any white four-wheel drives on the Hampton Road the other day when I saw you?"

"Why?" Johnno asked. "What do you want to know for?"

"I went out to Hampton after I saw you blokes and had a run-in with the shopkeeper out there. On—"

"That was you?" Macca asked incredulously.

"Me what?"

"Gave Henry a touch-up."

I nodded.

"Good, he's been asking for it for a while now," Macca said.

Something puzzled me about his comment. If the bloke had been asking for it, I couldn't imagine Macca and his brother letting it slide. "Why is that?"

"Damn crack head. Drug addict. Gives his daughter a hard time."

"You ever had trouble with him?" I asked.

"Once or twice," Johnno said.

"Give him a touch-up?"

"Him, no."

This puzzled me. "Why not?"

Macca snorted derisively. "For an investigator you sure don't know shit."

His comment got my hackles up a bit and my eyes narrowed. "How about you tell me."

"The guy has connections in the drug world," Macca said.

"He's just an Ice addict."

Macca shook his head. "No, it's more than that. Some guy a year or so back gave him a belting in the street. Couple of days later a couple of guys showed up looking for him."

"Henry?"

"No, the other bloke."

"What happened to him?"

"He disappeared," Johnno said, eyes wide for effect.

"It's just a tall tale," Happy said. "You clowns should know better than to spread bullshit like that."

"It isn't bullshit, Happy," Macca said. "You know it isn't. They turned up not long back when that other guy was asking questions."

"Whoa, wait," I said hurriedly before he could continue. "What blokes?"

"The guys in an Audi," Johnno explained.

An Audi? The one that I saw? "What colour?"

"Black."

Shit. "You said they came to town after the guy started asking questions. Which guy?"

"The bloke you were looking for," Macca said.

My mind whirled. These strangers sounded like hit men. But if Trent was taken out professionally, was it just coincidence that he ended up in the same place virtually as Inge Rasmussen? Or was her murder really tied to the other disappearances?

"Where did they come from?" I asked them. "Do you know at all?"

They shook their heads. "Has to be close for them to get here so quick."

"Or they flew. Maybe to Hay or Griffith and drove the rest of the way." I'd come for information about one thing and ended up with intel on another.

"Tell me this. Who is selling drugs out of the pub?" I asked.

"We figured it was Paul," Macca said eventually. "But he's not smart enough to be doing it on his own."

"You know how they're getting it into town?"

Macca smiled. All his anger towards me seemed to be gone. "That's something you'll have to work out for yourself."

"You weren't on drugs the other night, were you?" I asked them both.

Macca shook his head confirming my thoughts about the pair. "No, we don't touch the shit."

"Thanks for your time."

I turned away but Macca stopped me. "I still owe you for then," he said talking about the pub.

I spread my arms. "I'm here if you want me."

He chuckled. "You might be all right after all. Sing out if you need help with anything."

"I will. Thanks."

"And by the way, we never saw a white four-wheel drive."

———

Before I left Darling Station, I sent Nicole a message telling her I'd be home shortly and I needed to talk. What she sent back was that she'd been called back into work. Well, I'd have to go it alone.

When I arrived back in town I pulled up outside the pub and went inside. There were a few people there, but I was looking for Bluey and he was nowhere to be seen.

I walked up to the bar and spoke to the barmaid on duty where he was. She shrugged. "He left earlier and went somewhere."

"All right. You don't have a number I can reach him on?"

She reached under the bar and came up with a mobile phone. She gave me an apologetic look. "Sorry, he's left it here."

Damn it. "You weren't on last night by any chance?"

"Sure was."

There were two guys come in here in suits. Had a look of city folks about them. Did you, by any chance, happen to see them?"

"No, sorry."

"No worries, thanks anyway."

"You know where I can find Paul?"

"Sure, his place is a block back behind the pub. Twenty-four Hurst Street."

"Thanks again."

I left the pub and walked across the footpath towards the Isuzu. I placed my hand on the door handle and was about to get in when I changed my mind. Paul's place wasn't far away so I decided the exercise would do me good so I walked.

The house was easy to find. It was an older weatherboard style construction on stumps about a metre off the ground. I walked up the steps and knocked on the door. By the third knock it swung open by itself. It hadn't been properly secured.

"Paul? You home?" I called out.

No answer.

At this point, had it been a movie I was in, I would

have taken out a personal weapon and crept stealthily inside. But this wasn't the movies, and I don't carry a gun. Though it didn't mean I wouldn't go inside.

I made my way slowly along a hallway which fed two bedrooms, one to the left and another to the right.

At the end of the hall were another two doorways. One fed into the kitchen and the other the living room. I took the kitchen first but found it empty. There was a plate of partially eaten food on the table which appeared to have been sitting there since the night before judging by the flies which were crawling all over it. Beside it was a half-drunk beer.

That in itself didn't bode well.

The kitchen joined with the living room, so I didn't have to backtrack cross the hallway to reach it. That was where I found Paul. He was on the lounge with a syringe still in his right arm and his eyes wide in death. On the lounge beside him was an empty bag. The skin around his mouth was blue and a thread of dried saliva glistened from the corner of it. I studied the body for a moment. Whoever had done this had screwed it no end.

One: they left the food. Who stops halfway through the meal to shoot up?

Two: the needle was in his right arm. From what I'd seen in the bar he was right-handed.

For a moment I considered calling the police except that would cause me more problems than I wanted at that time. Besides, he was dead, there was nothing more that could be done.

Time to go.

I hurried back to the main street and climbed into the Isuzu. I thought again of Paul. His death had all the hallmarks of a professional job. A sloppy one, but professional none the less.

The question was, where did I go from here?

CHAPTER TEN

I went back to the pub. The same girl was still behind the bar, and I waved her over to me. I pointed to a CCTV camera which covered the bar. "Can I get a look at your footage from the other night?"

"I don't know," she replied. Her voice held an uncertain tone.

"What's your name?"

"Rose."

I took out my ID and said, "Rose, I could really use your help. I'm trying to track down someone who could be very dangerous."

"Are you like a cop or something?" she asked me, swiping one of her long dark hairs back from her face, putting it back in place with the rest that hung down her back.

I smiled to ease her tension. "Or something."

"Well, all right. But if I get into trouble with Bluey, I'm telling him everything."

"That's fine."

Rose took me back to Bluey's office. It was small and

cramped and it looked as though he had some kind of aversion to tidiness. Rose set me up on the computer and then went back to her job. I surfed through the vision from the previous night until I found what I was looking for.

Clicking the mouse, I froze the picture. The screen shot wasn't the best, but it would have to do. I pulled out my phone and took a photo of the two men. Then I made a call.

"What now?" Tia asked, her voice barely able to contain the resentful tone she used when speaking to me. She must have sensed a disturbance in the force or something as most Star Wars fans say.

"I need your help."

"To do what?" she asked testily. "I'm busy. Is your life in danger?"

I surprised her by saying, "It could be."

"What have you gotten yourself into now?"

"I'm going to send you a picture of a picture," I explained. "I think the guys in it are hitters."

"Mark—"

"From what I have been able to gather from a couple of sources they've been in town before. They were here when Trent disappeared."

"Why are you bringing this to me?" Tia demanded.

"Because you, I trust. This is all to do with drugs and I don't know who's caught up in it."

"Mark, this is only a small town. Why would any of the big boys be interested in it?"

"I don't know. Maybe we're looking at it the wrong way. What if the drugs are being funnelled through here in a different way?"

"You've lost me."

"What better way to bring drugs into the region than through a small, out-of-the-way town?"

"You mean Friar's Lake is the starting point of the operation?" Tia asked.

"It could be."

"If they were flying them in, they'd need an airstrip somewhere."

"There's plenty of flat land out here," I told her. "I thought the same as Trent, that they were coming in on trucks. But if what I think is true, then the trucks are the distribution mechanism."

At the mention of Trent's name, the conversation went quiet. It was a long moment before Tia said, "Is there any word?"

"Nothing." I thought about telling her about Paul but dismissed it. Instead, I said, "I have to go, Tia."

"Be careful, Mark."

I disconnected and closed the security vision. Then I sent the picture through to Tia who sent me a message to acknowledge receiving it.

Returning to the bar I thanked Rose for her help and went back outside. I was about to climb into the Isuzu when two men in suits approached me. "Mister Hayes, mind if we have a word?"

I saw Nicole standing behind them. I nodded. "Sure."

"Come with us to the station?" suggested one of them, a tall bloke with curly hair.

"Are you supplying the coffee?"

The other detective, a shorter, stockier man said, "I'm sure the senior constable can arrange something."

I shook my head. "No, I asked if you were going to do it?"

"I said—"

"Mate, I know all about people like you. Blow into town, think your shit don't stink. Get the little bloke to do your dirty work. Fuck off."

"Then I'll arrest you—"

"That won't be necessary," the curly-haired detective stated. "If it means that much to you, I'll make the damn coffee."

"Thank you. Now, how about we see those badges of yours."

————

They put me in the interview room. Made it all official with a camera recording everything that was said. Nicole excused herself and Tom came in to supervise while they carried out their questioning.

The detectives' names were Rogers and Ellis. Ellis was the good cop, Rogers the arsehole. So I was led to believe. They went through the preliminary bullshit for the recording before asking me questions.

"Why are you in Friar's Lake, Mister Hayes?" Ellis asked.

"I came looking for a fellow investigator."

"Was that Trent Jacobs?"

"Yes."

"You're a private investigator, is that right?"

"Yes."

"Who hired you?" Rogers asked.

"A lady."

"What lady?"

I said nothing.

"It's a simple question?"

Still nothing.

"We'll come back to that," Ellis said. I could see Rogers was pissed already. This was going to be fun. I don't mind detectives, I just dislike arseholes.

"What's your interest in the Inge Rasmussen case?" Ellis asked.

"Don't have one." It was a lie and I guessed they both

knew it. Which they did.

"Then why were you asking about it?"

"I figured the death of Trent and the girl might have been connected."

"In what way?" I could see he was curious.

"Drugs."

Over their shoulders I saw Tom frown.

Rogers said, "That's a big assumption on your part."

I shrugged. "Not really."

"Explain."

I took a sip of my coffee before saying, "Trent got side-tracked by the drugs and started asking questions about them. Then he disappeared. When I went out to where the girl's body had been dumped, I found a bag."

"That could have been dumped there at any time," Ellis pointed out.

"Or someone screwed up and missed it."

The barb struck home. These two were the investigators who caught the case.

"How did you know to look for the body where it was?"

"I used my nose." Which wasn't a lie. "Tell me this, how did he die?"

"Preliminary findings say he was shot."

"Where?"

"In the head."

"Professional hit?"

"You're not the one asking the questions," Rogers snarled. "We are."

"Let me make an observation, then," I said. "Trent was asked to come here to investigate a murder possibly linked to the Ten-Cent Killer—"

"That case is years old, you stupid knob," Rogers growled. "This isn't even his old killing ground."

I ignored him. "The killings of the girl and Trent are

linked through drugs. If you can't see that then you need a new profession. Also—"

"Here we go," Rogers mumbled.

"There have also been a number of girls gone missing around here in the past thirteen or so years. I found at least four—"

"You don't know that," Tom said from behind them.

My eyes narrowed. "Four. Two were reported, one left home and wasn't classed as missing. Another was an Aboriginal girl. Who knows what went on there? Maybe she just didn't fucking matter."

"Calm down, Mister Hayes," Ellis said in a low voice.

Shit, I was going to have to do this myself. These pricks were hopeless. "Do you have any idea who killed Trent?"

"We're following a couple of lines of inquiry," Ellis said without committing to anything.

I stood up.

"Where do you think you're going?" Rogers asked. "We're not done. You can't leave."

"I'm doing just that. If you want me, I won't be too hard to locate. Besides, you've got other things to worry about."

Rogers glanced at Ellis. "Don't leave town."

"If I do, I'll let someone know."

I walked out of the interview room and was followed by a less than happy Tom. She grabbed me by the arm and spun me around. "What the hell was that?"

"What was what?"

"That, in there," she snapped, pointing her finger toward the interview room.

"Those blokes are as thick as bricks. I've been in town a few days and I already know more than they do."

"Oh, yeah, well how about you tell me because this is

my fucking town and I want to know what the hell is going on in it."

I could see the fire in her eyes. "You know as much as I do."

I walked outside only to be followed by Nicole. "Are you all right?" she asked me.

"Yeah, I will be," I replied. "Do you have a moment?"

"Sure."

"I need to borrow your vehicle until tomorrow."

"Why?"

"I need to drive to Griffith to follow something up."

I could see she was conflicted. The drive would take the best part of four hours both ways. "Look, don't worry, I'll take the Falcon."

"No, no. It's all right. But I need to know what you're doing?"

"If I tell you, then I drag you into it and it'll put you on the wrong side with your boss."

Nicole's expression grew stern. "Tell me, Mark."

"I'm going to check out a couple of guys who I saw in town last night. They were at the pub. I think they could be the kind that make problems go away."

"You mean hired hit men?"

"Yeah."

"What makes you think that?"

"I was told that when Trent was killed, they were in town and there was another incident a while back and they were in town again."

"That could be a coincidence," she said.

"Tell that to Paul from the pub."

She looked confused. "What about Paul?"

Shit. "What I'm about to tell you, you never got from me. I don't have time to deal with the fallout."

"Just tell me."

"Paul is on his lounge right now dead as a dodo from someone giving him a hotshot."

At first, she looked at me like I was stupid. Then she realised I wasn't joking. "Jesus Christ, Mark, how do you know this?"

"I was in his house not long before you lot came and found me."

"Damn it," she said taking me by the arm. "We have to go back inside."

I shook her hand off and stood firm. "No. I can't go back in there. Make up a reason to go there and see for yourself. His needle is in his right arm. He's right-handed. There was half-eaten food and half a beer on the table which means they killed him last night. No one stops eating halfway through their meal to get high. When I went there to see him the door was open, so I walked in. So, I'm in the clear. I didn't kill him."

"I never said you did, but you didn't report it—"

"Damn it, Nicole," I cursed through gritted teeth. "I saw the two blokes at the pub last night and then again this morning. They drive a black Audi. They pulled up behind me when I was about to back out. At first, I thought that they stopped because I might run into them, but now I'm not so sure."

"So, you're saying these guys killed Paul?"

"That's exactly what I'm saying. Paul and Trent."

"Why?"

"It has to do with the drugs."

"What drugs? Listen, we have to tell the others."

"No." My voice was firm, almost harsh.

"Something is very wrong in this town, Nic. Don't trust anyone."

"What about Tom and Jace?"

"No one. I'll tell you more when I get back, all right?"

I think she was still confused about it all, but she

agreed. "I'll give you until tomorrow night. Then I go to Tom."

"Thanks, Nic." I don't know why I did it but for some reason I took her by the shoulders and pulled her close, kissing her on the lips. I stepped back and for a moment I was horrified by what I'd done. "Nic, I—"

She leaned in and kissed me back. "Be careful."

———

I was almost halfway to Hay when my mobile rang. I fumbled with it, tried to run off the road and into a ditch before gathering it and hitting the answer button. "Hayes."

"It's me, dopey."

"Tia, wonderful."

"Don't sound so happy to hear from me."

"I'm always happy to hear from you, babe."

"I'm going to puke," she mumbled.

"I take it that this isn't a social call to tell me how much you care?"

"I have an ID on those two men in your shitty picture."

"Already? I was just on my way to Griffith to see if I could dig up something there. I figured they would come in through the airport."

"Andrew Martinelli and Craig Phillips."

"Why do I get a feeling I should know them?" I asked.

"They work for Pete Agosti."

"Organised crime Pete Agosti? The biggest importer of 'vegetables' in Melbourne?" I was being sarcastic but what the hell. Agosti was about as dangerous as they came. He knew where all the bodies were buried because he put them there himself. "Shit."

"You're certainly in it this time around, Buster," Tia said.

"What I'd give to have a gun right now," I said.

"You need to get out of there, Mark. Just leave it."

"Can't do that," I said as I slowed to do a U-turn. "Thanks, Tia. I'll call you tonight."

"What are you going to do, Mark?"

"Something stupid."

"I was afraid of that."

Pete Agosti. Wow, that really changed the landscape. It looked like he'd branched out. I needed to get back and tell Nicole.

A car appeared in the distance. It was the first one I'd seen in a while. I looked down at my speed to check it automatically and saw the Isuzu was on a hundred.

The car came closer, grew larger. I stared at it and frowned. It was a dark car.

The distance between us closed until I could see it properly. The vehicle was black. A black Audi.

It flew past me at speed and looked to keep going. I felt a wave of relief wash over me. I looked in the side mirror and saw the taillights come on. The rear end seemed to lift from where the driver had stood hard on the brakes. Then the Audi turned and came after me.

My foot went down on the accelerator, and I felt the Isuzu respond. It shot forward at a steady rate, the speedo starting to climb. Looking in the mirror I could see the Audi closing like a black bullet. I was hopelessly outclassed.

It caught me in no time and began to pull up alongside. I looked out the driver's side window and saw that the passenger one on the Audi was down. The passenger's arm appeared out the window, pointing a handgun towards me. I stomped on the Isuzu's brakes just as he fired. The window beside me shattered, spraying glass everywhere inside the cab. I stomped on the brakes again, and the Isuzu slowed with a shudder. I was swearing out loud as I shifted my foot across to the accelerator and pressed down hard. The Isuzu shot forward once more.

Up ahead the Audi had stopped at an angle across the road, trying to block my path. The two men had climbed from the vehicle and stood near it. It took me only a moment to work out what they were planning to do.

They both opened fire at the same time. I could hear the bullets hitting the front of the D-Max. Making a split decision, I turned the wheel hard right and ran the vehicle off the road. It reared up as it bounced through a drainage ditch, and I hit my head on the roof. Thank God it didn't break an axle.

Next came the fence. The Isuzu punched through the wire and out into the dry paddock beyond. The shooters and their Audi fell far behind, still on the road. Me? I headed cross country. Where I'd end up, at that time, I had no idea. The main thing was that I was still alive.

CHAPTER ELEVEN

I picked up a gravel road I don't know how far away from the bitumen. I drove through another fence to get onto it and then turned right, the tail end of the Isuzu slipping to the left until I corrected it.

I followed the road until it met another which headed north, then it in turn joined a third which headed east again. I checked the fuel gauge and it looked fine. At least I had enough diesel for now.

The gravel road turned north and then back west as it did a large circuit. I passed a few houses on small farms as I went. I could have stopped and asked for help, but this was trouble they could do without. Besides, if they had children…

I kept checking my rear view. Not that it was much good because the large rooster tail of dust blocked out the view of everything behind me. The land either side of the road was flat. A lot of paddocks had sheep grazing lazily on the sparse grass, oblivious as to what was happening beyond the fence.

My phone rang. I looked at the screen, this time

without trying to kill myself. I pressed the decline button and tossed it on the passenger seat.

It rang again.

I let it go.

It stopped and started once more.

I reached across and accepted the call. "I'm a little busy right now."

"Mark?"

It was Nicole. "Yeah, it's me."

"Are you all right? You sound weird."

"It's the corrugations in the gravel road."

"What are you doing on a gravel road?"

"Those guys in the black Audi found me. Who did you tell I was going to Griffith?"

"No one, honest. Are you all right?"

"Yes, I'm just peachy," I replied. "They must have been watching me or—"

I hit the brakes and the Isuzu slid to a halt in the middle of the road.

"What was that, Mark?"

"I think they're tracking me," I said as I climbed out and started going around the D-Max. I still had the phone so I could hear Nicole.

"Where are you, I'll send some help?"

"I have no idea," I said checking the wheel arches. I mean, that's where they hide them in movies.

I found nothing. I looked in the cargo carrier and found it, just tossed in. I grabbed it and threw it into the ditch beside the road.

By now the dust was starting to clear and I could see back along the way I'd just come. There was a second cloud of dust reaching up into the blue sky. "Shit, shit, shit."

"What's wrong?"

"They've found me again."

"Mark, listen to me," Nicole said in a calm voice.

"You'd better make it quick because I'm about to have company."

"Look in the back seat of the D-Max."

"Nic, I—"

"Do it," she snapped.

I opened the rear door in the crew cab and saw a blanket on the floor. "Great, thanks. I'll have somewhere to hide."

"Under the blanket."

I lifted it and saw the gun case. It had a combination lock on it. I put Nicole on speaker in time to hear her say, "Four-eight-six-two-four."

I followed the instructions she gave me, and the lock popped open to reveal a well looked after rifle. Also, inside was a packet of Winchester 243 rounds. I lifted the rifle and opened the box of bullets. As I loaded the rifle, I asked her, "What are the sights like?"

"They're good. Just don't kill anyone with it."

"I guess we're about to find out."

Racing around the front of the Isuzu I used the bonnet for an arm rest. I worked the bolt and housed a round ready to fire. I brought the stock onto my shoulder and rested my right cheek on it so I could see through the telescopic sights.

Oh, how good this thing felt. Just because I didn't have a gun, did not mean I couldn't use one. I sighted the crosshairs on the centre of the windscreen. I wasn't aiming to kill them, but if it happened, then so be it.

I squeezed the trigger and the weapon slammed back into my shoulder. Through the sights I saw the bullet impact and the car swerve. It skidded to a stop and the front doors flew open. Martinelli and Phillips leaped from the vehicle and started shooting in my direction with their handguns. Fat lot of good that was. The bullets fell short, kicking up dust from the road.

I worked the bolt and housed another round. I shifted my aim and put a bullet into the closest front tyre. The Audi lurched as the air exploded from the tyre.

Working the bolt again, I was ready to fire once more. This time I put a bullet through the radiator.

By now Martinelli and Phillips realised how futile their firing was and were sheltering behind the stricken car. I shot the Audi once more just for the hell of it before climbing into the Isuzu which I'd left running and drove off.

———

"Sorry about your vehicle," I said. "It can be fixed."

Nicole and Tom looked at it, scratching their heads. "It's stuffed," Nicole replied solemnly.

"No, it's not. The engine and chassis are fine. It's just cosmetic."

"I knew letting you borrow it was a bad idea."

"At least we know who is behind this now," I said positively.

"Who?" Tom asked.

"Pete Agosti, the vegie king," I said. "They were his goons."

"You're lucky you're still alive," Ellis said appearing from inside the station.

"A little help from Mister Winchester helped."

"Speaking of that." Ellis said. "It'll need to be handed over."

Nicole nodded. "I'll bring it in and log it. What about the men who tried to kill Mark?"

"They were gone. The Audi was still there, and it's

being gone over as we speak. But obviously someone came along and picked them up."

"Great, I've still got a target on my back."

Ellis said, "We'll need a statement from you when you're ready. No rush."

The sun was going down in the distance, leaving an orange haze on the horizon. The others went inside, leaving Nicole and I standing by the D-Max. She looked at me. It was the first time we'd been alone since I'd gotten back. "Are you all right?"

I smiled. "I'm good. We trained for this shit at the academy."

"Mark—"

"I'm fine, really. What happened with Paul?"

"They're treating it as an overdose until otherwise proven."

"Why would they do that? Everything points to a homicide."

"He has form for drugs and apparently he'd over-dosed before."

"Great. These guys are as dumb as dogshit, fair dinkum," I growled.

"Just let them do their job."

"All right, all right. I guess you're going to impound your D-Max too, huh?"

"Something like that," Nicole replied.

"Looks like it's back to the Falcon."

Nicole looked at me sheepishly.

"What?" I asked, fearing what her answer was going to be.

"It went to the car tip, sorry."

I held a hand up to my forehead and wailed loudly. "What? Not my lovely new car. Do you know—"

She hit me in the ribs eliciting a grunt. "You're an idiot."

I smiled. "Truth be known, it is probably the best place for it. I'll just see Cyril and get another."

"Something a little safer this time."

"Yes, mum," I replied with a roll of my eyes. "You want to dine at the pub tonight?"

"You don't think that might be just a little dangerous?" Nicole asked.

"They're not going to come after me there," I said. "Besides, they're probably long gone by now. Plus, I have a policeman—correction—policewoman to protect me."

"I've still got a few things to do here but I should be able to knock off afterwards. Meanwhile you can give your statement."

I thought of Rogers. "Can you see me smiling?"

"On the inside, Mark. On the inside."

———

"I call shotgun on first shower," Nicole said as she went into her room.

"Have at it," I called after her. "I might have a beer if there is one in the fridge."

"There should be two, I think. Grab me one."

"All right."

I heard the water go on as I opened the fridge door. Removing two beers, I cracked the lid on mine and took a sip; it tasted good.

"Where's my beer?" Nicole called out from the shower.

I took the cap off hers and walked along her hallway to the bathroom. I opened the door slightly and passed the bottle through.

"You'll have to come in, I can't reach it from there."

Okay. I pushed the door open, keeping my eyes firmly fixed on the tiled floor. I walked forward in the direction of the shower and heard Nicole wipe the fog and water beads from the interior of the glass. "You're a goose."

I glanced up and saw that apart from the part she'd wiped, the rest of the screen was opaque. She cracked the door and slipped her slim arm through the opening. I gave her the open beer and she withdrew, taking a drink before placing it on a shelf. I turned to leave, and she said, "Where are you going?"

I turned and looked at the screen door. It was open again. Nicole said, "I thought you wanted a shower."

I cleared my throat. "Ah, yes, yes I do."

After the longest shower I think I've ever partaken in, we began dressing to get ready to go to the pub. Shrugging into my shirt, I was starting to pull it down when a pair of bare arms slipped around my waist. "Are you all right?" Nicole asked as she snuggled my neck.

"More than all right," I said as I turned around. We kissed twice before she pulled away.

"I'm starving," she said as she reached out to the back of a chair to grab a white singlet top. Her white sports bra was stretched over her full breasts. "You're staring," she said.

I looked up at her. "Sorry, couldn't help myself."

"Can you at least wait until we get back?" she asked with a sly smile.

"I'll try."

She came back over and kissed me again. "Try harder."

———

As I approached the bar to order drinks to go with our dinner, I noticed that Rose, the bar girl I'd talked to earlier in the day and who'd given me access to the security footage, was still working. She looked tired. "You're still here?"

"Yeah, I might get to go home sometime tonight."

"Where's Bluey?" I asked.

She shrugged. "I've no idea. He was only meant to have been gone a couple of hours and the bastard still isn't back."

"Does he do that often?" I asked.

"Always," Rose replied. "What'll it be?"

"Couple of beers."

I returned to the table where Nicole waited. "You look troubled," she said to me.

"Not so much troubled as curious."

"Why?"

"I came in earlier today before everything happened, to see Bluey but he wasn't here. I was just talking to Rose and he's still not back."

Nicole rolled her eyes. "Can you just shut down for one night and enjoy it?"

I smiled at her. "All right, you have my undivided attention."

Then the door to the bar opened and Macca and Johnno Pearce walked in.

———

They looked around the bar first before spotting us at the table. Macca turned to his brother and spoke, and they turned to walk in our direction. I heard Nicole mutter, "Good grief."

"Hey, dude," Macca said by way of greeting. "How's it hanging?"

"Straight up and down, Macca," I replied. "Straight up and down."

"Little bird told me you had some trouble earlier."

"Yeah, the same blokes you told me about."

"I warned you, didn't I?"

Out of the corner of my eye I saw Nicole straighten. "Yeah, like you said, they're bad blokes. I found out who they were though. Trouble shooters up from Melbourne."

"Seen anymore ghost lights out on the lake lately, Macca?" Nicole asked him.

He shook his head. "Nope. I already told you before. It happens just before the storms fill it."

"Could be something to do with the atmosphere," she said.

He shrugged. "Anyway, I'm off for a beer."

"Stay out of trouble," Nicole said to him. "Both of you."

"You know us, Constable, we're good boys."

"Yeah, I do know you."

They walked off, leaving us alone, and I looked at Nicole questioningly. But she got the first question in. "He's your source?"

"Turned out to be a good one too. He was the one who told me everything about Martinelli and Phillips. Not their names just that they were around at different times."

"Can we be honest with each other now?"

"Is that why we had the shower together?"

Nicole glared at me. "Arsehole."

"I'm sorry, it was a joke."

She picked up her beer. "Do you see me laughing?"

"He also told me that once before some guy gave Helen's father a going over. The next thing you know those two were in town and the guy vanished."

"Almost the same as Trent," she said drawing a line between them.

"Yes. Only he was asking about the drugs at the roadhouse."

"I suspect you have a theory?" Nicole commented.

"You really want to go down that rabbit hole with me?" I asked her. "It might get ugly."

She nodded. "I can do ugly."

I grinned at the mental imagery before stating my supposition. "All right, here goes. I figure Friar's Lake is the drug distribution centre for the Agosti Syndicate."

Nicole sipped her beer and put it on the coaster to stop the table getting wet. "I need convincing if you're throwing something that big out there."

"I think that Inge Rasmussen stumbled onto something she shouldn't have and paid for it with her life. Then Trent came along and stumbled onto it too. He dies. I know that the gruesome twosome were in town when he disappeared—"

"You only have Macca's word for that."

"It's been good so far," I pointed out. "I've been poking around and then they come after me. Paul is dead, and I'd say with him the link to the pub. However, I'm not sure why they would kill him."

Nicole took another sip of her beer. "All right, how do they get their drugs into town?"

"I'm going to go out on a limb and say a plane."

"They'd need a place to land."

"Plenty of flat stuff around here," I said.

"But they'd need a farm or something like that," Nicole said. Then her expression changed. "Or a flat piece of road."

My mind raced. Flat piece of road, a kilometre or so long. "Snake Creek," I said.

Nicole nodded in agreement. "I often wondered why that stretch was wider than the rest. It goes on for about a kilometre which is more than enough for a light plane."

"There would a lot of moving parts to pull it off," I said. "Roads department, council—"

"Police," Nicole said hesitantly.

I stared at her over the top of my beer. "What makes you say that?"

"For a plane to land on the road you'd need to shut it down long enough for a plane to land and then take off again after it was unloaded."

"Is there anyone else other than the three of you?"

She shook her head. "No."

Which meant one of the three of them was bent. "Who is it?"

Concern was etched on her face. "I don't know. And for all *you* know it could be me."

"Let's go back to your place where I can grill you," I said with a wink.

"This is serious, Mark."

"We need to tell one of the detectives."

"Which one?"

"Rogers," I said, taking her by surprise.

"I thought you didn't like him."

"I don't, but I think he's straight too."

"And you think Ellis isn't?" she asked.

"I don't know."

Nicole took her phone and punched in some numbers. Then she looked at me before hitting, call. "Last chance."

"Do it."

———

Rogers looked far from happy when he entered the pub. To try and ease the pain, I had a beer waiting for him. "What's the issue that can't wait until tomorrow?"

He sat his nuggety form down and I pushed the beer across in front of him. "Here, have a beer."

He looked at it and then at both of us. "Why the hell am I here? And no bullshit."

"We had to choose, and you won," I said.

"Won what?"

Nicole said, "There could be a dirty copper in our station, and we figure you're someone we can trust."

"Why me?"

"You're grumpy, arrogant, and take no bullshit. That makes you number one in my book," I said.

"I'm not sure how to take that," he said, narrowing his eyes at me.

"How about we find a corner table in the lounge?" Nicole suggested. "One where we can talk quietly."

We got up from the table and took our drinks with us, moving out to the lounge to find a quiet corner table. After we were seated, I glanced around the room and noticed Jeff Andrews. He was eating a meal with one hand. The other was swathed in a white bandage.

Once we were seated, Rogers said, "All right, tell me what you've got. It'll need to be good before I bring IA in."

"That's just it," Nicole said. "We're not sure."

"Tell me anyway."

We told him what we had and about the theory of a plane landing on the road out at Snake Creek. "It's long enough," I said. "And wide enough."

"All right, but we still need more," he said. "Has anyone seen planes landing? Anything like that?"

"We'd have to ask around," Nicole said. "But that could be hard."

"I could do it," I offered. "It would be better me anyway."

"Yes, but it's still thin," Rogers said sceptically.

"If I can prove that there is a plane coming in, will that help?" I asked.

"Yes, but to take it further I'll have to talk to Ellis."

"Can you not tell him until we find something further?" I asked.

"He's been my partner for three years, I—"

"Just until we find something further," Nicole repeated my words. "The less who know the better."

He nodded. "All right then. I don't like it though."

"What did you make of the OD?" I asked.

Nicole gave me a warning look.

"OD my arse. That—" He stopped and stared hard at me. "How do you know about that?"

He gave Nicole an accusatory glance. I said, "It wasn't Nic so don't go there, Rogers."

"Then who?"

"I saw it. I went there to question him, and I found him like that."

His face darkened. "I ought to arrest you right now."

"Do it later, just answer the question."

He glared at me than nodded. "All right, the guy was given a hotshot."

"How do you know?"

"What guy stops halfway through a meal to get high?"

"That's the same conclusion I came to. There was something else that convinced me," I said. "I'd talked to him a couple of times and noticed he was right-handed. Can you remember what arm the syringe was in?"

"The right one. Shit."

"What does Ellis think?"

"He's set on calling it an OD so we can concentrate on the murder and get out of here."

"Did you request this trip, Darren?" Nicole asked.

Darren? It was the first time I'd heard his name spoken.

"No. We were up to our necks in something else when this case came up. Mike volunteered us for it."

"That's why you were angry," I said.

"Damned right."

"What happened to the thing you were working on?"

"It was handed off to another team."

"Is that normal?"

"No."

I had a thought. "All right, answer me this. You were the team that did the Rasmussen case, were you not?"

"Yes."

"Were you assigned or was it requested?"

"Ellis—" He stopped.

"Ellis requested it," I said.

"Yes."

"How much do you trust him now?" I asked.

A pained expression crossed Rogers's face. "He's a good cop."

I glanced at Jeff Andrews's table. He'd finished his meal and gone. I said to Rogers, "Even good cops can go astray."

"What do we do now?" Nicole asked.

"Let me worry about Ellis," Rogers growled. "I'll make a few enquiries. Now tell me about this other thing you're pursuing."

"The missing girls?" I asked.

"Yes, it's got me partly intrigued."

"As you know, Trent was sent up here to find out if Inge Rasmussen was killed by Ten-Cent. Somehow, he got side-tracked and mixed up with the drugs. You know about the ones I found? And him talking to the truck drivers at the roadhouse?"

"Yes."

"So, when he disappeared, the woman who hired me —Marion Lawler—she came to me to carry on the investigation. I found out that at first he called her but after that the next few times were by text and then they stopped."

"I'd say he was dead by then," Rogers assumed.

"That would be my guess. When Nicole and I looked over the security footage at the roadhouse, the owner said that we weren't the first to ask about missing girls. We found out that two other people had been asking questions over the years." I shrugged. "Not much I know but I then went out to Porter Creek and found a flyer about a runaway called Eliza Carter. I asked the shopkeeper about her and found out that she gave the kid three-hundred dollars to get away from her father who used to beat the crap out of her."

"Where did she go?" Rogers asked.

"She came to Friar's Lake to get the bus. After that there is no record of her. I got my ex-wife who's a detective in Melbourne to search for her and she found nothing."

"She could have changed her name."

"That's what Tia said, but I don't think so. I went out to Hampton and found an old flyer with an Aboriginal girl on it. She went missing too. Except no one knows about her. Or cares."

"So you have four missing girls?"

I nodded. "Yes, but there could well be more."

"Why do you say that?"

"There's a pattern. All the girls are around the same age. Long hair and were either hitchhikers or possible runaways. Alone and vulnerable. Bluey, the owner of the pub, said he had backpackers work for him that were there one moment and gone the next. Just disappeared. Sure, some of them could have just moved on but I have an awful feeling that something isn't right."

"Your theories are sound," Rogers said to me. "Except for one thing."

"What's that?"

"The death of Inge Rasmussen and Trent Jacobs aren't linked."

I was suddenly confused. "Sure, they are. The drugs."

He shook his head. "Nope."

It was Nicole who could see what he was getting at. "She was killed differently. Trent Jacobs was shot. The hitman's main choice of weapon. Inge was strangled with the rope."

"Exactly. I've been doing this long enough to know what's what."

"You're certain?" I asked.

"Damn near."

"So, if the murders aren't linked then—"

"I'd say your serial killer theory has a lot of merit."

"Double shit."

Rogers took a sip of his beer and sighed. "Friar's Lake. Home to a drug distribution centre and a serial killer."

"I hate to rain on your parade," Nicole said. "But why would he drop a body out in the open like that? If he's been operating here all these years, then why not hide it like he obviously has done the others?"

"I guess that's something we'll have to find out," Rogers said. "One thing is for certain; we're going to need another detective out here. I'll have to call it in."

"You want me to find out about the plane theory?" I asked.

His gaze grew hard. "Do it quietly. If you get caught out, it'll mean both our arses."

I smiled mirthlessly. "Quiet is my middle name."

———

Nicole and I shared the same bed that night and after a time we slept. The following morning the air was clear, a midnight storm had blown through rattling the windows with some loud bangs. I awoke with a plan. It wasn't much of one, but it was somewhere to start. I said to Nicole over breakfast, "If I can get some wheels, I'm going out to Hampton."

Over the top of her glass of orange juice she gave me a look that told me she thought I was nuts. "Why?"

"I'll be halfway there anyway so I thought I might check on Helen."

"No trouble, Mark. It's not even a wise idea."

"It'll be fine, I promise."

"Where are you going to get a car from?"

"I figured I'll go see Cyril."

"If you're determined to go back there then I'm coming with you."

"All right, let's go."

"I'll just let them know I'll be a couple of minutes late."

CHAPTER TWELVE

"Come on, now, you're killing me," Cyril protested.

"You're lucky I don't arrest you for that last heap of junk you sold Mark," Nicole growled at him, her gaze hot.

"All right, keep your panties on," he growled. "Follow me. I might have something to suit."

He started to walk away, and I glanced at Nicole. "I'd rather your panties came off but who am I to complain?"

She rolled her eyes and punched me in the arm. "Just follow the man."

Cyril took us out back to a shed. He opened the door and I almost fell over. Sitting there was a HX Monaro GTS sedan. It only had a top speed of just over a hundred miles an hour, but the car was a classic, a beast.

"It's had a couple of modifications," Cyril said. "It now runs on unleaded, and it'll top out at almost a hundred and sixty miles an hour."

"Did you put a jet engine in it?" I asked touching the blue exterior to make sure it was real. "Man, they don't make them like this anymore. How much?"

"Ten."

I did some calculations in my head and nodded. If I didn't eat for a week and slept in the car, then it should be right. "I'll take it."

"You want to test it out first?"

"As long as it runs, I'm happy."

Nicole slapped me on the back. "It looks like you don't need me anymore. Shall I expect you tonight or will you be making out with the car?"

"How about I make out with you, in the car?"

"In your dreams, Buster," she replied with a grin.

"It would be something like that," I assured her.

Meanwhile Cyril had climbed into the car. He turned her over and it fired almost straight away. The burble coming from the twin exhausts was amazing.

Nicole put her mouth near my ear. "I'm going, be careful."

I looked at her. "You're not staying for a better look?"

She kissed my cheek. "No."

Cyril backed the Monaro out of the shed then climbed out. "She'll run good for you. I've looked after it while it's been in there. If you come over to the office, we'll sort everything out."

I finished all the necessary details involved and Cyril handed me the keys to make it all official like and then we shook hands. I was about to turn to walk out when I had a thought. "Cyril," I said, "where can I buy a rifle?"

I honestly could not help myself, as the black marks on the street outside the caryard driveway will attest to for some time to come. My foot went down on the accelerator and before I knew it, the tyres had lit up and smoke was coming from the rear of the Monaro as it laid a good chunk of rubber on the bitumen.

On the rear seat lay a Winchester 1886 Model rifle that Cyril had brought in from the US. It was chambered for a 45-70 round which would stop a Grizzly Bear and was more than a match for a human, or hitman. When I hit the Hampton Road, I opened the throttle and felt the power of the Monaro coursing through the car as it sat on a hundred and sixty. That's kilometres an hour for the uneducated.

Reaching the Snake Creek crossing, I slowed down and pulled off the side of the road. Sitting for a moment or so to let the dust cloud overtake the car, I climbed out and walked slowly up the centre of the road. I glanced at the bridge railing when I reached it and frowned, knowing there was something different but I couldn't quite put my finger on it. Changing direction, I walked across and stood next to it for a few minutes, trying to work out what it was that puzzled me. A red Ford flew past and beeped its horn at me. My response was automatic as I raised the middle finger of my right hand. Then I went back to my contemplation.

It took several more minutes before realization dawned. The rail was lower than normal. I took a picture of it and then walked further along the road towards where the new met the old. When I reached it, I turned back and stood there looking, cicadas in the trees actively trying to deafen me with their buzz, and the galahs flying in their erratic way across the road in front of me before landing in a large gum in the paddock opposite the one they'd just left.

It was the burnout which helped me out in the end. Long and winding. However, there were other black marks which drew my attention. I started forward until I reached the first one. It was short, indistinct. Another was maybe a couple of feet ahead of it. Another to the side, and still another three feet further on. I kept walking until they stopped.

They definitely weren't from burnouts, that was for sure. Then I remembered where I'd seen something similar. Tullamarine Airport on the runways where the planes landed.

I took out my mobile and took pictures of the rubber marks. Placing my phone in my pocket I looked up to see another vehicle approaching. It wasn't until it got closer that I saw the lights on top and realised that it was a council truck. It pulled over and came to a rattling stop near the bridge and two men climbed out.

"You all right, mate?" the guy called from the passenger seat.

I gave him a wave. "Fine, fine. Just having a walk around. Not feeling the best."

"Yeah, the bloody heat will do that to a bloke."

As I watched on, the two of them put out a couple of signs and some traffic cones. Not long after, another ute pulled up. This one carried road safety technicians. Or stop and go people. I heard one of them say, "Couldn't you blokes wait for us?"

"No. You're too fucking slow."

"Get it up your arse."

And right then, as they kept the banter going back and forth, I realised that there were other ways to stop traffic. "Shit."

———

Hampton was just as dead as it had been the first time I'd visited it. I half expected the spectacle of my entry in the Monaro to draw some kind of audience but no such luck. I pulled up outside the store and climbed out of the car. After shutting the door, I was walking towards the shopfront when Helen's father, Henry, appeared in the doorway. The swelling in his face had gone down and all that was left was the bruising. "You're not welcome here, get lost."

A crow cawed from its perch upon a light pole, as though it were echoing the man's thoughts. "I'm here to see Helen."

"She don't want to see you."

"Maybe she does, maybe she doesn't," I said. "How about we let her make up her mind?"

He looked nervous, jumpy. His eyes darted everywhere as though he was looking for a way out. Licking his lips nervously, he said, "I know people. I can have you killed. Just like that." He nodded his head as if to say, "so there".

"Was it you that called people before who tried to kill me with your daughter in my car?" I asked him, keeping an even tone.

Again, licking his lips. "No, that wasn't me. I called no one."

"You're a liar, Henry," I told him frankly. "A junkie and a liar."

"It's true," he wailed, spittle flying from his lips. "Yeah, I called someone, but they never tried to kill you with my kid in the car. That was someone else."

"Who?" I asked angrily.

"I don't frigging know. Maybe it was someone else you pissed off."

"Where are the guys they sent? The killers?"

"How should I know?"

"They killed a man I knew, and a girl, Henry," I said hoping he was unhinged enough to bite.

"They didn't kill no girl," he snapped.

There it was. "How do you know that?"

"They weren't even here when she was killed."

"Then who was it?"

"How the hell should I know? The same one who's been killing the others."

My blood ran cold. "What others?"

"The backpackers, the dark girl you was asking about. Others."

"How do you know this?"

"I hear things. Shit, over the years people get to talking, have their little conspiracy theories." He got a smug expression on his face. "You think that she was the only Aboriginal girl to disappear? They're not white so you don't hear about them."

"How many, Henry?" I asked. "Over how long?"

He seemed to calm down some as we talked. I guessed as long as I didn't approach him, he was fine. He shrugged. "Maybe over ten years I suppose. I don't know how many, you'll have to ask Grandma Mary."'

"Who is Grandma Mary?"

"She lives in a house down the road that way." He pointed towards a crossroads.

"All right, I'll go and see her," I said. "But when I come back, I want to see Helen."

The words agitated him. "No, you can't see her."

"Thanks for the information."

As I walked away, he yelled after me, "Don't come back, you hear?"

I climbed into the Monaro and drove in the direction he'd indicated. There were four houses in the street. Two were rundown and boarded up. Another looked like it had suffered fire damage, and the last had a manicured garden and looked loved. I pulled up to the kerb and climbed out. The gate squealed at me when I swung it open, the hinges stiff. I walked along the cracked path between two rows of some kind of red flowers I'd never seen before.

"You lost or something?"

I looked up to see a well-rounded Aboriginal woman standing in the doorway of her home. She wore a plain dress, and her hair was iron grey in her later years.

"Are you Grandma Mary?" I asked.

"Might be. Who are you?"

"My name is Mark Hayes," I said. I dug into my pocket for my ID. "I'm a private investigator."

"Like Kojak?" she asked.

I smiled. "No, like Jim Rockford."

"You don't look like him."

"I'm not as old as him," I replied.

"What do you want to ask me about?"

"I want to talk about the missing girls," I said.

"I don't know nothing," she said abruptly and turned to go back inside.

"Wait, please. It's important."

She looked back at me.

"Please," I said again.

She seemed to get angry. "No good can come of it."

"Don't you want to know what happened to them?"

"I know what happened. They're dead. Leave it be."

"How do you know?"

"I've seen them. They come to me in my dreams. They're all drowning."

"Please, just a few minutes?" I implored her.

"No."

"At least tell me this. How many are missing?"

She hesitated then said, "Five. Five girls."

"Was it reported?"

"Why would we do that?" she sneered. "They're just black fellas. He didn't care."

Grandma Mary went back inside and slammed the door leaving me standing there contemplating what she'd just said.

I climbed into the car and went back to the shop. As soon as I pulled up, Henry was back out there and started yelling, "Get away! You can't see her! Fuck off."

"I just want to see that she's all right and then I'll go."

"She's fine," he screeched at me.

"Show me."

Helen pushed past her father. "I'm fine, Mark. Honest."

"He hasn't hurt you?"

"No."

I nodded. "All right." I reached into my pocket and took out a card. I held it out. "Take this."

Helen came towards me and when she was within reach, she took the card with my number. "Are you really all right?" I asked softly.

"Yes."

"Are the men around?"

"No, they're somewhere else. They have a house."

"OK."

"What are you whispering about?" Henry demanded.

I looked at him. "I'm just making sure she's all right."

"She bloody said so, didn't she?"

"I guess she did."

Helen left me then. Walked back to the shop, pushed past her father, and went inside. Henry just stared at me, waiting for me to leave. I returned to the Monaro and started the motor. I sat there unmoving while the engine burbled. Still staring at him, I shifted the car into reverse before backing up. A minute later the echo of the V8 engine could still be heard as I drove towards Friar's Lake.

———

I sent a message to Rogers saying I needed to see him. He sent me one back saying that he'd be at the pub that night with Ellis eating dinner. He'd find me there.

On the way back to town I thought about what Grandma Mary had said. How the dead girls came to her and that they were drowning. I tried to figure out what she meant but drew a blank. But what she'd said was disturbing indeed. Five girls missing, added to the others and that was far too many. And she'd said 'he didn't care'. Who didn't care?

I was about a kilometre past the bridge at Snake Creek when I came across a dirt road which turned off to the right. I jammed on the brakes of the Monaro and slammed the shift into reverse. The wheels spun as I gave it too much juice and had to ease off. Once the car was backed up far enough, I turned onto the road.

I followed it for about five kilometres before a homestead emerged from the heat haze. I passed through a gateway and over a cattle grid with a thump-thump. Upon reaching the yard I found a man, maybe fiftyish, waiting for me wearing a long-sleeved cotton shirt, jeans, and the customary Akubra hat. I climbed out and he looked at me. "You a city folk?"

"That easy to tell, is it?"

He shook his head. "It is when you don't get many visitors. The only times most people come here is if they're lost. And then they're mostly from the city."

"How about, I am from the city, but I'm not lost?" I asked.

"Then I'm not interested," he said and turned away.

I was confused. "Wait. What do you mean?"

"I mean you must be the other kind we get here."

"What kind is that?"

"The kind that wants to sell me something."

"Oh, that," I chuckled. "I can promise you I'm not one of those."

"What do you want then?" he asked then pointed at a machinery shed. "I got a tractor to fix."

"My name is Mark Hayes," I told him introducing myself, holding out my right hand.

He came forward and took it. His hand was rough, dry.

"Bill Turner," he replied.

"Pleased to meet you, Bill." I took out my ID. "I'm a private investigator. Can I ask you a couple of questions?"

His guard shot up immediately. I didn't blame him; here was I, a bloke he didn't know from Adam, and I wanted to ask him questions. "Well—"

"Not about you," I said hurriedly. "About things that may have gone on out on the Hampton Road."

"What things?"

"I'm not sure. Has it ever been shut down of a night?"

Bill took his Akubra off to reveal a mop of dark hair. He wiped sweat from his brow before replacing it. He looked at me, his head cocked to the left. "Not that I recall. Most nights we're in bed early around here anyway. Up at sparrow fart of a morning."

"Sure, I understand. What about a plane? Did you ever hear a plane of a night?"

"Around here? No. Not me, I—wait here a minute."

He hurried off towards the house leaving me to wonder what he was up to. While he was gone, a Red Kelpie came out of the shade of the shed and walked lazily over to me. It sniffed around my legs and feet then looked up at me as it sat in front of me. I reached down and patted its head, rubbing it between the ears. "What about you, pup? Have you seen a plane of a night?"

"He won't answer you," Bill said as he emerged from the house with a woman in a floral dress. She looked to be about his age with greying hair. "This is my wife, Gwen."

"Gwen," I said smiling at her. "Nice to meet you."

"You too, Mister—"

"Hayes. Mark Hayes."

"Tell him about the plane, Gwen," Bill prompted her.

This was interesting.

"All right, don't rush me," she growled. "Okay. One night a while back—maybe a couple of months—I woke up in the middle of the night and I thought I heard a plane."

"Is that all?" I asked her.

"Uh, huh. I told Bill about it, but he said I must have been dreaming. But I know what I heard."

"I believe you, Gwen. I really do," I said to her.

She turned to her husband and nodded as if to say, I told you so.

"What is it about with these questions anyway?" he asked.

"It's just something I'm investigating," I explained as I handed over a card. "If you hear one again, Gwen, please, give me a call."

"Any time?"

"Day or night," I said. "Even if it's two in the morning."

She looked uncertain. "Well, all right. Just don't go getting all shitty when I do."

I smiled at her reassuringly. "I promise I won't. Thank you for your time."

CHAPTER THIRTEEN

Arriving back in Friar's Lake after lunch, I was hungry so I found a little café in the street that served the best hamburgers. Eating healthy wasn't a big thing for me. I ran a lot, so I figured that compensated for it. My running was not the exercise kind though; mostly it was away from whoever was chasing me. Even the odd bullet or two.

I hid the Winchester under a blanket that Cyril had given me before I went inside. After I had placed my order, I walked over to the wall where there was a small notice board. You can learn a lot from these things, providing the information is all there. Like someone was offering to be a babysitter, three years ago. Someone else was trying to sell a horse, four years ago in 2016.

"I wouldn't take too much notice of what's there, Mister," the lady behind the counter called out across the room. "I've been trying to get my husband to clean it up for so long now my jaw hurts from asking."

I smiled at her. "Don't take this the wrong way, but why don't you do it?"

"If I do it, then he's won, hasn't he?" she said then

went on to try and explain her logic. "See, if he thinks he's won he'll never do anything again. But by me not doing it then it's telling him that he hasn't won, and I won't do everything for him."

"Okay," I said sounding unconvinced. "Tell me, do you have council offices here?"

She looked at my strangely. "Of course."

"Sorry, just because Friar's Lake is small, I wasn't sure."

"Yes."

"Could you tell me where?"

"On the north side of town, you can't miss it."

"Thanks."

We chatted some more and by that time the burger was done. I must say, if I've had better burgers then I can't remember when. I hate to say it, but they were even better than Mort's.

I found the council offices quite easily. A brick affair which looked reasonably new. I found myself wondering why they weren't built closer to the centre of town.

A man greeted me at the counter. He was dressed in a suit and had thinning hair on top. He gave me a look of inconvenience as I stopped at the counter. He said, "If you're after something you'll have to wait until Glynis comes back from lunch."

"That's all right," I replied. "Do you know much about the road works that go on out on the Hampton Road at all?"

His eyes narrowed. "Why? Who are you?"

"Mark Hayes, private investigator."

"We've got no time for the likes of you," he said abruptly.

"I only have a couple of questions."

"And I'm busy. The door is that way," he said pointing to the exit.

"All right, I'm going. Thank you for your help."

As I walked out, I heard him mumble, "Fucking smart arse."

————

Rogers looked through the pictures I'd taken on my phone before giving it back to me. The dining room in the pub was almost deserted, an elderly couple the only others there. "They could be what you say they are," he allowed. "Not hard evidence, though."

"I also have a wife of a station owner saying that she heard a plane one night."

"Still not enough."

"Shit," I growled, and Nicole reached out her hand, placing it on my arm.

"We'll get it," she said.

"Did you make any headway?" I asked Rogers.

"Ellis is still adamant that the OD was an OD and he's got me running around chasing my tail on this other thing," he replied. "There has been no sighting of the two men we're after at all. It's like they've vanished. Then I mentioned about getting a second homicide team out here to look at the girl's death and Ellis canned the idea."

"Why would he do that?" Nicole asked.

"Too many coppers make it harder to cover shit up," Rogers said.

"While I was out at Hampton today, I learned two interesting things," I started to explain. "The first is that your two killers are still around. I wouldn't be surprised if they're hiding out there somewhere. Lean on the store owner."

"I'll look into it."

"The second thing was I had a brief conversation with a lady called Grandma Mary."

"Oh, God," Nicole breathed. "You didn't listen to her, did you? She's a lovely lady but a little bit out there."

"She seemed pretty adamant to me," I said.

"Come on, Mark. Drowning are the dead? They come to her in her dreams."

"She also said he wouldn't do anything," I replied. "I'm yet to work out what she means by that."

"Have I missed something?" Rogers asked.

"There's an indigenous woman out at Hampton who says dead girls come to her in her dreams," Nicole enlightened him.

"She says that over the years five girls have gone missing," I told Rogers.

"Five?"

"Wait," Nicole said perplexed. "I only heard that dead girls came to her in her dreams. No one ever said anything about missing girls."

Rogers said, "So that is possibly eight—nine missing girls?"

I nodded.

His face grew grim. "Wait here."

He got up and walked away, and Nicole leaned towards me, saying, "This is going to come back and bite you on the arse."

"Why?" I asked innocently.

"Because the woman is batshit crazy, that's why."

"I don't think so."

"I guess we'll find out then, won't we?"

Rogers returned with Ellis. "Tell him what you told me about the girls."

I told him the same story and he listened in silence until I was finished. Then he said, "She sounds crazy."

"That's what I said," Nicole agreed.

"I think it could be worth another team to look it

over," Rogers said. "That makes at least eight girls who have gone missing over the past years."

"Suspected, Darren," Ellis said. "Look, we've got a current case we're working on that's going nowhere fast so let's just concentrate on that."

"What about the girl? Inge Rasmussen?"

"It's been weeks and we've got nothing."

"What if they are connected? Her and the other missing girls? Another team can't hurt."

"No, that's it. No more."

Rogers was about to argue more when Tom hurried into the dining lounge. "We've got a lead on our two killers out at Hampton. All hands on deck."

I got to my feet and Tom gave me a hard stare. "Not you."

Nicole gave me a sympathetic glance and followed the rest of them out the door.

"Where's the fire?" Bluey asked as he stuck his head through the door to the bar.

"Hampton, apparently," I replied.

Surprised he said, "Really? That's the last time I say something stupid like that."

"No, there's no fire."

He came over to the table. "Mind if I sit down?"

"Sure, what's up?"

He took a seat. "You're in good with the cops, yeah?"

"I wouldn't go that far."

"Well, with one of them, anyway."

"I'll admit to that," I said.

"Is there any word about Paul?"

I frowned, curiously. "What do you mean, Bluey?"

"They said he died of an overdose, but I don't believe it. He'd cleaned himself up."

"Do you know that for a fact?"

"Sure do, I seen him do it."

"What do you think happened?"

"I think it has something to do with those blokes the other night who came looking for him. The same ones that tried to kill you."

"They came looking for him?"

"Yeah, why do you suppose they did that?"

"You haven't heard the stories, Bluey?" I asked.

"What stories?"

"That Paul was supposed to have been selling drugs out of the pub?"

"What?" he gasped. For a moment I thought I saw genuine shock on his face. Right before it was replaced by anger. "That's bullshit!"

I grabbed his arm across the table. "Take it easy."

He shook it free. "I already told you, he was clean. Unreliable, but off the drugs."

"It doesn't mean he couldn't have been selling them."

His shoulders slumped. "I guess you're right. That would be why those arseholes came looking. They didn't have to kill him."

"We don't know they did," I reminded him.

"I do," he said. "I damned well do."

I suddenly realised that Bluey had a point when he inferred that Martinelli and Phillips had come looking for Paul to kill him. If he'd been selling the drugs when he wasn't supposed to, skimming as it was called, then the boss would be far from happy.

"Bluey, who were Paul's closest friends?"

He shrugged. "No one really."

"Think, there must have been someone?"

I could see his mind ticking over. "If there was anyone, it would be Terry Smith."

"Who is Terry Smith?"

"Works on the council," he explained.

"He wouldn't be part of the road crew, would he?"

The pub owner cocked his head to one side. "How did you know that?"

"Wild guess. Do you know where he lives?"

"Yes, I do."

———

I knocked on the room door and waited. From within came the sound of movement. I looked at Bluey who nodded. "I told you he'd be there."

The doorlatch rattled and the door swung open. The man filling the void glanced at me and then focused on Bluey. "What's up, Blue?"

Smith wore jeans with no shirt. His hair was long, and he was unshaven.

"We need to have a talk," Bluey said.

"Can't just at the moment. I'm busy."

"Terry—"

I kicked the door back and he lost his grip.

"What the hell, man? What are you doing?"

I walked into the room. Helga sat at a small table. She too was shirtless with no bra. It didn't seem to worry her, however. She was too busy trying to get rid of the drugs on the table and saying, "Oh, God. Oh, God."

"What the hell is this?" Bluey snarled. "You're doing drugs in my hotel as well as my barmaid, arsehole."

"Get the hell out!" Smith shouted. He took a swing at me which I avoided easily. I grabbed it and twisted hard. He cried out and buckled at his knees.

I placed my mouth near his left ear and said, "We're going to have a quiet chat. If you try something like that again, I'm going to break your frigging arm."

"All right, all right, let me go."

I released Smith and gave him a shove towards the bed. "Take a seat."

"Screw you."

Bluey grabbed Helga's shirt and tossed it to her. "Out."

She snatched it up and began putting it on. Once the buttons were mostly done up, she grabbed her bra and headed for the door.

Now that we were alone, I could ask the questions I wanted to. I stood over Smith and said, "What was Paul doing?"

"What?"

"What was he doing that got him killed?"

"I don't know what you're talking about."

I stepped closer. "He was skimming drugs and selling them, wasn't he?"

"You're crazy man; back off."

"You think that they killed him for fun?" I asked him. "They killed him for a reason. Word is he was selling drugs from the pub. If the drug bosses got wind of those activities, they would have thought he was putting their operation in danger. The only thing for them to do was kill him."

"It was an overdose, man," he griped.

"No, it wasn't, and you know it. He was clean. Were you in on it, too?"

"What? No way, man, that was all him. I told—" He stopped cold.

"You told him what?"

"I told him if they caught on, he'd end up taking a dirt nap, but he kept telling me, it's cool, no worries, they make heaps anyway, that kind of shit."

"Well, they caught on and gave him a hotshot," I said.

"I told him."

"Who else is involved?" I asked hopefully.

He shook his head. "I don't know."

"You don't know? Or you won't say?"

"I don't know. All I did was shut down the road for the plane."

I glanced at Bluey before saying, "And that's it?"

Smith nodded. "I'd get a call and they'd tell me they needed the road shut down for thirty minutes while the plane landed and then took off."

"Surely you saw faces?" I asked.

"Nope, everyone wore masks."

"So you have no idea of any of the individuals involved?"

"No."

"Were you the only one stopping the traffic?"

Smith said nothing.

"Come on, don't stop now," I barked at him.

"I'm not saying no more," he said, shaking his head. "I do, and I end up getting a bullet in my head like that other bloke."

"You mean the guy under the bridge at Snake Creek?"

"Yeah, that's him."

"You can be protected," I told him.

He snorted derisively. "By who? The police? They're in this up to their eyeballs."

"Who? Which one?"

"Nope, I'm done. No more."

"All right, but if I were you, I'd get out now while the going is good."

Bluey and I left Smith sitting on his bed. Once out in the long hallway the pub owner said, "That was informative."

I was about to answer when my mobile phone rang. I looked at the screen. Bluey said, "Nice ringtone."

"I'd like to choke the shit out of it."

"Change it then."

"I don't know how."

I answered the phone. "Yes, my love, what can I do for you?"

"Shut up and listen would be a good start," Tia said to me.

She really does love me. "I'm all ears."

"I reached out to some guys I know in the drug squad. Word is that Agosti has a clean-up order on Martinelli and Phillips."

"How do they know this?"

"They have an informant on the inside of Agosti's organization. He's worried that they screwed up and will take him down with them. Their faces are all over the news so there won't be many places they can hide."

Hide? It hit me like a freight train. "Tia, I have to go."

Without waiting for her to reply I hung up and called Nicole. "I can't talk right now," she said.

"Are you on speaker?"

"No."

"Listen. Agosti has put a clean-up order on Martinelli and Phillips. Be careful. All right?"

"Got it," she replied and hung up.

As I put my phone back in my pocket, I couldn't help but feel that things were about to go from bad to worse.

———

The call came through around two in the morning. The damned rooster dragged me from a deep slumber, and I awoke telling Tia to chop its bloody head off so we could eat it. It wasn't long after that I realised I wasn't dreaming and reached out to grab the blasted thing. I looked at the screen, but it told me nothing. Pressing the accept button I said, "Hello?"

"Mark Hayes?" It was a woman's voice. Croaky, old. No, elderly.

"Yes, who is this?"

"It's Grandma Mary, I have a child here that needs your help."

"Who?" I asked before realising there was only one person in Hampton I gave my card to. "Helen?"

"The child is in trouble, Mister Hayes. She says you are the only one she can trust."

"All right, I'm coming."

"You will have to come the long way by Porter Creek. We will meet you by the old service station out on the road where you come in. The police have the town sealed off."

"What's going on?" I asked suddenly concerned about Nicole.

"I will tell you when you get here. We will meet you."

The call disconnected and she was gone.

I don't think I've ever dressed so quickly before. I clambered out of bed, threw on my clothes and boots, before running for the door. I climbed into the Monaro and kicked the engine over. It fired first time and I thanked Cyril for looking after the machine so well. I let it idle for a moment while I called Nicole. Her phone went straight to voicemail.

As I drove out of Friar's Lake, the crackling Monaro did its best to wake the sleeping town At my back, lightning streaked across the sky from a storm as it made its way northeast. Once I reached the edge of the town limits, my foot went down. I really hoped there were no kangaroos on the road. If there were, it was going to be a disaster.

———

I made it before three-thirty. The Monaro had been floating on the road as I had the hammer down most of the way. She handled it perfectly and if there were any kangaroos, I didn't see them.

I found the old servo without any problems. I killed the headlights and coasted to a stop on the concrete driveway which was overgrown with weeds. I climbed out of the car and opened the back door, pulling the Winchester from beneath the blanket. I worked the lever should any surprises come my way. The old servo was far enough from town to be out of sight. I walked towards the front door when a torch light appeared from around the left corner of the derelict building. "Over here."

I could tell by the voice that it was Grandma Mary so walked towards her. "Follow me."

I did as she said, and she led the way inside through a side door. She pushed it open and even before I entered, I could smell the remnants of old oil and grease.

Inside, she shone the torch around until I noticed Helen hiding in what had been a darkened corner. I walked over to her, my boots crunching broken glass under their soles. "Are you all right?"

"No." Her voice was soft, childlike.

"What happened?"

"The two men came to the shop," Helen said. "They were waiting for someone."

"How do you know?"

"I overheard them talking."

I nodded. "Keep going."

"Three other men came. There was shooting. The two men were killed."

"Who shot them?"

"The man. He was smaller than the others."

"Then what happened?" I asked as I tried to process what she'd already said.

Helen remained silent.

"Helen?"

"Tell him, dear," Grandma Mary gently urged her.

"Then he—he shot my dad."

Shit. "What happened next?"

"He put the gun in my dad's hand."

Hell, they planted a gun on him. I tried again. "Do you know who the man was?"

"I don't know."

"Helen?"

She hesitated again. "I—I can't say. I won't, they'll kill me too."

"You need to get her somewhere safe," Grandma Mary said. "Away from this place."

"The police—"

"No," gasped Helen. "I heard the man say that the police would take care of it. One of the detectives, I heard the short man say."

My mind raced while I thought about where to put her. Then I came up with an idea. "I think I know where she can go," I said.

"Don't tell me," the old woman said. "What I don't know, I can't tell anyone."

"All right." I looked at Helen. "Will you come with me?"

"Yes."

"Let's go."

CHAPTER FOURTEEN

"What do you want?" Jeff Andrews asked me grumpily. He'd not long been out of bed by the look of him and probably hadn't had his morning coffee.

"Can we come in?" I asked him.

He frowned at me. "We?"

I waved at the Monaro parked outside his house and Helen climbed out. She hurried through the gate and up the path. "What's going on?" he growled.

"Can we come in, Jeff? Please?"

He stepped aside and we moved into the house. He closed the door and followed us into the living room. "Now, how about you tell me what is happening."

"Helen needs a place to hide," I told him.

"What for?" he asked frowning at me, puzzled at my words. "Why can't you go to Tom?"

"Because police are involved in this, Jeff."

His face grew grim. "Then you'd better sit down and tell me about it."

By the time I was finished, he knew what I did about the drugs. "This sounds bad, Mark," he eventually said. "Really bad."

"I don't know who I can trust. At least if Helen is safe then she can be used as a witness later on."

"This is a Melbourne drug syndicate, you say?"

"Yes. Pete Agosti."

"I knew there was something bad going on in my town," he said firmly.

"So, can she stay here until this gets sorted out?"

"Sure. I've got a spare bed."

I looked over at Helen who'd slipped into a deep sleep on the lounge listening to the monotonous drone of our voices. Beside her I saw a small picture of a girl in a frame on a side table. Maybe seventeen, long dark hair, pretty smile. "Who's that?"

"What?" Andrews asked.

"The picture? Good-looking girl."

"Granddaughter."

"Really. I thought you said you never married?"

"Mistake. One of the times I left him to soak too long," he explained.

"Oh, sorry. She lives here?"

His expression changed as though he was reminiscing. "No, she lives in the lake."

I cocked my eyebrow. "In the lake?"

"Lake's Entrance in Victoria."

"Wow, nice place to live. Holidayed there once. Loved it. When was the last time you saw her?"

I could see him calculating the time in his head. "Probably not long after the picture was taken. Ten years ago."

"You haven't seen her for that long?"

He shook his head. "No. Long story."

"Shame," I replied. "I should wake Helen and get her into bed."

"Leave her there," Andrews said. "I'll see to her when she wakes up. What are you going to do now?"

"I have no idea."

———

I went back to Nicole's for a shower. I figured she wouldn't be home, and I was right. The water was as hot as I could stand it which felt like needles piercing my skin. Once I was dry and dressed, I called Tia and told her what had gone on the previous night.

"Jesus Christ, Mark, you have to get that girl into police custody," she stated disbelievingly.

"I know, Tia. What I don't know, however, is who to trust. There's at least one bad copper here."

"But they don't know you have a witness," Tia said.

"That's right. Maybe you could make a call to Sydney?"

"Sorry, Mark, I've got no connections there. I could ask around but—"

"You wouldn't know who to trust," I finished for her.

"Sorry. What does concern me is the appearance of those three men. She said one of them was shorter than the others?"

"That's right."

"Agosti is short," she said out loud.

"Shit. Can you get the Drug Squad to check if he's still in town? He could be here closing everything down."

"If he's doing that you can expect the body count to rise. I'll see what I can do. Just stay out of trouble."

"You know me," I said tongue in cheek.

"Yes, I do. You attract trouble like flies to crap."

After she disconnected, I messaged Nicole. She sent one back which virtually said, don't expect me home anytime soon. Then I sent her one telling her that Agosti was possibly in the area. Hers came back, be there shortly.

Ten minutes later she turned up, tired, and looking a little worse for wear. "I know, I look like shit," she said wearily. "I think you should go back to Melbourne. Ever since you showed up it's been nothing but trouble."

I was about to go into my story when I heard the door open, and Tom walked in. Nicole looked at me apologetically. "I had to tell someone."

"And that someone was me," Tom said. "Now, what's this about Agosti?"

"There's a good chance he's in the area. I have an eyewitness which puts him—sorry—puts someone of his stature at the scene of the crime last night with two other men. Possibly bodyguards."

"Good grief," Tom sighed angrily. Her eyes developed little pinpricks of fire in them, something I'd seen more than once in Tia's eyes. "What the fuck were you doing out there last night? I told you to stay here."

"I got a phone call early this morning. Around two. It was a call for help and the person who made it trusted only me."

"Who?" Tom snapped. "Who's the witness?"

"I'm not going to say."

"Damn it, Hayes. You tell me or I'll arrest you for obstructing a police investigation."

"Not going to happen. Just be happy that the witness is safe and saw the murder of three people. And I might add overheard a conversation stating that the crime scene would be taken care of by police."

"It's Helen Miller, isn't it? That's why we couldn't find her last night."

Nicole said, "You have to tell us where she is, Mark. She could be in grave danger."

"That's why it's better if you don't know," I told her. "If Agosti is still around and he hears word of her, he'll go all out to find her and kill her. As it is, word on the street in Melbourne is that he's jumped into clean-up mode."

"What do you mean?" Tom asked.

"It means you can expect more bodies to drop."

"Who's giving you all this information?"

My phone rang and Tom rolled her eyes. I looked at the screen and took the call. It was Tia and I put her on speaker. "Go, Tia, you're on speaker with Senior-Constable Nicole Berger and Sergeant Tomika Rains."

"What happened to not trusting anyone?" Tia asked.

"I had to start sometime."

"Okay, it looks like you've got a fox in the henhouse. Agosti left Melbourne yesterday for places unknown. My guess is he's there with you."

"Are you sure?" Tom asked.

"It's a good possibility since it looks like he's starting to clean house."

"Great, that's all we need."

"Can you send a picture of him to my phone, Tia?"

"Sure, I'll do it as soon as I get off the phone."

"You're a doll. Do you know who his bodyguards are?"

"You'll love this." I could hear the chuckle in her voice. "You thought the other two stiffs were bad. These guys are worse. Donahue Walsh. Former Australian Army, dishonourably discharged three years ago and walked into a job with Agosti. The other one is even more special. Kent Collins. He's a former Drug Squad detective. He was forced out a couple of years ago suspected of shaking down couriers and pocketing bribes. It is believed—but can't be proven—that he was responsible for a low-level dealer who wouldn't come across with a payment."

"Thanks, T. When you send a shot of Agosti, throw them in as well, could you?"

"Sure. Take care, Mark."

She disconnected and Tom gave a long sigh. "Of all the towns in New South Wales, why pick this one? How are they even getting it in?"

My phone pinged. I looked at Nicole. "You want to do the honours?"

Her voice was full of sarcasm. "Thanks."

While Nicole filled Tom in, I checked the pictures that Tia had sent. Agosti was a short man with dark hair and solid build. Walsh and Collins were both larger as expected. Walsh had red hair, while his partner Collins's was dark brown. Both were as ugly as a hat full of arseholes.

When I finally tuned back into the real world, Nicole was just finishing up giving Tom the short version about the drugs. "And all this is happening under our noses?"

"Yes."

"I have something to add," I said. "While you were all out last night, I had a chat to a person who was a good friend of Paul's. He works for the council and was part of the crew shutting down the road for the plane to land."

"Who?" Tom demanded.

"Terry Smith."

"We need to bring him in," Nicole said.

"The last I saw of him he was under advisement to leave. So, I'd be quick about it."

Tom said, "We'll go and see if we can find him. Maybe he'll be able to give us some information and roll on the others involved."

"Don't hold your breath. They all wore masks, so no one knew the identity of the others. Paul was skimming off some drugs and selling them on the side. That's why they killed him."

Tom gave me a funny look. Nicole said, "Let's go, I'll fill you in while we drive."

Tom gave me a hard stare. "You, stay out of trouble. And give some serious thought about what you're doing with Helen Miller."

"You find out who the bad apple is, and I'll gladly help."

Tom's mobile rang. She checked the screen and looked over at Nicole. "It's Jace."

She answered it and listened for a few moments before saying, "We'll be right there."

When she hung up, I could see the concern on her face. "It looks like your theory was right. Only we won't be able to talk to Terry Smith. It appears as though he's killed himself."

"What's he doing here?" Ellis asked looking in my direction as I leaned against the front quarter panel of the police Nissan.

"He's helping us with our enquiries," Tom replied.

I noticed Rogers glance at me before he went back to his work. Terry Smith hung from a thick branch of a tall redgum. His limp body dangled from a branch, flies swarming his already decomposing corpse. Beneath his feet, tipped on its side, was an old twenty litre oil drum. Supposedly what he'd stood on before he took that last plunge.

I swatted at a fly which buzzed around my ear. "The dead guy is over there," I muttered.

Ellis looked at the corpse and I heard him say to Tom, "Definite suicide. Tied off the rope, stood on the drum, and stepped out into nothing. The question is why?"

"Your guess is as good as mine," Tom replied.

"Did he have any debts, suffer any mental illness, lost love?"

"Not that I'm aware of."

Ellis said, "We'll need a list of close friends, relatives, just so we can get to the bottom of it. What about drug use?"

"I don't know."

"He used drugs," I said, interrupting.

They turned and looked at me. Ellis frowned. "I beg your pardon?"

"I said, he…used…drugs."

"And you know this, how?"

"When I went to talk to him last night, I found him using."

"You went to talk to him?" I could see the angry surprise on his face. "What about?"

"About his friend, Paul who supposedly overdosed."

"Weren't you told to stay out of this investigation?" Ellis demanded.

Rogers came sauntering over. "What's going on?"

"Mister Hayes here has been interfering in our investigation. He—"

"No, he hasn't," I corrected him, lying through my teeth. "I've been trying to find out what happened to Trent Jacobs which is exactly what I was hired to do. I can't help it if some things intersect."

"That's bullshit and you know it," Ellis snarled losing some of his previous cool exterior. Now, how could I chip more of it away?

I said, "Detective Rogers?"

He stared at me. "What?"

"Could you indulge me and stand that drum up under the corpse?"

"What?"

"The drum. I'm just curious about something."

He looked at the old oil drum. "What about it."

"Get back to what you were doing, Darren," Ellis snapped. "Take no notice of him. He needs to leave."

It was Nicole who stepped forward to do what I'd asked the detective. Ellis saw her move and said, "Stop right there, Senior Constable. You're contaminating the scene."

In all my romantic life I seem to attract the headstrong women. I wasn't about to let the side down now. Nicole ignored the detective and stood the drum up under the corpse. There was at least a six-inch gap between the top of it and the toes of the shoes above it.

"Oops," I said. "I guess he must have shrunk while he was hanging there."

No one said a word.

———

Another day, another homicide investigation. When I left the crime scene, Rogers and Ellis were arguing about getting more bodies to help investigate. I was sent back to Nicole's to be under some kind of house arrest while I waited for Rogers to come and interview me.

I'm not really sure what happened after that. I remember having a shower and putting on some clean clothes. But then I lay down on the bed and went to sleep.

Then came the dreams.

At first it was Tash, walking along the highway, thumb out, looking for a ride. She was picked up by someone in a white 4x4. The same one that hit me.

She was waving at me, smiling—no she was calling for help. I tried to run after her, but I couldn't move. I looked down and my feet were stuck in mud. I tried to get them free, but they wouldn't move. Hands were reaching up from the stinking mess sucking at my legs. A face appeared. I'd seen her before. It was Eliza Carter, the runaway. *Help me. Why didn't you help me?*

The ooze sucked her back down, her scared face disappearing beneath it, muck filling her nose, her eyes, and open mouth, cutting off her cries for help.

I looked desperately around for help, but no one was there, just the kookaburras in the trees, laughing at me.

The dead are drowning. The words echoed when I heard them. *You must help them, they're drowning.*

I saw Grandma Mary pointing behind me. I turned and saw the lake. It was full of water. "Who?" I shouted. "Who is drowning?"

"The dead, you must save them. Save them. Save them."

"I can't see them," I shouted.

Save them before the storms come!

"What storms?"

Lightning streaked across the sky above me, grey clouds boiled violently. I took a deep breath and dived into the water. Except there was no water. It was just the lake bottom. Dry, baked hard from the sun.

Something caught my eye in the cracks. A card, plastic, shiny. Sun glinted off it. I reached out to pick it up with trembling fingers. I turned it over and looked at the face on it. It was Tash. She wasn't smiling this time. Her face was different. Concerned. Scared.

I stood up and looked about me at the barren landscape of the lakebed.

"Tash!" I shouted. "Tash! Where are you?"

Here. Down here.

Looking down I saw her face. It poked up through the lakebed surrounded by the hard earth. *Help me, Mark. Help me.*

I dropped to my knees and clawed at the earth around her face, desperate to free her from her tomb. I scraped and scratched while she pleaded with me to go faster, but the more I did, the less I was clearing. I held my hands up and looked at the bloody stumps my fingers had become.

At my knees, Tash's face disappeared below the lakebed, and I threw back my head and called her name—

I leaped awake, Nicole's hand on my shoulder.

"Holy shit, you scared the crap out of me."

"Sorry, you were having some kind of nightmare."

"You could say that," I said with a sigh of relief.

"What was it about?"

"I'm not really sure."

She nodded. Sometimes dreams take their time getting their meanings to you. "Rogers is here to talk."

"All right."

"I'm going to have a shower while you get interrogated."

I gave her a wry smile. "What? You don't want to join the fun?"

"Maybe tonight."

"I'll look forward to it."

I found Rogers waiting for me in the kitchen. "This won't take long, Mark. I'll make it as painless as possible."

"I'm used to pain."

"Huh. Tell me what you know about the dead guy."

I ran through the events of the night before.

"And after that, you left?"

"Yes, I came back here and went to bed. Listen, Rogers, that guy was responsible for shutting down the road so the plane could land."

I could see the curiosity flash in his eyes. "How do you know that?"

"He told me."

"I don't suppose he told you any names of who else was involved."

"He said he couldn't even if he wanted to. Everyone wore masks."

"So one can't lead to the next," he surmised.

"I expect so," I replied.

He sighed. "We know how they're getting them in, but we don't know who is heading the distribution part of the operation."

"If you don't hurry up you won't find out either," I told him.

"What do you mean by that?"

"My ex-wife told me that Agosti is shutting down his operation. What you've seen is him cleaning house."

"You mean he's cutting ties with anyone who can link the whole thing back to him?"

"Permanently."

"Shit."

"Word also out of Melbourne is that he left there yesterday for an undisclosed destination," I continued.

Rogers's eyebrows raised. "You mean, he's here? Is that what you're saying?"

"The mortality rate has climbed within the last twenty-four hours; you put two and two together."

"Damn it."

"Is there anything else?" I asked.

He shook his head. "Just keep an eye out for Ellis. He wanted you locked up for interfering with the investigation. I managed to talk him down but if you keep putting your nose in so blatantly, he'll try to chop it off."

"Understood," I replied.

"Make sure you do. And if you come up with anything else, anything at all, let me know."

"I will."

Rogers stood there as though expecting me to say more but I remained silent. He nodded. "Fine, I'll be seeing you."

By the time the door closed, Nicole was done in the shower. She came out wearing a clean uniform and had just finished putting her hair up. "How did that go?" she asked.

"All right, I guess. He just warned me about Ellis."

A strange look came to Nicole's face. "What is it?" I asked her.

"I'm not sure. Something isn't right."

I chuckled dryly. "Nothing is right about any of this."

"What are you doing after I leave?" she asked me, moving into my arms. I could smell the soap she used and the freshness of the shampoo on her hair.

"I'm going to see Helen and show her the pictures I have. If she will Identify them, we'll know what we're up against."

Nicole stood there staring at me. "Was there something else?" I asked.

"The nightmare?"

"Oh, that."

"Yes, oh, that."

"I'll tell you tonight."

"Fine," she said and kissed me on the lips. She stopped. "I just realised something. Soon you'll be gone, and I'll be still here."

"Enjoy the time we have," I said.

"Oh, I intend to."

CHAPTER FIFTEEN

"Is Helen awake?" I asked Andrews when he tentatively opened the door later that afternoon.

"She's awake," he said grudgingly. "Though I don't think she feels like seeing anyone at the moment."

"I need her to look at some photos. It'll only take a few minutes."

He nodded acquiescence. "All right, come in."

Helen was sitting at the table. Andrews had made her something to eat which looked like a cross between scrambled eggs and an omelette. She'd smothered it in pepper and tomato sauce which I gathered was a habit, or the food tasted bad. "Hi, Helen. How are you doing?"

She looked up at me and gave me a wan smile. "I'm all right, I guess."

I sat down beside her and took out my phone. "I want to show you some pictures, is that okay?"

"I guess."

The first one I showed her was of Agosti. "Was this the man who shot your father?"

No words just a slight bob of the head.

I showed her two more and got the same reaction.

Climbing to my feet I placed a hand on her shoulder. "Thanks, Helen. I'll leave you in peace."

"Mark."

"Yes?"

"Could you stay a while?"

I glanced at Andrews. He gave a non-committal shrug and I smiled at the girl. "Sure."

———

After I texted Nicole confirmation of Helen's sighting, I was driving through the main street when I saw Macca and Johnno's 4X4 outside the pub. I pulled into the park next to it and climbed out. Looking at my watch I could see that the time was three-thirty. I had one more job on my list to do but it was getting late. I went inside and found the two larrikins perched up at the bar with a beer each in front of them. I nodded to Bluey and said, "I'll have a beer please, Blue."

"Coming right up."

"You blokes finished for the day," I said.

"Yeah," Macca replied. "Time to let the dog off the chain."

"I've been meaning to ask you about the lights on the lake."

Macca put his beer on the bar. "Here we go, you're going to call us crazy like the others, aren't you?"

I took the ice-cold beer from Bluey and slipped him a ten-dollar note. The glass was already gathering droplets of condensation on the outside and they soon began they downward trek in rivulets to the bar mat below it. With a shake of my head I said, "No. I'm just curious."

"All right, but if you laugh at us, I'm going to walk right over you and shit down your throat."

"You want to ditch that crap?" I asked him. "It's me you're talking to."

"Fine. Johnno and I saw lights out on the lake a couple of years ago. When we mentioned it, we were laughed at."

"What's to laugh at?"

"We saw them at the east side."

"So?"

"Most years when the lake goes dry, the east side has quicksand sinks. It may look good, but if you put one foot out of place, you're in deep shit. So, no one goes there."

"But you think someone has been?"

"The lights didn't fly there, that's for sure," Johnno said.

"I've seen where people drive onto the lakebed," I told them.

"Sure," said Macca. "Everyone does. It's just that no one goes—"

"To the east side," I finished.

He held up his beer. "Now you're beginning to understand. If you drove down there of a night, you'd just disappear. Which is why they think we're crazy."

"What about the shore? Could there have been someone there?"

"No, there's no track around that side," Macca explained. "It's part of a national forest. It's not big but it is protected. More of a patch of scrub, really."

"How many places are there to get onto the lake, then?"

"A few."

"So, you didn't see where whoever it was came off?"

"We were there, and we didn't see them come off the lake. They must have turned their lights off," Johnno explained. "Which is just fucking crazy."

"Dead-set crazy," Macca said, agreeing with his brother.

The dead are drowning.

"Can I get you blokes to show me around there in the morning?" I asked them.

Macca gave me a WTF look. "Haven't you heard what we were just telling you, mate?"

"I heard."

"And you still want to go?"

"Yes. It'll be fun."

"Fun my arse," Macca growled.

"I'll buy you blokes a carton of beer for your trouble," I said cheerily.

They looked at each other and then back at me. "What time?"

———

"Don't ask me about the investigation," Nicole said to me later that night. "I'm under strict instructions to tell you nothing."

"I can understand that," I replied.

"What did you do for the rest of the day?"

"I went and had a beer with Macca and Johnno," I told her.

Nicole raised her eyebrows. "I'm impressed. You blokes are becoming best friends."

"They're going to show me around, tomorrow."

Now, this did make her suspicious. "What are you up to?"

"Nothing too bad. They're going to take me out to the lake and show me a couple of things."

"Nothing out there to see," she said. "A few dry patches is about all."

"What about the sinks?"

"You'd do well to stay away from that area," Nicole told me in a stern voice. "They could swallow you up and you wouldn't ever be found."

"I promise I'll be careful. Now, what am I not allowed to ask you?"

"Damn it, Mark," she growled at me.

"I take it that there has been no news on the Agosti front."

"No."

"What about Terry Smi—"

"Quit it."

I held my hands up in mock surrender. "All right, all right. I'll say no more."

"Good. Have something to eat and then you can take me to bed."

"I like the sound of that."

"You can give me a back massage, Dick Tracy. It's as stiff as a board."

"Probably just like—"

"You finish that sentence, and you can go back to the motel."

I smiled. "You're a harsh woman, Senior Constable Berger."

"Just you remember it."

———

We arrived at the lake the following morning. The brothers in their 4X4 and me in the Monaro. The high humidity in the air indicated that a storm was possible later in the day. Both Macca and Johnno were hungover which was to be expected. Especially the way they were putting the beers away when I left the pub the previous day. I made sure the Monaro was locked before I left it.

With the Winchester in the back, I wasn't prepared to take any chances.

I said to Macca, "Are we taking your vehicle?"

He shook his head. "Nope. We walk. You want to go over to the east, we do it on foot."

"All right," I said with a shrug of my shoulders. "We walk."

The lakebed was still dry but with the storms coming through and a cyclone on the horizon off the coast of northwest Australia, it would only be a matter of weeks before the lake would start taking water. When the cyclone crossed the coast up north the remnants would feed down through the centre of the country as it moved east.

"Where does the lake get its water from?" I asked.

"Snake Creek feeds it. When it gets full it overflows to the east not far from where the sinks are."

The bottom of the lake was bone dry with a cracked surface, and the heat from the sun kicked up mercilessly from it. The hard-baked earth crunched under our boots as we walked. A constant heat haze shimmered in the distance, and to the west a band of storm clouds were already building. I pointed them out to the brothers. "They're backing up early," I said.

Macca looked at the clouds and said, "This early, it's going to be a bad one. We need to do whatever the hell it is you want then get off this hardpan or we'll be like mobile lightning rods."

That was something I hadn't considered and didn't fancy.

Thirty minutes of walking put us close to our destination. Macca stopped. He turned to me and said, "Just watch where you put your feet. The crust could give way under you at any time."

Our pace slowed as Macca and Johnno zig zagged

their way to a patch of discoloured lakebed. "There's a sink there," Macca said. He bent and picked up a rock from the lakebed. He threw it forward and the ground made a wet slopping sound as the stone disappeared.

"Nasty stuff," I muttered.

"You're not wrong," Johnno said. "There's another there, there, there, and there."

I looked where he was pointing and saw the discolorations. "That's why it's crazy to come out here of a night. Especially in a vehicle. Some of them are large enough to swallow the whole thing."

"Anyone fallen into that trap?"

"Only one bloke. There's an old Land Rover in one over there somewhere," Johnno said pointing at one of the bigger ones. "Over there where that thing is shining."

I frowned. I started walking towards it. "Watch where you're walking," he called after me.

I walked slowly, my eyes darting left and right, making sure I wasn't about to fall into the sucking depths of a sink. I reached the spot where the shining item was and bent down to pick it up.

I was bending over whatever it was when the first shot came. The was a crack and a thump as the round hammered into the ground near my feet. "Shit, get down!" I cried out. "Someone's shooting at us."

Diving onto the hard-packed earth I felt the roughness of the coarse dirt take skin off my knuckles. I ground my teeth together against the nagging pain. Another shot rang out and the impact was almost as close as the last.

I turned my head and looked back the way I'd come. The two brothers had followed my lead and were also on the ground. I started to crawl towards them like a commando on a battlefield.

More shots came and slapped into the ground. I tried to pinpoint them as I moved, and the best I could figure was that they were coming from the west side of the lake. Then I caught the flash of sunlight on glass. Whoever it was, they were using a scoped rifle. I was starting to wish I'd brought the Winchester. It might not have been accurate over the distance, but it would have made me feel good to shoot back.

"Who the frigging hell is that?" Macca yelled at me from where he and Johnno lay.

"I don't know."

"Follow us. It's not far to the scrub from here."

I watched them get to their feet and start running towards the eastern edge of the lake. Following suit, I took a deep breath and did the same, trying to follow their weaving route between the sinks as more shots pounded the lakebed around us.

The east bank of the lake was surprisingly steep. Ahead of me the two brothers were scrambling up it, utilising tree roots as handholds. I followed them up it, a bullet punching into the bank beside me. Throwing myself over the rim, I rolled into the brush beside Macca Pearce. "That got the blood pumping," he said breathing heavily.

"Hangover's gone," Johnno said.

WHACK!

Splinters flew off a branch above me. "Time to get out of here."

We slipped further back into the scrub and started to circle back around toward the vehicles. The shooting had stopped which gave us some relief. Macca looked at me as he stepped over a fallen branch. "Who do you figure that was?"

There was only one person I *could* think of that would be shooting at me. Agosti. "Someone who wants me dead." But when I thought about it, it didn't gel. The shooter was using a rifle with a scope. If they were any kind of capable marksman—or woman for that fact—I'd be dead on the lakebed.

We reached the vehicles, and I opened the back door of the Monaro, pulling the Winchester out from beneath the blanket and slammed the door.

"Whoa, lookout, it's John Wayne," Macca said surprised. "What you doing with that, Pilgrim?"

"I'm going back out there."

"Holy shit, Johnno, our private investigator friend has lost a couple of sheep from his top paddock."

"Dumb as dog turds, Macca," Johnno said agreeing with his brother. "What the hell do you want to go back out there for?"

"Someone doesn't want us to find whatever there is out there to find."

"You're a stupid galah, Hayes, you know that, right?" Macca said to me with a shake of his head. "Whoever it was could still be out there."

I tossed him the keys to the Monaro. "Here. You and Johnno take off. Find somewhere to park for a while. That way our friend out there with the rifle might think we've left. Wait for an hour and then come back for me."

"This is a stupid idea," Johnno growled. "You could have let me drive the Monaro. Macca drives like shit."

"Watch where you step," Macca cautioned me.

"Get out of here."

I watched them leave and waited for another few minutes before starting to circle back through the scrub to where we left the lakebed. I waited, watching for a tell-tale flash that the shooter was still there. When nothing came, I moved to the rim and slid down the bank to the lakebed.

My thumb cocked the hammer as I moved further out into the open. It was a case of watching the west and watching where I put my feet. One missed step out here on my own and there was no coming back.

At one point I froze when I thought I saw a flash of sunlight on glass. I brought the Winchester up to my shoulder and waited. When nothing happened, I kept going. The bush was eerily silent, dark clouds were still building to the west but as yet there was no thunder.

I reached the spot where I'd seen the shiny object on the ground. I looked around but couldn't see anything at first. I moved back a little trying to see if the sun would catch it again and pinpoint its position. Nothing doing.

I did it the hard way by walking a grid pattern without trying to kill myself. And after ten minutes, there it was. I bent down and picked it up. It was a chain with some kind of medallion on it. I put it in my pocket. For now, all that I needed to do was to get out of there before something happened.

———

The brothers were waiting for me when I returned. "You find anything?" Macca asked me.

I dug into my pocket and held up the medallion. "Only this."

He took it from me and said, "St. Christopher."

"How do you know that?"

"I'm not a complete dill," he gave me a scathing look. "Just because I come from the country doesn't mean I don't know anything."

"I never said you didn't."

"It's got a name on the back of it."

I took it from him and had a look. The engraving was partly obscured by mud, so I spat on it before rubbing it on my pants. Holding it up I could read it more clearly. "Ingrid."

"There used to be a girl at the pub called Ingrid," Johnno said. "She worked behind the bar."

"What happened to her?" I asked.

"Same as all the backpackers. She moved on."

"How long ago was that?"

"Not that long. Couple of years I guess."

My mind ticked over. "Did she come out here with anyone? Seeing anyone from town?"

Johnno shrugged. "Don't know. She was a bit of all right though. Hot little number."

"Shut up, Johnno," Macca said. "One of the boss's sheep is a bit of all right to you after a dry spell."

"But she was," Johnno insisted.

"All right, just shut up."

"Let's head back to town," I said. "There's some things I need to do."

"Shouldn't we go to the police and tell them what happened?" Macca asked.

"I'll take care of that," I told them.

"Fine. We'll go to the pub. We'll be there all day if they want us."

I reached into my pocket and took out a hundred dollars in fifty-dollar notes. "Here, a couple of cartons as I promised. "

Johnno took one. "That'll do."

Macca said, "Just remember, you need help, we'll be there somewhere."

CHAPTER SIXTEEN

I went to the station in search of Nicole. She was there along with Tom and Jace. The two detectives were off doing what they did, detecting shit. "Any news on the Agosti front?"

"You look like you've been rolling in the dirt with the pigs. What are you doing here?" Tom demanded.

I looked down at my clothes and for the first time saw how unclean they actually were. "Nothing much. Just thought I'd come in and report a shooting."

That kind of got them to stop what they were doing. "Who and where?" Tom asked.

"Out at the lake," I informed her. "Someone was shooting at me and the Pearce brothers."

"The Pearce brothers I can understand," she replied. "Maybe even you too."

"I have that effect on people."

"Come in and let Nicole take your statement."

"That's it?" I asked. "No calling out the cavalry or anything like that?"

"Not until we get a full understanding of the situation," Tom said.

Nicole took me aside to her desk. "Are you all right?"

"Yeah, I'm fine. I don't think the shooter was trying to kill me, just scare me off."

"What were you doing out at the lake?" Tom called over to me.

"Following a dream," I replied.

She stabbed a finger at me and growled, "That there is why someone is trying to shoot you."

"It's true, I was following a dream."

Tom shook her head. "Whatever. Give Nicole your statement. We've got way more important shit to be working on."

"Tell me what happened," Nicole said.

I did. Everything that had occurred. Except for the part about the chain and the theory I was working on in my head. She said, "Dangerous place the sink holes."

"It is when some prick is shooting at you," I said.

"What was this dream you had?"

"Basically, it was Grandma Mary telling me to rescue the girls who were drowning. I figured the only place they could drown was out at the lake."

"In case you haven't noticed, it's dry out there."

"It is, isn't it."

"Is there anything else you can tell me?"

"Not really."

She stared at me for a moment. "Are you sure?"

"No. I didn't see any cars, four-wheel drives, anything like that."

"All right, I guess someone will go out there and look around."

I nodded. "Is there somewhere I can get access to a computer this time on a Saturday?"

"You have to be joking," Nicole said. "You'll have to wait for Monday to get in at the library."

My mind went to Miss Melody, AKA Judge Judy. I winced. "Bugger."

Nicole said, "Go home."

I reached into my pocket and felt for the medallion. "Maybe I will. After I have a beer first."

"You do that. Do you have any idea where I might find the Pearce brothers?"

I leaned my head to the side. "It's Saturday."

Nicole nodded and sighed. "Yeah, silly question."

———

I went to the pub to look for Bluey. As I walked up to the bar Macca called out to me. He raised his beer and shouted, "Come and join us, Hayes."

I shook my head. "You'll get me into trouble."

He winked at me and went back to his beer. Rose came along the bar and asked what I wanted to drink. I said, "Nothing, thanks. I'm looking for Bluey."

"He's upstairs *helping* Helga," she replied with a roll of her eyes. "He's been out all damn morning and now he's taking more time off."

Thinking nothing of the eyeroll I asked her, "What room?"

"Four."

I pulled away from the bar and started for the stairs. My boots thudded loudly with each step. I went along the hallway to room four and was a bit surprised to find the door slightly ajar. Voices filtered out through the opening. The first one I heard was Bluey's.

"Stroke it, nice and slow."

"Is that good?" Helga.

"Beautiful, darling. Just beautiful. Now, put it in your mouth."

I frowned; my hand reached for the door.

"I don't like it."

"Just try, darling."

I could only imagine what was happening and for a moment I considered walking away. Then I heard, "I don't like the way it tastes."

Bluey's voice grew a hard, menacing edge. "You'll get bloody used to it. Don't stop."

I'd heard enough. I pushed the door open and said in a loud voice, "Rose told me you were up here helping out."

"What the fuck?" Bluey blurted out as he tried to hurriedly stuff himself back into his pants. Helga was sitting in front of him on the edge of the bed. Her shirt was beside her, leaving her in only shorts and bra. She hurriedly grabbed the shirt from the bed and got to her feet, donning the piece of clothing as she hurried to the door.

"You haven't heard of knocking?" Bluey demanded, his eyes flashing with anger.

"The door was open."

"Yeah, well, it shouldn't have been," he growled. "What do you want?"

"You had a girl named Ingrid working here?"

"You come up here to ask me a bullshit question like that?"

I shrugged. "Pretty much."

"Bloody hell. Sure, Ingrid worked for me."

"What happened to her?"

"She left like the others did. Anything else?"

My opinion of Bluey was about rock bottom by now. The once happy, customer-friendly owner was now nothing more than the stuff left behind in the sewer after all the shit has passed along. "No. Not a thing."

I went back downstairs and saw that Helga had returned to the bar. I walked along to a corner and signalled to Rose. She came down. "You want a beer, now?"

I reached into my pocket for the St. Christopher Medallion. "Have you ever seen this before?"

She looked at it then nodded. "Sure, it was Ingrid's."

"Who was Ingrid?"

"Ingrid Parker."

"Thanks."

"Is there a problem with her?"

"No, I'm sure she's fine," I said. "Does Bluey try it on with all the bar staff?"

The question surprised her. There was a moment of indecision as she looked around the bar. She nodded. "Pretty much. But I never told you that."

"Has he tried it on with you?"

"Once."

"What happened?"

"Arsehole wanted me to suck him off."

"How'd that go?"

"I punched him in the balls."

"And yet you're still here?"

"He can't sack me, he's my uncle."

This was a surprise. "Did he try it on with Inge Rasmussen?"

Again, another hesitation. "Yes."

"Is that why she left?"

"Yes."

"Thanks."

Alarm came to her eyes. "I didn't tell you that."

"Tell me what?"

Sunday came and went. I spent it laying around with Nicole who had the day off. When I wasn't laying around with her, I was trying to put two and two together from my notes.

Two cases nagged at me. What I knew from the original one was that:

- Trent had been murdered by hitmen working for Agosti, because he got too close.
- Drugs were being flown in and the road at Snake Creek was being used as an airstrip.
- Someone in town was distributing them.
- Agosti had his hitmen kill Paul because he was skimming drugs, and he killed his hitmen because they made a mess out of killing me. He also killed Helen's father.
- Helen was a witness to that, which made her important.

Still with me?

- Now they were cleaning shop, and they would need a good place to lay up while they did it.

Two questions nagged me though about the case:

- Who killed Terry Smith and was Ellis the dirty cop? We still didn't have hard evidence on that one.

Then came the girls:

- There were at least eight or nine missing, possibly more.
- Inge Rasmussen's death wasn't related to the drugs, so it was almost safe to assume she was killed by someone else.

- Why hadn't Jeff Andrews done anything about the missing?
- Why had only two been reported?
- Was Bluey involved?
- Had he ever been reported to the police?
- What was the secret of the quicksand sinks out at the lake?
- Who tried to kill me out on the Hampton Road?
- Who shot at me?
- Why was the medallion out at the lake, and what happened to Ingrid?

I looked at the notes and quite frankly it did my head in. All that information just staring back at me made my brain hurt. Then I remembered an old instructor at the academy had once said, "Son, if you have too many questions, break it down and do it one at a time."

So, I underlined the one question I thought I could answer first.

What happened to Ingrid?

Monday arrived and I went to the library to use one of their computers hopefully without incurring the wrath of Miss Melody. "You may use it for one hour," she told me in her certain way. "After that someone else is booked on it."

I thanked her and set about my search for answers. My first port of call was Facebook. See, I know some things. There were five Ingrid Parkers on Facebook, but only two in Australia. There were probably more but that was all I could find.

I clicked on the first one and found a picture of a

young redheaded woman who looked to be in her late twenties staring back at me. I scrolled down a few pictures to make sure the person in the picture belonged to the page. Once I was certain, I backed out and went to the second.

Clicking on it brought me to the page of a younger woman. This one would have been twenty at the most. She had long dark hair and olive skin. I started to scroll and stopped. The first picture I came across was of her standing out the front of a building. I looked at the sign behind her. It read, Friar's La— It was definitely the right girl. I looked at a few more pictures. She looked happy. One was taken out at the lake. It was dry. I looked at the date and noted that it was taken almost two years ago, exactly.

To get around she obviously had friends in the town. I made a note to ask Rose at the pub.

I went back to her posts and saw that not long after that day, she stopped posting.

Going back through her posts I saw that she had posted something most days. At least three or four times a week. So, for her to stop so abruptly like that, something wasn't right.

I Googled the name and came up with a lot of pictures of different women, which proved useless.

What to do next?

When in doubt, go to a great source.

Looking around the library, I took out my phone, punched in a number, and waited.

"What?"

"Thought you might have missed me," I said to Tia in an innocent voice.

"I'm busy, Mark."

"Got yourself a stiff?"

She gave a heavy sigh. "Yes."

"The butler did it."

"Shut up and tell me what you want."

"I've been trying to run down the girl whose St. Christopher medal I found. I Facebook trailed her and—"

"Stalked."

"What?"

"Facebook stalked her."

"Right," I said, rolling my eyes. "I Facebook *stalked* her and her posts end abruptly two years ago. About the same time that she left here."

"Shit, Mark, you want me to do all your work for you? You're a private investigator, investigate."

"Give me a password or two and I'll gladly do it, Tia," I replied a little testily.

"That's it, Mark, I'm hanging up."

"No, wait, Tia. Please. I'm sorry. I'm frustrated and didn't mean to take it out on you."

"Yeah, well keep it up and see what happens."

I looked around for the wicked witch of the west, but she was nowhere to be seen. I waited patiently for Tia to come around. "All right, Mark, give me a full name."

"Ingrid Parker."

"All right. I'll see what I can do. But it could be a couple of days."

"Thanks, Tia. Can you run someone else for me too?"

The sigh returned. "Give it to me."

"Bluey Edwards."

"Bluey?"

"Yes. Wait a minute."

I looked around for Miss Melody but still couldn't see her. I cleared my throat. Loudly.

And there she was. Glasses on, frown on her face. I gave her my best smile. "You wouldn't know Bluey Edwards's first name, would you?"

She looked down her nose at me, and for a moment I thought she wasn't going to tell me. "Nathan."

"Thank you, Miss Melody, you're a wonderful lady. If I wasn't already involved with someone, I'd scoop you up myself."

"Whatever," she grunted and left me to it.

"Did you get that, Tia?"

"You're involved with someone, Mark?" she asked me.

"Not now, Tia. Did you get the name?"

"Yes. Who is she?"

"Goodbye, Tia."

"Don't you hang up on me, Mark Hayes, damn it."

"Love you."

I disconnected before she could say anymore.

I went back to my notebook.

———

Being a Monday morning, the pub was reasonably quiet. I looked around the bar and wasn't surprised to find it empty. The smell of stale alcohol and cleaning fluids was heavy in the air. There was no sign of Bluey, but he wasn't the one I'd come to see. The roar of the vacuum cleaner masked my approach to Rose who was working it furiously.

I turned the machine off because I had no intention of startling her with her unaware of my approach. When the noise suddenly died, she muttered a curse under her breath and turned to see me standing there. "Oh, it's you. Bluey isn't here."

"No matter. It was you I came to see anyway," I replied.

"You keep this up and I'm going to think you fancy me."

I smiled. "Maybe if I was ten years younger."

"You know," she said, "age doesn't count for much out here."

There was a look in her eyes that said, you can have me if you want me. "I'm sure it doesn't. I needed to ask you some more questions about Ingrid."

For a second I thought I saw a hint of disappointment, but if there was, it quickly vanished. "What do you want to know?"

"Who were her close friends here in town? She had to get around somehow while she was here. I saw where she was out at the lake one time on her Facebook page."

"She didn't have many. I was one of them, until—" She stopped.

"Until what?"

She looked nervously around the bar. "She came to me and told me that Bluey had come onto her."

"What did she mean, come onto her?"

"He told her if she didn't do what he asked, he'd fire her."

"Just like that?"

She nodded.

"What did you do?" I asked.

"I accused her of lying to her face," Rose admitted. "You have to understand, at that time, he hadn't tried it on with me. But by the time that he did, it was months later, and she was gone. I sent her a message, but she never answered it."

"How long after that did she leave?"

"The next day."

"How did Bluey take to her leaving?" I asked Rose.

"He couldn't give a stuff," she said bitterly.

"Is there anyone else in town who knows what he's like?"

"I doubt it, he's always so nice to them. One of the blokes."

"Why don't you leave and go somewhere else?"

"And go where? There is nowhere else. My parents are dead and I've no brothers or sisters. Only that monster who owns this place."

I found myself feeling sorry for her. I said, "If you think of anything else, will you let me know?"

"Sure."

"Thanks."

———

I walked out into the main street and found Ellis, Rogers, and some other guy I'd never seen before waiting for me. "Just the guy we were looking for," Ellis said, a snide look on his face.

"I'm not too hard to locate."

"You'll be even easier to locate locked in a cell," he said harshly.

"Okaay."

"Where is the witness you've got hidden away?"

Shit. "Witness?" I said innocently.

"Don't be an arsehole, Hayes. We know you've got Helen Miller stashed away somewhere."

"You need to bring her forward, Hayes," Rogers said. "She needs to be in police custody."

"Who told you?" I asked.

"That doesn't matter—" Ellis started but my crisp words cut him off.

"Bullshit it doesn't."

"I beg your pardon."

"You heard me, Ellis. I said, bullshit."

"Then we'll lock you up until you tell us."

Sometimes the best defence is offence, so I went on

the attack to try and put them off balance. "I'll hand her over as soon as you get an IA person out here." My eyes diverted to the newcomer. He was thickset, tall, and carried himself with an air of arrogance. Just what I needed. "You aren't IA, are you?"

"Drug Squad," he grunted. "Senior Detective Rick Byers."

"Then you won't do."

"We're not calling IA out here, Hayes," Ellis stated. "Not for you or anyone else."

"Then you don't get the witness."

"What?"

"That girl saw Agosti shoot his two hitmen as well as her father. She also overheard the bastard say that the detective would take care of it. Now do you understand why I—"

"Oh, grow up," Ellis snarled. "Turn around and put your hands behind your back."

"Wait a minute," Byers said in an authoritative voice. "This is my case now. Remember. Mine and my team. You two are to keep on with the death of the bloke you found hanging."

Ellis muttered something under his breath. Byers's gaze grew hard. "What was that, Detective?"

"On our way, sir."

"Good. I can take it from here."

Ellis and Rogers left, leaving me there with Byers. "You'll have to trust someone, you know? Eventually."

"You asking me to trust you?"

"I'm as good as the next person."

"Who called you?"

"What?"

"Were you sent out here just because the job came up and was getting out of hand or did someone ask you to come?"

He looked at me, a wry smile on his face. "I heard you were a cop once. You should have stayed one."

"Who?"

"Rogers."

"How many on your team?"

"Me and two others," Byers replied.

"Can you get her out of here today?"

He nodded. "Yes."

"You sure?"

"I can promise you she'll be gone today."

"You're not Drug Squad, are you?"

He shook his head. "I'm part of a larger taskforce that deals with police corruption in organized crime."

"You mind if I see your ID?"

He flashed his badge at me. "All right I'll take you to her."

"Wise move, my man."

"Just you, no one else."

"That's fine."

"We'll take my car."

Byers nodded. "Again, fine."

We climbed into the Monaro. "Nice ride," Byers said. "Where did you get it?"

"Here in town."

"Did the rifle come with it?"

I stopped what I was doing and looked at him. "Since I've been in town someone has tried to kill me three times."

"Is it registered?"

"I'm sure it was at one time."

"Good thing I didn't see it then. Otherwise, I'd have to arrest you."

"Definitely," I said and turned the key.

The engine roared to life and the car vibrated with the

power surging through her. I backed out of the park, and we drove to the Andrews residence.

———

"I'm not going with him!" Helen shouted. "No way at all."

"But you'll be safer with them," Helen," I told her. "He works for a special taskforce."

"I don't care."

"You're better off away from here," Andrews said. "I'm not good company for you."

Her gaze settled on me. "I'm scared."

"Sweetie," Byers said, "I know this is way out there but there's no other option. It isn't safe for you, here. Not anymore."

"No."

Byers looked at me. "What do you suggest?"

I reached into my pocket and took out my phone. I punched in a number I memorized and waited until it was answered. "Are you busy?"

———

"Where is she?" Tom asked as she came in through the door.

I indicated the lounge where Helen sat quietly staring at the floor. Tom said, "Everybody out."

"Tomika—" Andrews started.

"Sorry, Boss, but I need to talk to her alone."

Andrews threw his arms up in the air. "Fine. It's not like it's my house anyway."

When we went outside, I saw Nicole leaning against the front quarter panel of one of the Nissans. She smiled at me and said, "This is a good thing, Mark."

Still full of uncertainty, I said, "I hope you're right, Nic. I really do."

I stood beside her in silence, a lot on my mind. She reached up and placed a hand on my shoulder and said, "What's wrong?"

"I think—" A car with a hole in the exhaust roared past and I had to stop so I didn't need to shout. We were apart from the others but trying to get above the noise would have them hearing everything I had to say. I started again after the sound had faded into the distance. "I think I've found another missing girl. I'm just waiting on Tia to do a search."

"That woman must be sick of you by now."

"Probably."

"Tell me about the girl."

"She was in town until an incident a couple of years ago," I informed her. "After that she left. I checked her social media profile and her Facebook page stops getting posts at the same time."

"How did you come about all of this?"

"I found a medallion out at the lake. It had a name on it and the Pearce brothers gave me the full name of the girl who'd worked at the pub. Rose filled me in on the rest."

Nicole gave me a concerned look. "What rest?"

"Bluey put the hard word on her, and she cleared out the next day. He told her he'd sack her if she didn't do as he asked. She refused. She told Rose, who didn't believe her. Then sometime later, he tried it with Rose."

"His niece?" Nicole said, disbelief on her face.

"Yes. I went looking for him before I knew all of this and I found him upstairs with Helga, the new barmaid and he was trying the same with her."

"The bloody arsehole."

"He's that and more. He just shot to the top of my suspect list."

"Suspect for what? The missing girls?"

I nodded. "Rose said he tries it on with all the girls."

"I have a feeling there is an 'and' coming."

"He tried it on with Inge Rasmussen which was why she left."

"I thought there was another reason for that?"

"So did I."

"We're going to have to bring her in for a chat," Nicole said.

"I expect you will."

Tom and Helen appeared in the doorway of Andrews's home. They came down the stairs and Tom said to Byers, "She's agreed to go but I'll come so far with her."

He nodded. "I'll set the wheels in motion. The problem we have is that she has to be driven to an airstrip somewhere. The longer she's out in the open increases the risk of exposure to danger."

"I know of somewhere," I said.

Tom looked at me. She nodded knowing where I was going with it. "It should be long enough."

"What are you talking about?" Byers asked.

"Snake Creek," she told him.

"What's Snake Creek?"

He hadn't been told about the strip. I said, "Agosti had someone from Main Roads widen that section, when they built the new bridge, and it's about a kilometre long. They've been using it to land drugs before distribution."

"Why wasn't I told about this?" he growled.

I shrugged. "That's something you'll have to take up with your fellow officers."

"All right, it sounds like we've got a place. It'll take a

few hours, but we'll get her out of here. I'll advise the bosses that we have a witness and a plan."

Everyone seemed satisfied with that. Everyone except me. You see, there's something to be said for the best laid plans. Something always comes along to screw them up. This time was no exception.

CHAPTER SEVENTEEN

Nicole and I had a quick bite of lunch at her place while Tom kept an eye on Helen at Andrews's house. The Drug Squad detectives were working out their end of things while trying to figure out where Agosti and his goons were. Ellis and Rogers were off questioning all possible links to Terry Smith.

"I'll go and speak to Rose after I've finished my lunch," Nicole said to me around a mouthful of salad sandwich.

I winced. "How can you eat that stuff?"

"What stuff?" she asked with a curious frown.

"That bloody rabbit tucker."

She smiled. A broad grin that revealed some of the contents of her mouth. "It's yummy."

I shook my head in disgust.

"Give me a kiss."

"You're a bloody animal, Nic. Fair dinkum."

The rooster crowed. I took the phone out and looked at the screen. It was Tia. I put her on speaker. "Hey Tia, you're with me and Nic."

"Nic, huh?" Her voice held an edge of suspicion.

"Oh, shut up," I growled. "I take it you have something for me?"

"Yes, and it's all bad news, I'm afraid."

"Let me have it."

"Ingrid Parker went missing two years ago about the same time her Facebook posts stopped."

"Makes sense," I said.

"But get this. She was reported missing, and her last known sighting was Cobar."

I frowned. "All right."

"No one there remembered seeing her. Every time she posted something, the page had her location as Cobar, so it was assumed that that's where she disappeared from."

"So, it's possible she wasn't?"

"Yes."

Nicole said, "Did the investigators even check out Friar's Lake?"

"Not that I'm aware of."

"Shit," I hissed.

"Now for the other bad news," Tia said to me. "I checked out your publican. Nathan 'Bluey' Edwards was once a resident of the great state of Victoria. Around St. James outside of Benalla. He ran the pub there. From all reports, he was up to the same vile acts that you said he is doing now."

"I gather he was investigated."

"Yes, but nothing came of it and he left."

"I think I know where he went from there," I said in a gruff voice. "Any reports of missing women in that area?"

"Nothing around his time but it doesn't mean he couldn't have escalated once he left. I think this needs to be taken further, Mark."

Nicole said, "I'll inform the detectives on the case of Inge Rasmussen."

"This guy should be at the top of their list."

"I agree."

Tia hung up and Nicole stuffed down the rest of her monstrosity. "I'm going back to work, now. Try to stay out of trouble."

"Always."

She leaned in and kissed me. It felt and tasted good, in spite of the remnants of rabbit tucker lingering on her lips. I was starting to develop feelings towards her, and I wished in a way I could stop. I hadn't felt like this since Tia and I began going out.

"Stay safe," I said to her and watched her walk out the door.

———

It was about three in the afternoon when the proverbial hit the fan. I heard the siren and hurried out the front door of Nicole's place to see one of the Nissans approaching. Nicole was driving and I guessed she was headed out of town. Something told me whatever had happened was bad, so I ran back to close the door before running for the Monaro.

Days later you could still see the black marks on the road where the muscle car had peeled rubber on the street as I took off after her.

Heading out of town on the Hampton Road the needle on the speedo was touching seventy. That's miles per hour.

The machine tore along in the wake of the Nissan that had lights going and Nicole had her foot pressed to the floor. I looked down at the speedometer and the needle sat on eighty. The intense speed cut down the travel time to where we were headed.

Something caught my attention in the rear-view

mirror. I glanced up and saw another police vehicle behind me. I figured this to be Jace.

He was driving the worked highway patrol Commodore I'd seen at the station when I'd first arrived. It blew past me like I was standing still and did the same with the Nissan.

A short time later, we all came to a stop at Snake Creek amidst a scene of utter carnage.

The first thing I noticed was the plane. A light aircraft, possibly a Cessna. I wasn't too sure because the main thing I like about flying is the wheels touching the ground when the damn thing lands. Then there were the bodies. Four on the ground. Three Drug Squad cops and the fourth was Tom. Nicole was already bending over her talking frantically. It was like the scene out of a bad movie. I took a step forward and my boot crunched on something. I looked down and saw the spent casings on the ground. Someone had stood where I was and let rip with an automatic weapon.

"Mark!"

Looking up I saw Nicole waving at me. "Mark, over here."

I hurried across and looked down at Tom. She'd been hit twice in the torso and had obviously lost a lot of blood. Her eyes were open, and a thin trickle of blood ran from the corner of her mouth.

"Mark," Nicole said to me in a calm voice. She could obviously see that my mind was running faster than the Monaro had been on the way out. "Mark, take a breath and put pressure on this wound."

"Which one?" I asked dumbly, looking at the one under the ribcage.

"The one here on her chest," Nicole said. "Under my hands. It's bleeding worse than the other."

I knelt beside Tom and Nicole lifted her hands,

releasing a fresh wash of dark red from the hole I could see through the fabric. I placed my hands over it and started to press down. Tom screamed and bucked under the pressure. I tore my hands away from her as though stung by a bee.

"Get them back there, Mark," Nicole snapped. "Put pressure on the wound or she'll die."

I placed my hands back on the wound. Tom's screams were less intense this time and she soon went quiet. Nicole said, "That's it. The ambulance will be here in a minute. I need to check the others."

"What happened?" I asked her.

"Agosti took Helen."

Nicole climbed to her feet, and I could see the wet stains on her knees where she'd been kneeling in Tom's blood. I looked back down at the wounded sergeant and could see that her colour had changed to a pasty grey. Her eyes were open, and she stared up at me. Her bottom lip quivered as she tried to speak. I spoke first, "Hang in there, Tom. You'll be fine."

The sound of the ambulance siren was faint but becoming louder as it closed the distance to our position. "You hear that," I said. "They're almost here."

"B—Byers," Tom managed.

"He's been shot," I told her.

"N—No."

"Take it easy."

"Byers," she grated using whatever strength she had left. She choked, coughed and said, "Byers did this."

Tom's breathing stopped and her head lolled to one side. I felt rage well up inside me and tears come to my eyes. My head fell to my chest and my hands stopped their downward pressure. The screaming siren was unbelievably loud and suddenly went silent. The ambulance had finally arrived. Too late for Tom.

I sat on the edge of the road, my rage building to a simmer like a slow cooker. The sun was going down in the west and things were still happening all around me. At one point I thought I heard Nicole say that there was a whole police taskforce headed our way. The final tally had been four police officers dead as well as the civilian pilot who had been supposed to fly Helen and one of the Drug Squad cops back to civilisation.

The surprise came when Nicole walked up behind me and advised me that one of the dead was Detective Darren Rogers. Tom's last words had been proven right. There was no sign of Byers anywhere. He'd been in on it.

"Did Tom say anything else before she died?" Nicole asked me for a fourth time. Or was it the fifth?

"No."

I looked over to where Tom lay, a sheet over her. "This is fucked."

Nicole reached down and grabbed my shoulder. "I know. But no one could have known Byers was bad."

Staring at Nicole I asked, "Why would they take Helen? Why not just kill her here?"

"I don't know."

"What do you make of it?" I asked her.

"I'm no detective but it looks like they waited until the plane landed before hitting them."

"He must have told Ellis which is why Rogers is here," I said. "The automatic weapons would be Agosti's men."

Nicole nodded. "The crime scene guys, and Homicide will piece it all together."

"I thought you said they were sending a taskforce?"

"They will but they'll send an advance team from Dubbo first to get started."

"How's Jace taking it?" I asked her.

"He's a bit like me," she replied. "Feels numb. Shock."

"Yeah."

"What I can't figure out is where they were hiding. It had to be somewhere close by but out of the way."

I nodded.

"There's plenty of that out here," I said climbing to my feet. I looked down at my hands. They were dark with dried blood. Tom's blood. "Shit."

"Wait there," Nicole said to me before hurrying off.

When she returned she had a bottle of water. "Here."

She tipped it so I could wash off the blood. With that done I flicked off the excess water and left them to air dry at my sides. "I'm going back to town."

"Are you all right?" Nicole asked.

"Yeah. It's just not every day you watch someone die right in front of you. Not someone you know, anyway."

She nodded knowingly and I wondered what kind of inner turmoil was wrenching at her guts. She looked stoic on the outside, but I figured there was something she was fighting to keep compartmentalised. "I'll see you when I see you."

"I'm starting to wish I had never taken this bastard job."

Nicole's reply was a wan smile.

I walked back to the Monaro and climbed in. For a moment I just sat there breathing deeply before turning the key. The engine gurgled to life, and I put it into reverse so I could turn around. On the move once more, albeit a bit slower, I drove back towards Friar's Lake.

———

I stomped on the brakes and the Monaro shuddered to a standstill in the middle of the road. I looked out the driver's side window and stared at the dirt road. There was something about it that had caught my eye and it took a few moments before I realised what it was. The marks on it. Someone had taken the turn at a rate of knots so that the rear of the vehicle they were driving had fishtailed.

Turning onto the road, I stopped and climbed out. The motor was still running, and the chug-chug seemed louder than normal as I stood beside the car. Reaching back in through the open window I flicked the key off and the motor died.

The silence was eerie. In the orange glow of the late afternoon, I could hear nothing apart from the tick of the engine cooling. Not even the wind. My first step was a loud crunch of boot on gravel. The second seemed softer. Suddenly a galah flew past, ducking and diving, making its raspy shrieking call.

I stopped and looked down. A vehicle had definitely gone through here fast. A frown crossed my face. The skid marks on the gravel didn't add up. I traced each one with my eyes and then realised there were two sets. Two vehicles.

Raising my gaze, I stared along the gravel road. I knew of only one place that they could be going. It was off the beaten track and secluded enough to be private. "Bastard."

I reached into my pocket and took out my phone. No signal. A kookaburra laughed. Maybe it knew something I didn't.

———

The Monaro chugged to a stop near the gateway. I climbed out and took the Winchester from the back along with a box of shells that I placed in my pocket. Gone was the heat haze of the day as the sun began its hurried slip below the horizon. Another twenty minutes or so and it would be dark.

I sat and waited on the hood of the car. I was almost certain they knew I was there. The flatness of the land would have ensured that. But if it hadn't given it away, then the plume of dust from the gravel road would have.

A figure appeared near the house. It stood there for a moment, and I guessed whoever it was might have had a set of binoculars. Checking me out. They disappeared back inside before reappearing. Whoever it was began walking towards me along the gravel driveway. It took several minutes to reach me and once within normal eyesight range I confirmed that it was Byers. I let him get to about thirty metres out before I said, "That'll do you."

He stopped. "You shouldn't have come here, Hayes."

"There's a lot of things I shouldn't do," I allowed. "However, you bastards kind of pissed me off. Where's the girl?"

"She's fine for the moment."

"What about the Turners?"

"We've no argument with them."

"Where are we at, Byers?" I asked.

He looked around. "As far as you're concerned, we're at the gates of Hell. Get back in that piece of shit and go away. One time offer."

"Give me the Turners and the girl and I might just do that."

"This isn't a negotiation," Byers said calmly.

"Never thought that it was."

"Last chance, Hayes. Like I said, this is a one-time offer."

"I guess I'll pass."

Rather than expecting him to try to kill me then and there, I thought he'd head back to the farmhouse, get Ellis or one of the others, an automatic weapon, and then come after me. Which was why his next move took me by surprise. It almost cost me my life.

While we'd been talking, his right hand had been moving slowly behind his back. When it reappeared, the weapon filling it was moving quickly into line and snapping a shot at me. The bullet fizzed past me and ricocheted off the top of the Monaro.

The Winchester I was holding needed no convincing (okay so maybe it was me who made the decision), and had travelled the short distance it needed to snap into line with the Drug Squad cop. I depressed the trigger and the weapon bucked in my grip as he fired a second time.

I've never professed to being an expert marksman, but I can generally hit what I aim at. The same couldn't be said about the cop I'd just shot though, as his second round flew wider than the first.

The Winchester could stop a grizzly so you could imagine what it did to a crooked cop from the city. The bullet punched into his chest and blew a fist-sized hole in his back, ruining his suit. Byers dropped into the dust and gravel of the drive. Even though I wasn't that close to him I could imagine the dry earth beneath him drinking greedily at the thick liquid. I worked the lever and jacked another round into the breech just in case he was still alive. As it turned out I needn't have worried. Not about him, anyway.

There was a sharp crack as a bullet came from long range. The boom of the shot was close on its heels. The round passed close and rolled off the Monaro's hood and onto the gravel road behind it. Someone was shooting at me with a rifle.

Another round came in and I heard the bullet smash into the other side of the vehicle. I ground my teeth together. Didn't these pricks know anything about classic cars?

Another shot, another hit. I wriggled around to put the engine block between myself and the farmhouse.

The shooting stopped, and I looked skyward. It was darkening and I saw the evening star already up. I'd decided to give it a while before going in after them. Not considering myself a super brave or heroic kind of guy, I knew that there was no way that the girl inside that farmhouse, depending on my actions to rescue her, would be left to fend for herself. I couldn't let her down. Plus, I still had no reception with the phone.

I waited. Just thirty metres from where I huddled behind the Monaro, the last flies of the day feasted on the dead cop.

———

The sun had been down for an hour, and I still hadn't moved. Neither had they. Not that they had to. They were the ones sequestered away in a prime defensive position.

Waiting a further ten minutes before I moved, I left the cover of the Monaro and started towards the farmhouse via a circuitous route. Once through the gateway and across the cattlegrid I moved to the fallen Drug Squad cop and took his handgun, tucking it into my jeans. Then I went left, keeping low as I tried not to skyline myself against the flat horizon. As far as I knew there were still four men inside.

Crossing the open ground had me exposed, and with each step I felt as though someone was drawing a bead on my back and about to open fire with an automatic weapon. Thankfully, the feeling was only my fatalistic imagination, and it didn't eventuate. I reached the machinery shed and slid along the corrugated iron wall towards the front where it was open and exposed to the elements. I edged into the shadows and jogged across to the tractor.

A low growl greeted me, and I froze. Turner's dog. "Is that you, pup?" I asked.

The animal seemed to recognise my voice and gave a whimper before coming out from underneath the farm equipment, wagged his tail and nuzzled my leg. I reached down and rubbed it between the ears. "What are those bad men up to, pup, eh?"

The dog whimpered some more then crawled back beneath the tractor. While I was there, something occurred to me. This was a working station. Where were the station hands? Then I realized that Turner was a crop farmer so would do most of the work himself.

Moving out of the machinery shed, I saw the two vehicles that Agosti and his goons were using. A snap decision made, I nodded my satisfaction and aimed the Winchester at the first. I fired. Bullets punched into the tyres I could see. I shifted aim to the next one and repeated my actions. Both vehicles had flats by the time I backed away and disappeared into the shadows.

Shouts emanated from within the farmhouse and figures soon appeared. One of them had a torch and they shone it on the cars. I heard someone mutter a curse as they started back towards the house.

"Ellis?" I called out.

Sudden automatic weapon fire erupted, spraying bullets in my general direction. Luckily however, I'd taken shelter behind a water tank beside the machinery shed. It might have been made of poly but there was no chance the bullets could make it through all that water (I was hoping that the tank was close to full) to get to me.

The firing stopped. "Ellis?" I called out again.

"I'm here, Hayes."

"Send the girl and the Turners out and I'll let you leave."

"Like you're in a position to give orders," Ellis shouted back.

"The police are on their way," I lied.

"Fuck off, there's no mobile reception."

I guessed he wasn't totally dumb then.

"Is Byers dead?" he called out to me.

"Dead enough for the crows to eat."

"Shame. He was a good partner back in the day."

So, that was their connection.

"Is Agosti with you?" I called back to the crooked cop.

"Yeah, he's here."

"What's he want with the girl?"

"What do you mean?"

"The girl. She saw him kill her father but he's keeping her alive. Why? I'd have thought he would have just killed her with the others."

"You don't know, do you?" Ellis's voice seemed to have a chuckle to it.

"Know what?"

"Her mother isn't dead. She's in Melbourne. Her being dead was just a story that the father put around because he couldn't accept that she left him and the kid behind."

"She left him for Agosti?"

"Sure. That's where the money was."

"So, why now? Why come after the girl?"

"It was either take her or let her be part of the clean-up."

"Damn messy clean-up if you ask me," I said tightening my grip on the Winchester.

"Blame yourself for that. One man brought the whole

thing crashing down. We're going to have to leave the bloody country now."

"I can see how you might want to," I replied.

The dog growled.

I swung around and saw the shadow looming up in the darkness. I was too late to bring the Winchester around to fire so I did the only thing I could. I threw myself to the packed earth just as the shooter opened fire.

The weapon in the shooter's hands rattled to life. It was an automatic and bullets fizzed all around me. It had been one of those moments by rights that I should have died with at least three or four holes in me, my life's blood draining away as I breathed my last. However, the shooter was a piss-poor shot or I was just lucky.

I rolled and brought the Winchester around. As soon as the barrel centred, I tugged on the trigger. I didn't hit the bastard, but I made him think twice. He seemed to flinch.

I threw the rifle away and reached for the handgun I'd taken from Byers's body. I could use the rifle proficiently but in my class at the academy I was top two using a handgun. Second only to the girl I married. I still think she cheated.

The weapon in my fist bucked three times and I heard the shooter cry out in pain. He doubled over and tried to backpedal away from me. I fired twice more and with a whimper he sagged to the ground and died, curled up in a ball.

I came to my feet and taking the rifle, moved further into the shadows. I heard Ellis call out. "Walsh? Did you get him?"

When no answer came, Ellis's voice grew in pitch. "Walsh? Answer me."

"He can't hear you," I called out.

"Christ, Hayes. Why don't you just die already?"

"Bit busy to be doing something like that, Ellis. Mind you, I'm willing to go away."

"You know where the gate is."

"And you know my price," I called back.

A long silence ensued, and I shifted nervously unsure whether someone else was trying to sneak up on me. I transferred the rifle to my left hand and took the handgun from my pants once more. At least I had the dog watching my back.

A couple of minutes later, Ellis's voice came to me. "Agosti said he'll give you the farmers, but he keeps the girl."

"What if I refuse?"

"Then he'll shoot the woman."

There was that.

"If I agree then I walk out of here with the Turners?"

"That's right."

He obviously wasn't going to kill the girl. And letting me go just like that? Something wasn't right. "What's the catch?"

"What do you mean?"

"You let me go and that's it? I'll have the cops back here in no time. No, there's something else."

"You can, but by then we'll be gone. The choice is yours, Hayes."

"All right, send them out."

Minutes later, the Turners emerged from the darkness. Bill had his arm around his wife's shoulders. "Are you all right?" I asked them.

"About as good as can be expected," Turner said.

"Did they hurt you in any way?"

"Not really."

"Mrs. Turner, are you all right?"

"That poor child," she sobbed. "We can't just leave her there."

"I don't intend to," I said quietly.

"Well, Hayes?" Ellis called out.

"We're going."

I ushered the Turners through the machinery shed and out through the shadows of the yard until we were retracing my steps to the gate and the Monaro. Once I was sure we were out of earshot I said to Turner, "Tell me what happened."

"They showed up late this afternoon. I was out in the yard. I'd not long come in from the north paddock. By the time I worked out they were trouble I had two guns pointed at me."

"Is Helen all right?"

"Yes. They were given orders by their boss not to hurt her."

"Did you hear anything about what they're planning to do?" I asked.

"I didn't hear anything," Turner said.

"I heard them talking about a plane," Gwen said.

I knew that the road they always used was off the table, so what was another option? "Where would they land it?"

"Nowhere around here," Turner said.

We reached the gate and stepped across the cattlegrid. The moon was up by now and it lit the darkened landscape enough for us to see. When we reached the Monaro, I took the keys out of my pocket and gave them to Turner. "What do you want me to do with these?" he asked.

"Take your wife out to the Hampton Road and head to Snake Creek," I explained. "The police are there. Tell them what's happening."

"What about you?"

"I'm going back for Helen."

"On your own?"

I was about to speak when I heard a sound in the distance. It started out a low thud-thud-thud. But as it grew closer the sound changed to a clearer whop-whop-whop. I looked to the darkened sky and saw the flashing light in the distance. At least now I knew how they were going to get away. I turned back to the Turners. "Hurry. Go now."

"Is that a—" Turner started.

"Yeah, a helicopter. That's how they're getting out of here."

————

The Monaro spun its wheels on the gravel as it took off back towards the Hampton Road. I was headed in the opposite direction as I jogged towards the farmhouse. In the sky the helicopter was beginning its final approach and I needed to get to wherever the hell it was going to land to try and stop it.

As I came around the side of the farmhouse, I could see figures hurrying towards a blazing fuel drum which was obviously being used as a beacon of sorts for the helicopter to land. The sound of the machine grew deafening as it approached. I didn't want to shoot the helicopter down, just scare it off. I brought the rifle up and opened fire at it. I knew at the time I was hitting it. But that pilot wasn't deviating from his course.

Undeterred myself, I continued to fire until the tubular magazine on the Winchester was empty. That was when the others started firing at me. The first indication was the sound of a bullet passing close to my head as I was reloading the rifle from the box of rounds I had in my pocket.

That really caught my attention.

Through the swirl of dust and debris being kicked up

by the helicopter, I could make out the figure no more than thirty metres from where I stood. Whoever it was had broken away from the others to deal with me, cutting short my attempt to prevent them from getting away with Helen.

I dropped the rifle and took out Byers's handgun. Another bullet snapped close as it cut through the dirty haze. Grit and shit were starting to get into my eyes, and I had to squint to keep it out. I pointed the weapon in my fist at the rapidly disappearing figure before me and squeezed the trigger until the slide on top latched back indicating that there were no more rounds in the magazine.

Then everything went dark as the cloud of debris grew thicker. I realised then that I wasn't going to stop them from getting away with Helen. I dropped to my knees and buried my face inside my shirt so I could breathe without filling my lungs with dirt.

Then the whine of the rotors increased in pitch once more and the blustery gale became even more intense before decreasing again as the helicopter lifted into the sky and flew away.

I came to my feet and looked up into the darkened sky at the fading flashing lights of the machine. I muttered a curse under my breath, feeling defeated and deflated. Looking around I could see the body of the shooter lying on the ground, illuminated by the still burning fuel drum. I walked over and looked down at the still form. The shooter was lying on his back, and I could tell by the flickering orange light that it was Ellis.

Great, I'd now shot two cops. They were really going to love me.

In the distance I could hear the sirens. The cavalry was on the way. Just too bloody late.

CHAPTER EIGHTEEN

For the next couple of days, I was questioned incessantly about my part in what had transpired and the deaths of the two detectives. I was almost certain they were going to charge me with something good. Murder, manslaughter, assault with a deadly weapon, prostitution, credit card fraud. Maybe all the above. In the end everything around me seemed to go away, after a meeting with a high-ranking officer from Professional Standards Command.

His name was Stewart Higgins. That's all he gave me. No rank, just his name. He then proceeded to question me about everything I knew.

"Name?"

"Mark Hayes."

"Occupation?"

"Private Investigator."

"What were you doing in Friar's Lake?"

"Looking for someone."

"Who?"

The guy was starting to rub me the wrong way. He had a permanent look of disdain on his face and gave off the impression that he had no time for any human being apart from himself. "Someone a client asked me to find."

"Did you find him?"

"Yeah. Dead under a bridge."

Higgins stared at me. "Why didn't you leave then?"

"I wanted to know what happened to him."

"You leave those things to the police."

"The crooked ones you lot sent here?" I asked taking a cheap shot.

He asked a few more questions covering a range of things from my first encounter with Paul the bartender, to finding him dead, then Terry Smith and the finding of his body. The questions also got around to the relationship I had with Rogers and the one with Nicole.

Then, Helen Miller.

"Why did you hide her?"

"She called me for help."

"That wasn't the first time, was it?"

He was referring to the car accident. "No."

"So why do it again?"

"The girl had seen her father murdered by Agosti," I said. "Have your lot found anything yet?"

"Did anyone else know you had her hidden away at former Senior Sergeant Andrews's home?"

"Not at first."

"Why not?"

"Isn't that obvious?"

"Who did you tell?"

"Tom and Nicole."

"Sergeant Tomika Rains and Senior Constable Nicole Berger?"

"That's right."

"Then Senior Detective Rick Byers?"

"Eventually."

"What happened with the detective?"

"Byers?"

Higgins nodded stiffly. "Yes."

"I killed him."

"Not then, before. With the girl."

"I took him to see the girl—Helen. He wanted her to go into protective custody. She didn't want to."

"Then what happened?"

"I had Tom come and talk to her."

"Sergeant Tomika Rains?"

"That's what I said." My voice was curt.

"Then what?"

"She talked Helen into going into custody."

More questions ensued and then we got to the part about the incident at Snake Creek. He said, "When did you become aware about the incident at Snake Creek?"

"When I saw Nicole driving out of town in a hurry."

"Senior Constable—"

"Yes, that's right," I said cutting him off.

"Nicole Berger."

I remained silent.

"Answer for the tape."

"Yes."

"What happened after you saw her driving out of town?"

"Do I need a lawyer?"

He looked at me as if I were stupid. "You're worrying about that now?"

I shrugged.

He shook his head. "Answer the questions and we'll discuss the other later."

I nodded. "I followed her out of town."

"Senior Constable Nicole Berger?"

"Yes." Christ he was annoying.

"And then?"

"When I reached the site of the incident, Senior

Constable Berger was leaning over Sergeant Rains trying to stop her bleeding out."

"Sergeant Rains had been shot."

"Twice."

"Continue."

"Nicole—"

"Senior Constable Berger."

"Senior Constable Berger asked me to keep pressure on the main wound while she and the other constable saw to the others."

"And was Sergeant Rains unconscious or awake at this time?"

"She was awake."

"Did she say anything?"

I nodded. "She said Byers did this."

"Meaning what?"

"Meaning he was responsible for the ambush."

"Did she say anything else?" Higgins asked.

"No. She died."

Higgins paused. I could virtually see his mind ticking over. Then he said, "Let's skip forward to the farm. Why did you think they were there?"

"I saw the marks on the gravel road."

"But they could have been made by anyone."

"But they weren't."

"Again, why did you think they were there?"

"I had a feeling."

"Uh, huh." This was the first time he'd deviated from the questioning. A grunt. "Why didn't you try to call someone if you had a feeling?"

"There was no reception."

"So you took it upon yourself to keep going instead of going to the police," Higgins said, his voice taking on a condescending edge.

"I was thinking of the girl," I shot back at him.

"Helen Miller?"

"Yes."

"So, you got to the farm and then what happened?"

"I stopped at the gate and sat on the car bonnet waiting for it to get dark."

"Just sat there?"

"Yes."

"At what point did you get the rifle from your car?" Higgins asked me.

"About that time."

"They obviously saw you," Higgins surmised.

"They did."

"And?"

"Byers came out to talk."

"What about?"

"About me going away."

"What did you say?" Higgins asked.

"I told him I wasn't going anywhere."

"What did the detective do then?"

"He tried to kill me. Missed and hit my car. Pissed me off."

"Is that when you shot him?"

"That's right."

"Was he dead then?"

"If they kill bears, they'll kill a dirty cop."

"What happened after that?"

"I waited for dark."

Higgins nodded. "Then you went where?"

"I took Byers's weapon as backup and walked around the house to the machinery shed. I found their cars and shot the tyres out so they couldn't go anywhere."

"That helped a lot," Higgins said with sarcasm.

"Hey, I didn't know there would be a bloody helicopter at the time," I replied heatedly.

He ignored my outburst. "What did they do after you did that?"

"They tried to kill me again," I told him. "Ellis kept me talking while one of their goons tried to creep up behind me and shoot me in the back. If it hadn't been for the dog, I'd be dead right now."

"So, you shot Byers and then Walsh," Higgins said.

"I didn't know it was Walsh at the time," I explained. "The same with Ellis."

"We'll get to Ellis. Tell me what happened next."

"They offered to give me the Turners but not the girl if I'd go away."

"And you accepted the deal?"

"Only after Ellis explained a few things," I replied.

"Explained what?"

"That Helen's mother was still alive and living with Agosti. I couldn't figure out why they hadn't killed her. That told me all I needed to know. They wouldn't hurt her. The Turners on the other hand were a different kettle of fish."

"And they released them?"

"Yes. I took them to safety and then went back after I worked out that Agosti was waiting on a helicopter."

"You went back for the girl?"

"I wasn't going to leave her there."

"Can you remember anything about the helicopter?"

"No, except that it was big."

He nodded slowly once more. "Tell me about Ellis."

"Like I said, I didn't know it was Ellis at the time. The helicopter was landing even after I'd shot it a—"

"Wait," Higgins said. "You shot the helicopter?"

"Yes, for all the good that it did. The pilot just brought that damned thing in and landed anyway."

"Did you tell the investigators you shot at the helicopter?"

"Should I have?"

"It's possible that the pilot had experience flying in a combat zone," Higgins explained. "A normal civilian contractor possibly would have aborted the landing once he'd noticed the aircraft getting hit. So yeah, you should have. Keep going."

"As the helicopter was landing there was all this dirt and shit flying around. Ellis—I didn't know it was him at the time—came out of the crap and shot at me. I shot back, he died. The helicopter took off. There was nothing I could do about it. I found out that the dead shooter was Ellis after the helicopter was gone. By then, the Turners had informed the police what was happening, and they turned up not long after."

"Is that it?"

"As much as I can remember. Did you find the helicopter?"

"Yes."

"What about Agosti? Helen?"

"They've left the country."

My heart fell. "Do you know where they went?"

"Not yet. But they'll be found eventually."

"What happens to me now?" I asked.

"You're free to go," Higgins said, taking me completely by surprise.

"What?" I couldn't help it. Here I was expecting them to throw everything including the kitchen sink at me and all I got was 'you're free to go'.

"There are some higher up than me who think we have enough problems with the New South Wales Police Force without adding to it with the spectacle of a public trial. After all, they see you as having done them a public service."

"Won't it all come out eventually when you catch up with Agosti?"

He went silent.

Suddenly I realized what was going to happen. They would make a token effort to bring back Agosti, but that was all. The families of those who had been killed would never get closure. It then dawned on me why I wasn't going to be charged. "Me not being charged is a way of keeping me silent, isn't it?"

"That's what is assumed," Higgins said. "But if all the details—or any for that matter—find their way into the public domain, the New South Wales Police Force will come down on you like a ton of bricks and you'll never see the outside of a prison facility again."

"What about Helen?" I asked him.

"Like you said, they won't hurt her."

And that was it. Investigation over. I stayed in town for the funeral of Tom which was held a couple of days after the investigation wound down a week later.

It was a somber affair with some officers from Police Command in attendance. After that they disappeared before any questions could be asked.

The following day I watched Nicole dress as I lay in her bed. She paused and turned to look at me. "You're leaving, aren't you?"

I'd only just made the decision that I was, but somehow she'd picked up on it. I nodded. "Yes."

She looked sad. "I knew this was coming but I guess in a way I'd hoped it wouldn't. That maybe you'd change your mind?"

"I've been putting it off, but I have to get back."

"What about the missing girls?"

"You can handle that," I said. "I'll leave you everything I have before I go. Although I think Bluey looks good for it."

"But you've done so much."

"I'm sorry, Nicole. I'd stay here with you in a heart-beat. But I have to get back to work."

"Will you visit?"

"Count on it."

She climbed back onto the bed, and we kissed. Then she continued getting dressed. "Do you know when they're sending you a new sergeant?" I asked.

"They're not. I'm getting a constable."

"You? They're putting you in charge?"

"And giving me a promotion. I guess you weren't the only one offered something to keep quiet?"

"How do you feel about that?"

"Like shit," she said. "Come and see me at the station before you go."

"Sure will. I'll drop the notes in that I have."

———

It was just after midday when I drove out of Friar's Lake in the Monaro—minus the rifle. The vehicle thundered as it went past the town limits sign. As I drove past the roadhouse, I saw a couple of unmarked police cars near the fuel pumps. Somehow, they had worked out that Bruce the owner was part of the town's drug business, as well as the guy I'd met at the council offices. Oliver, I think I'd heard his name was. Dickhead was more appropriate.

The afternoon was hot, and the heat haze stretched as far as the eye could see. Clouds were building up in the west. There was a cyclone up north which had crossed the coast and was expected to track down through the heart of the continent bringing rain with it. Maybe within the next few days the afternoon storms would develop into a constant deluge to fill the rivers and dams for miles around.

I thought of the lake and of the St. Christopher's medal I'd found. Anyway, I'd left it all with Nicole.

The Monaro blew down the road past a dead kangaroo on the gravel verge. Its legs were stiff and its body taut with gases trapped within its already decomposing carcass. The grass alongside the verge was green from the runoff of the afternoon storms. Emus and wild goats were starting to migrate towards the new feed in the paddocks away from the road where they'd been getting most of their sustenance from.

I switched the radio on and got nothing but static. Carelessly I fiddled with the dial as I tried to find something to listen to. The Monaro drifted dangerously all over the road. Muttering a curse, I glanced up, saw nothing, and went back to the damn thing. However, the next time I looked up I saw a person standing in the middle of the road. I stood on the brakes and the wheels on the Monaro locked up. The rear of the car began drifting sideways as the arse end came around.

All the while the car continued its forward motion toward the figure in the middle of the road. And the closer I got, the clearer the figure's face became. It was Grandma Mary, and I was about to kill her.

I closed my eyes and waited for impact.

———

When I opened my eyes again the car was sideways across the road. My heart raced wildly, and my knuckles were tight from where I'd been holding the wheel in a vise-like grip. Sweat broke out upon my brow as I tried to regain my composure with several deep breaths. I was staring out through the front window at a once barren paddock now flecked with the green of new growth.

The bang, I thought. There hadn't been a bang. You

hit kangaroos, debris on the road, anything like that there is going to be a bang. But there'd been no sound.

I climbed from the car still dreading what I would find. I circled it but found nothing. Sucking in a deep breath I got down on my knees to look under the car.

There was only bitumen there.

Climbing back to my feet I looked up and down the road, seeing nothing. Had I been imagining it? Then Grandma Mary's voice came to me. *Help them. They're drowning. Only you can save them.*

Shit. This bloody place wasn't finished with me yet.

I climbed back into the Monaro and turned it around, headed back towards Friar's Lake.

CHAPTER NINETEEN

I drove through town and kept going until I reached Darling Station. I found Johnno Pearce in the yard, loading a truck with hay. I climbed from the Monaro and closed the door, waiting for him to finish what he was doing. He climbed down from the tractor and grinned at me. "Hey, it's Gary Cooper."

I got the reference but let it go. Instead, I said, "I need you and Macca to help me with something again."

"Are we going to get shot at?"

"I hope not. Where's your brother?"

"He's out checking sheep. Won't be back in until late."

I looked up at the storm starting to slide northward as it approached. "I guess it can wait until tomorrow. When you come to meet me bring a rope with a hook on it. A heavy hook."

"Where we going?" he asked me.

"Fishing."

———

"You didn't get far?" Nicole said to me when I walked into the police station. "Forget something?"

"Saw something," I replied.

She frowned at me. "Care to elaborate?"

"Meet me at the pub after you're done, and I'll fill you in."

"All right. I suppose you'll want a place to stay?"

"I thought the pub—"

"Like hell," she growled. "You'll be bunking with me."

"With you?"

"Yes, with me." She reached into her pocket and dug out her house key. She tossed it to me. "Here."

"Thanks."

"And watch your step at the pub. We brought Bluey in and questioned him this morning. I think he knows it was you that put him in."

"Thanks for the heads up."

"I'll see you after."

"Bet your arse you will."

I left the police station and went to Nicole's. Unloading my gear, I put it inside then looked at my watch to check the time, noting that it had stopped. No doubt the battery was flat. I took out my mobile and frowned at the screen. There, staring at me was the little icon telling me I had a message. Shit, it could have been there for days as far as I knew. Besides, it was a number I didn't know so I'd never gotten around to looking at it. I went to see who it was from when the phone rang.

Damn rooster startled me that much I almost dropped the damned thing. Maybe I should have, hoping it would crap itself. As it was, I had to press the answer button and deal with Tia and her anger.

"Hey, Tia."

"How far have you got?"

"Why?"

"I just want to know when we can expect your dead-beat arse home."

She still loved me; I could tell. Which was why my next words broke her heart. "I'm still in Friar's Lake. I need to wrap something up."

"Of all the stupid—"

I held the mobile phone away from my ear as she went on an expletive-laden rant full of love and concern. At one point I thought she'd finished and placed it near my ear.

"—arsehole you are. Not bloody caring—"

Nope.

A few minutes later the tirade stopped. "Are you done?"

"Yes," she replied. "Tell me, Mark. What are you up to?"

"The girls."

"I thought you handed everything over?"

"I did. But I can't let it go."

"Damn it, Mark. Let it go. Leave it up to the proper authorities."

"I can't, Tia. I just can't."

"You be careful then."

"I will."

"Before I forget, Bluey Edwards can't be your man. At the time one of the girls disappeared he was here in Victoria at the funeral of his brother."

"Oh, shit."

"You got that right."

"You looked into it?"

"Your girlfriend called me and asked if I could have a quick squiz."

"Have you told her?"

"Yeah. Called her a couple of minutes before I called you."

The penny dropped. "You already knew I was still here, Tia, didn't you? That's why you frigging unloaded right off the bat."

"Bye, Mark."

She hung up and left me shaking my head.

―――――――

"You! Get out!" I stared at Bluey Edwards as he came from behind his bar carrying a cricket bat. "Get out or I'll frigging knock you out, you lying bastard."

"Calm down, Bl—"

"Calm down bullshit," he raged. "You told the cops that I was taking advantage of the girls who work here. Then they asked me if I killed Inge Rasmussen."

"Calm down, Bluey. Don't make me take that bat off you."

"You want to do it? Come on ahead. I'll take your frigging head off."

"Put the bat down."

I turned to see Nicole standing in the doorway. She had an angry expression on her face which made Bluey lower the bat straight away.

"That's better. Now I suggest you go and serve your customers."

"Yeah, well he's not staying." He stabbed a finger at me. "Neither are you."

"Come on, Mark," Nicole said to me. "I've got beer at home."

Bluey came closer to me, invading my space. "Yeah, frog off. And take your mole with you."

The clenched fist I thrust out never travelled far. But it sure as shit had some force behind it. It buried itself in the soft middle of the pub owner, doubling him up and making him gasp for air. As he coughed and retched trying to gain his breath, I leaned down, placing my mouth near his ear. "I ever hear something like that come out of your mouth again, I'm going to break your damned neck."

I felt Nicole's hand on my shoulder. "Come on, Mark. It's time to go."

I straightened and looked around at the rest of the room. There were a lot of eyes on me, including those of Rose from behind the bar. For a moment I thought I saw a smile touch her lips. However, if there was one, it vanished in an instant.

My body trembled with the anger I felt towards the publican. But before I did anything else stupid, I turned and headed for the door, Nicole right behind me.

———

"Why did you come back?" Nicole asked me before she took a sip of her beer.

I told her.

"Do I need to do a drug test on you, Mark?"

"What?" I asked in disbelief.

"Hallucinating is one of the signs."

"Bullshit. I don't touch anything like that. You know it."

She nodded. "Yes, but someone could have slipped you one without knowing."

"Not a chance."

"Are you sure?"

"Sure, I'm sure."

"Have an early night just in case," she said.

I moved closer to her and put an arm around her slender waist. "I hadn't planned on it."

Nicole's eyes narrowed. "If you think I'm going to let you put some of your demon seed in me, Mister Hayes, you've got another thing coming."

"They'd be good looking spawn," I joked, a stupid grin on my face.

"Don't even joke about it. Now, sit down and I'll find us something to eat."

We ate, we showered, then went to bed. The night on my part was spent mainly awake thinking and trying to process the meaning of the dream. I think I was actually too scared to close my eyes early on just in case the dream returned.

By the time the sun came up I was ready to get the hell out of bed and meet the day head on. But the peaceful calm of the morning sunrise was shattered by the bloody rooster.

"Yeah?" I answered gruffly.

"They told me you came back," the voice on the other end said.

I swung my legs over the edge of the bed. Behind me, Nicole was coming awake. "Grandma Mary?"

"They told me," she said again.

"Who told you?" I asked.

"The girls. At first, they told me you were leaving. Then last night they came to me and told me you'd returned."

I looked at my watch. It was five-thirty. "All right."

"You don't have much time," she said urgently. "The rain will be here soon. Then they will be gone again."

"Are they at the lake?" I asked her. "Is that where they are?"

"They are drowning, Mark. They are drowning and you are the only one who can save them and stop him."

Shit. "Who? Stop who?"

"The killer man. He is the one."

"Who? Who is he, Grandma?"

"You know him," she replied. "Save the girls."

The call disconnected.

I glanced around at Nicole who was sitting up in bed. "What was that all about?"

Frowning, I said, "I'm not sure."

"It sounded like something," she said.

"She said they came to her."

"Who?"

"The girls. They told her I was here."

"What girls?" Nicole asked.

I gave her a WTF look. She raised her eyebrows. "The dead girls?" she asked sceptically.

"So she said. She said I needed to be quick because the rain was coming. If I wasn't, they would be lost again."

"Do you think she was talking about the lake?"

"Possibly," I replied.

"What are you going to do?"

"I'm headed out there this morning with Macca and Johnno Pearce."

"Remember to be careful."

"I will. I suppose I can't get my rifle back?"

This time it was her turn for the WTF expression.

"I didn't think so."

———

Macca and Johnno met me out the front of Nicole's. It appeared as though they'd had a big night, but it was Macca who said, "We were out Roo shooting last night for the station dogs. Never got in until two this morning."

"Did you bring what I asked?"

"Sure did," Johnno replied. "It's in the back."

"Show me."

"I made it up special yesterday afternoon after you left," Johnno explained. He took out a hook he'd welded together a lot like an old grappling hook.

I nodded. "Looks good. Rope?"

"In there too."

"Cool, let's go."

"Where to?"

"Out to the lake."

We drove out of town and followed the Porter Creek Road. Once we reached the turn off, I slowed down and took the gravel road into the lake. I parked and the brothers pulled in beside me. The heat haze on the lake was shimmering, making it look as though a body of water lay in the region where Snake Creek ran into it.

The brothers clambered out of their vehicle and grabbed the hook and rope. I looked at Macca. "You wouldn't have a rifle, would you? Just in case?"

"No."

"Oh well, it was just a thought."

We walked out onto the lakebed and Macca called at my back, "Where are we going?"

"The sinks," I answered.

"What are we going to do there?"

"Fish."

"For what?"

A Sulphur Crested cockatoo flew across my path, screeching its protest at our intrusion. I waited for him to bugger off before saying, "I'm not sure."

We reached the sinks and I looked out across the lake again. It was then I realised that what I thought was heat haze was indeed water. "Has Snake Creek started running?" I asked Macca.

He shrugged. "Wouldn't be surprised. The storm that went north of here last night looked to be big. If enough of it fell in the catchment it would certainly start an inflow."

"We need to get moving then," I said grimly.

When we reached the sinks, Johnno tied the rope to the handmade hook and passed it to me, saying, "Here you go, Rex Hunt. Good luck."

"Yeah, right."

I started at the closest one and threw the hook into the centre. It made a slopping sound when it landed and for a moment it just sat there. I thought maybe it wasn't heavy enough but then it slowly dropped below the surface.

I stood there waiting for it to sink down, the rope slowly, almost painfully trickling through my hands. The three of us stood there watching for what seemed like an age. The cicadas were humming, and the sound was almost deafening. The heat of the day was climbing quickly which possibly signalled another storm coming that afternoon.

"How deep are these things?" I asked Macca.

"How long is a piece of string?"

"Yeah, I've heard that before."

The rope stopped.

I let out some more and walked around to a point where I had to drag it across the sink. Then I began pulling the hook in. I brought the rope in slowly, hand over hand. It snagged. I pulled it harder, and it came free. I kept going.

It got heavy; the hook obviously snagged on something. I looked at Macca and Johnno. "I've got something."

They looked at me apprehensively. "I hope it's not what I think it is," Johnno said.

Me too, I thought to myself.

After a couple more minutes the hook broke the

surface, the base of a large branch in tow.

The three of us let out a collective sigh of relief. I unhooked the branch and quickly threw the hook back in.

For the next three hours we worked on four sink holes but came up empty. I moved around to the northern part and tried another larger one. I threw the hook and waited patiently for it to sink down. This one, however, seemed shallower than the others. Once the hook was on the bottom, I circled the rim of the sink and began the processing of dragging it across.

It came towards me slowly as I retrieved it once more, hand over hand. It snagged momentarily then started to move once more. This time it was heavier. A lot heavier.

A few minutes later, when the hook broke the surface, I found out why. Even though it was covered in muck, the outline was immediately identifiable. It was a backpack.

"Holy shit," Johnno gasped.

I unhooked it and cast the hook back in and while waiting for it to sink, we looked the backpack over. I said, "It's been in there for a while."

The material was soft and easy to tear. It was unbelievable it had remained in one piece during the haul to the surface. The muck covering it stank worse than I could ever believe. Carefully I dug through it pulling out the remnants of clothing and other items. However, there was nothing in there that could identify the owner of the backpack. "This is bizarre, man," Macca breathed as he watched me go through it.

I nodded. "Yeah."

I got to my feet and looked around. "Johnno, pull that hook for me, would you?"

"Sure," he said but there was apprehension in his voice. "What else you figure we're going to find?"

"I don't know."

"You don't suppose there's a body down there, do you?"

I looked at him. "I'll be back in a minute."

Johnno looked at his brother. "He didn't say no, Macca."

The older Pearce boy's face grew grim. "He didn't, did he?"

Leaving them beside the sink I walked further away from where the holes were. Once I was about forty metres from them, I began walking an invisible perimeter, not taking my eyes from the surface of the dry lakebed. I'd walked a further twenty metres when I saw the tyre marks. They were almost obliterated by the last lot of rain, but they were still faintly visible. I stood between them and looked left and right. I called out to Macca. "What's up that way?"

"Not much," he shouted back.

"Can you get onto the lake from up there?"

"There's an old track that hasn't been used for years. It's all washed out."

Well, someone was using it.

I turned and faced back towards the sinkholes. Then I walked a straight line towards them until I came to a stop before another medium-sized muck hole. "Try this one."

The brothers moved positions to the new spot, and as the hook went in, we waited while it sank. Once again, this one wasn't as deep. It was Macca who dragged the hook along the bottom. And it was Macca who got lucky. Or unlucky depending on the way you look at it.

He grunted and said, "I've got something, Hayes."

I watched and waited as he hauled whatever it was to the surface. It was an expectant silence. The only noises, apart from several grunts by Macca, were the cicadas and that was it.

When the hook appeared, it had what looked like a strap caught over it. Macca lifted it free with a grunt and there it was. Another backpack. However, this one was in better shape than the last. A lot better shape. Evidence that it hadn't been down there as long.

I walked over to where it had been dumped and wiped some of the muck off with my hand to reveal the fabric beneath. We had colour.

It was red. I stared at it for what seemed like an age. I'd seen that thing before and the more I studied it the surer of it I became. Macca must have noticed the colour had drained from my face because he said, "Are you all right, mate?"

"I think I've seen it before."

"Bullshit," Johnno said. Nothing derogatory, just disbelief. "That could have come from anywhere."

"It hasn't been in there long. I need to get a look inside."

The backpack had buckles which made it easier to get into. Supposedly. However, my shaking hands made me fumble which made it awkward. Eventually I got them open and I began digging through the contents. Everything was wet and dirty, but unlike the last one, it wasn't degraded.

The first thing I came across was a mobile phone. It was pretty much had it. I kept going through the backpack until I found a purse. I took it out and opened it. Inside were a couple of coins and a small pocket containing some cards. I slipped them out and started to pick through them.

I stopped. A pain suddenly knifed through my heart as though it was being torn apart. This couldn't be happening. There had already been so much death and now this.

"Hayes, are you all right?" Macca asked hesitantly. "You look awfully pale."

I said nothing, just stared at the card with the picture on it.

CHAPTER TWENTY

"Are you sure it's her?" Nicole asked.

I looked at the picture of Tash and nodded. "Yes, it's her all right. We found another backpack there as well. If I had to guess, I'd say the sinkholes are a dumping ground for our killer."

Nicole could see that I was upset. She put a hand on my shoulder. "I'm sorry, Mark."

"It just doesn't stop, Nic. Made worse by them being kids. I don't know the others but this one is different. Tash, I knew her."

Nicole just nodded, there was nothing she could say that made me feel any better. I said, "I'm going back to your place. Is there anything you need from me?"

She shook her head. "I don't think so. I've sent Jace out there to seal it off, the homicide detectives are on their way; they'll probably want to talk to you and the Pearce brothers."

I made a point of telling her about the water already running into the lake. Then I said, "I think those boys were better off before I came to town. They've had more visits from the police than ever."

"They had their fair share before you came along, don't worry about that." She cocked her head to the side. "Can I make a suggestion?"

"What's that?"

"Don't try to ride this out on your own. When you get the chance, see someone. Okay?"

"You mean a shrink?"

"Yes."

"I'll think about it."

"I'll see you later then. I don't know what time I'll be home. I need to reach out for some more bodies."

I glanced at her.

Realizing her mistake, she covered with, "Sorry, too soon? I worded that badly. I meant getting some help."

I headed for my car and I climbed in, kicking it over but sitting for a minute, thinking. When I pulled out, it wasn't in the direction of Nicole's place. I'd had an idea and was going to follow it through.

I pulled up outside the roadhouse and turned the motor off. As I climbed out, I could hear thunder in the distance as another storm rolled across the outback. It wouldn't be long, and the lake would be inaccessible for months. Depending on the wet season up north, it could even be longer. And if the killer got a hint that their dumping ground had been discovered they'd be in the wind as soon as they could.

I went inside the roadhouse. One of the staff was behind the counter, seeing as Bruce was under lock and key for his part in the drug ring. The attendant was a middle-aged woman with wire-framed glasses. I forced a smile and told her who I was. After showing her my ID, she told me her name was Betty. I said, "Would it be possible to get a look at your pump cameras please, Betty?"

"Can I ask why? We're not supposed to—"

"I'm looking for a missing girl."

Even so, she was loath to let me look. "I don't know. Bruce would have a foal if he found out."

"I don't think you'll have to worry about him for a while, Betty. Do you?"

"I—I guess you're right."

She ushered me out the back and into Bruce's office and the first thing I noticed was that there was no computer. "Shit."

"The police took it. Do you need it?"

"All of the camera files were stored on it," I said solemnly. "Yeah. I needed it."

The monitor in front of me kept flicking between the cameras. There were five of them. "I guess the only feed you have is from the last few days?"

She nodded. "That's right. Can you use it?"

I shook my head. "No."

"The police took virtually everything. Computers, diaries, files. The only thing they left behind was the extra recorder for the hidden camera outback near the toilets."

My head snapped around so fast my eyes spun. "What camera?"

"He had one installed near the toilets because the backpackers were using them as their own private bordello. Often someone would go out there and find them, pants around their ankles, the bird bent over the sink while her man was pounding the shit out of her.

"In the end he put up one of those little spy camera thingys. He often said it was so he could keep an eye on them but the only eye he was keeping on them was his damned trouser snake. Ellen Gray came in here one evening and found him watching the footage, tugging on his pudding. Ghastly sight it was, she said."

The mental imagery was now in my mind and I shuddered. "Can I get a look at it?"

"Sure. He keeps the disks in the back of the cash register."

I gave her a puzzled look. "Why would he—"

"I don't know."

I followed her back out into the main service area and she opened the register. "You'll need a computer to look at them," she said handing them over.

"I'll find one."

"When you've finished with them, throw them away."

"If you say so."

"That dirty prick won't need them."

"Consider it done."

———

I fired up Nicole's computer and found I needed a password. I called her and said, "What's the password for your computer?"

"Why?"

"I need to look through some footage from the roadhouse."

"Mark—"

"If I find anything, I'll let you know."

"I thought the Drug Squad took virtually everything electronic from there."

"They missed the hidden camera."

"What hidden camera?"

"I'll tell you when you get home."

"If you find anything, you let me know immediately," Nicole growled firmly.

"I promise."

"The password is…" She stopped.

"You still there?"

"The password is Teddy5432Bear. Capital T, Capital B."

I let out a long breath as I memorised it.

"What?" Nicole asked.

"Nothing."

"That wasn't a nothing sigh."

"Who sighed?"

"You did. It's the password, isn't it?"

"No."

"It is. I knew I shouldn't have told you."

"Nic, the password is fine."

"Then what is it?"

"Nothing. I have to go."

"Arsehole."

I hung up.

For the next two hours I looked through the footage. I saw backpackers come and go, sometimes alone, other times together. I saw truck drivers, travellers, and even the staff from the roadhouse. But there was no sign of Tash.

I kept at it and after another half an hour started to feel my eyes burning from staring unblinkingly at the screen.

Rubbing at my eyes I almost missed it. From where the camera was situated it covered two angles, mostly the entrance and part of the outside, but it also caught inside where the handbasin was situated. It was in the top right corner of the screen that I glimpsed a pair of legs and hanging down beside them was a red backpack.

I clicked the mouse to pause the feed. Once again, I found myself staring at the screen, focussing on the backpack. It was her, it had to be. I ran the feed forward. She was talking to someone. They walked away out of frame.

"Shit."

I looked at the time stamp. It was a couple of hours after we'd arrived in town. I ran the feed further forward. Stopped. Rewound. Stopped again.

There.

It wasn't much. A front tyre of a four-wheel-drive and part of the quarter panel above it. A front *white* quarter panel.

The killer had gone to all kinds of lengths to remain undetected, but he hadn't known about the hidden camera.

I had my first good lead.

————

I went to see Cyril. If anyone in town knew who owned a white 4X4 it would be him.

I pulled up in his yard and he came out to meet me. "You been in a lot of trouble since we last met, mate."

"It follows me around," I replied grimly.

"What can I do for you?"

"Can we talk in your office?"

A puzzled expression crossed his face. "All right. What's it about?"

"I'll tell you in a minute."

His office was air-conditioned and was a welcome relief from the afternoon heat. We sat down and Cyril waited patiently for me to ask my questions. "Who around Friar's Lake owns a white four-wheel-drive?"

"Bloody hell," he breathed. "Who doesn't? You'll have to give me something more."

"Knobby off-road tyres, looks like a black bulbar that wraps around the front quarter panel."

"Narrows it some but you still need to be more specific."

I reached into my pocket and took out the disk. "Let me show you."

Five minutes later, the screen was frozen on the image of the departing 4X4. Cyril stared at it and then looked at me. "It's a town vehicle."

"How do you know that?"

"If it was from one of the farms that part of the quarter panel would be covered in dust and shit."

I nodded. He was right. I don't know why I hadn't thought of it.

Cyril continued. "It looks like a Hundred Series Land Cruiser. There are five in town that I know of."

"Can you give me the names of the people who own them?"

He balked.

I said, "It's important, Cyril. The driver of that vehicle is a killer. He'd picked up a girl only minutes before what you're seeing there."

His eyes widened. "You're trying to find her?"

I shook my head. "No, I'm pretty sure she's dead already."

That darkened things a bit, but I was being realistic. The chances of finding Tash alive were non-existent.

"I'll write out those names," Cyril said.

A few minutes later I had the list in my hand.

Eddie Fisher.

Jack Warren.

Mavis Burke.

Alma Harris.

Jeff Andrews.

I immediately eliminated the two women from the list. It wasn't impossible that one of them was responsible, but it was highly improbable. That left the three male names on the list.

My gaze lingered over the one at the bottom. Jeff

Andrews. Former cop, been in town fifteen or so years. High profile.

The next name was Eddie Fisher. "Tell me about Eddie Fisher, Cyril."

"He lives in town. Married, two daughters. Works in the local IGA supermarket."

"How old?"

"Forty."

"How long has he been in town?"

"Four years."

Scratch him.

"Jack Warren?"

"Rabbit? He is a delivery driver around the area. Not married, late forties, been in town around fifteen years. Used to travel to Cobar to work in the mine early on."

Possible.

"Jeff Andrews?"

"Local copper—"

"I know that. I also know how long he's been in town. Tell me something I don't know."

"Not married. No family. None to—"

"Wait," I interrupted. "Did you say he had no family?"

"That's right."

"No daughter? Granddaughter?"

"No."

"Are you sure?"

"Yes."

I put the list and disk in my pocket. "Thanks for your help, Cyril."

The car salesman put out his hand for me to take. When we gripped, he stared me hard in the eye. "Everyone is talking about what happened out on the Hampton Road and at Turner's place. I just wanted to say thanks for everything you've done for our town."

I gave him a grim smile. "Don't take this the wrong way, Cyril, but I really wish I'd never heard of this place."

He let my hand go. "That I can understand."

He walked me outside and I climbed into the Monaro. "How's it running?"

My smile was a broad one. "She's a beast."

"Good. Be seeing you around."

"Count on it."

———

"What do you know about Jeff Andrews?"

I saw Nicole stiffen. Her gaze had a troubled look about it as though she were about to witness something go horribly wrong. "Why? What are you up to?"

I told her what I'd found on the disk and my visit with Cyril. She nodded slowly. "And Jeff Andrews has shot to the top of your list? Are we about to have a repeat of Bluey from the pub?"

She was becoming angry; I could see it in her eyes and hear it in her tone. Plus, I had experience with these things. Married, remember? "It's just a line of inquiry—"

"Bullshit," she hissed. "Lines of inquiry are what cops follow. You're kicking over rocks to see what you can find."

"Sometimes that works."

"No matter what it takes, huh?"

"I get it, Nic, I do. You know him and worked with him. But—"

Nicole bristled. "You don't know shit, you patronizing prick."

"Does he have any family?"

"What?"

"Did he have a wife? Kids?"

"No."

"Are you sure?"

"Oh, fuck off. Of course, I'm sure."

"Then why did he tell me that a photo he has was his granddaughter?" I snapped.

"What?"

"I saw a picture he had on display. I asked him who it was, and he said it was his granddaughter. Said she was a mistake and lives in Lake's Entrance in Victoria."

Nicole looked confused. "That's not right."

"Then he lied."

"Why would he lie about something like that. Maybe you got it confused."

I shook my head. "No, not at all. He told me straight to my face."

"Why would he lie like that?" Nicole demanded.

"I don't know but it makes me want to find out what else he's lying about."

"What are you going to do?" she asked suspiciously.

I stared at her. "It's best if you don't know."

"Damn it, Mark—"

"Stop," I told her. "If I tell you, you'll try to stop me. And then I'll do it anyway. Save yourself the worry. I'll be home for bedtime."

"I'll make up the spare bed."

So that's how it was going to be. "All right. I'll see you later."

I started to walk out. "Mark?"

I turned. Concern had replaced the anger on her face. "Be careful."

"Always."

————

The Monaro came to a stop a block away from Andrews's home. I sat there and waited, hoping that it would be pub night. It was, and just before seven, Andrews left home for the pub and the meal that awaited him.

As soon as he disappeared, I climbed from the Monaro and walked the block toward his house. I went in through the front gate and up to the front door. Making a show of knocking, I looked around as though waiting for the door to be answered. All the time I was looking to see if anyone was watching. Once I felt certain that I hadn't been observed, I reached into my pocket and retrieved a set of lockpicks that I always carried. Tools of the trade.

The door snicked open and before I went inside, I took one last look around.

Breaking into places was one of my least favourite things to do as a private detective. So many things were left to chance. You could break something, someone might be there you hadn't figured on, there might be a dog, the smaller, the more likely it was to bite you, or the owner might return home. None of them made for pleasant experiences.

I found what I was looking for. The picture of the girl. I took out my phone and took a picture of it.

Any normal person would have taken the photo and left. Not yours truly. I was curious as to what else I would find there. I started to go through drawers and knew instantly it was a waste of time. Everything was so organised. I went into his bedroom and found more or less the same. Hell, if he was taking girls, there was no way he was going to bring them here. He needed somewhere he could take them. Somewhere out of the way.

But it wouldn't stop him from having little keepsakes. I walked back out into the living room and looked around again.

There was a noise from outside and I hurried across to the window to look out. Andrews's car was in the driveway and he was getting out. In his hand was a bag of some descript. He'd gone and picked up takeout.

I rushed to the front door and locked it then hurried towards the back one. It was locked but it was easy enough to relock it on the way out. As I went out, I heard the front door close. I shut the back door as quietly as I could and keeping low, slid along the side of the house and out the front onto the street.

When I reached my car, I found that I was breathing heavily and my heart was racing. I flicked open my phone and looked for the picture. When I found it I stared at it. There was only one way I would find out who she was and that was to have Tia run a search for me.

"No." There was no hello, what do you want, or piss off.

"Tia—"

"No. All I seem to be doing for you lately is your job. You should be in Melbourne after what you've been through. So, get your arse back here—"

"I've got a suspect."

"Another one. Who is the poor bastard this time?"

"If I send you a picture, can you run it for me?"

"Shit, Mark."

"Please, Tia."

She went quiet. "What's going on, Mark? You sound different."

"On the way up here, I picked up a girl. She was hitchhiking. I think he's killed her."

"Haven't they got police there?"

I explained the events of the past day.

"You're a shit magnet, aren't you?"

"I think they'll find Tash and other girls in those sinks, Tia. If this has been going on for as long as I think, they'll find too many."

"All right, send it. Give me a day and I'll see what I can come up with."

I sent the picture to her phone. "Where did you get this?"

"I took the picture with my phone."

"Where?"

"In the suspect's house."

"You break and enter?"

"No, the door was open."

"Sure, after you picked the lock. What's so important about it?"

"I believe he killed her."

"And left the picture out for display?"

"Yes."

"Where was it sitting?"

"On a side table," I replied.

"Were there other things around it?"

"Yes."

"Like what?"

I closed my eyes and tried to picture the side table. "Just a few knick-knacks."

"Would you say they were something your suspect would normally collect."

I paused as I tried to focus. "No."

"Think carefully before you answer this question," Tia said to me. "Would they be for a male or a female?"

"Bloody hell."

"I'd say you've got your man."

"Okay, where would he keep the girls?"

"Somewhere out of the way, quiet. What's that thing from the movie Aliens? 'Space, where no one can hear you scream', or some shit like that."

"There's plenty of that out here," I replied.

"Well, he must have somewhere."

"Would it be close to where he dumps the bodies?"

"Not really. Probably further the better."

"Opposite side of town?"

"Depends. How far away is his dumping ground?" Tia asked.

"If it's where I think it is, maybe twenty kilometres from town."

"Then no. I'd stick within a ten-kilometre radius. The last thing you want to do is travel too far with a body in the back. Shouldn't you be discussing this with your girlfriend?"

"Long story," I replied. It wasn't really but I just didn't want to get into it with her. "Talk later."

"Take care, Mark."

CHAPTER TWENTY-ONE

When I got back to Nicole's she was still awake, watching some cop show on the television. "Getting some tips?" I asked, trying to lighten the mood.

She ignored me. Angry again.

I went into the spare room and started to gather up my things. I may be a male, but I can still gather when I'm not wanted. I walked back out and Nicole never even batted an eyelid. I guessed that was it. Good while it lasted but—oh well.

By the time I backed out of the drive it was dark. I headed towards the motel. Once there I had to ring a doorbell to get service. The owner looked surprised to see me. "You got a room?"

"Sure. Here."

He gave me a key and said, "Fix me up in the morning. Have it as long as you want."

"Thanks."

I climbed back into the Monaro and drove along to the room I'd had last time. Grabbing my gear from the trunk, I let myself into the room and stowed it beside the bed. I decided the pub was a good place to be.

Walking there, I figured on having more than my quota to numb the pain I was feeling about Nicole. I thought I'd be fine but her not talking to me had hurt more than her scorn.

Rose was behind the bar when I walked in. She gave me a wary look. "You're game. I'd keep my head down if I was you."

"Where is he?"

"I'm not sure, but he could be back anytime."

"Get me a beer, would you?"

She nodded. "It's your funeral."

She got me a stubbie and put it on the bar. Handing her some money I took a pull at the beer. "Is the kitchen still open?"

"I think so. What do you want?"

"Steak would be good."

"I'll see what I can do."

The door to the main bar opened and I saw Macca Pearce come in. He spotted me and came over. "What the fuck are you doing here?"

"I could ask you the same thing."

"The boss sent me into town to get some things. What about you? Shouldn't you be at home with that little copper?"

I grunted.

"Trouble in paradise?"

"Not anymore. You want a beer?"

Macca smiled. "Does a bear shit in the woods?"

I looked up and saw Rose coming back. She said, "Your steak is cooking."

"Thanks, Rose. You couldn't get us another beer, could you?"

She winked at Macca. "Hey, beautiful," she said.

"The usual, please, love."

She walked off to get him a beer. I glanced at Macca

and he caught me. "What?" he asked.

"You and Rose, huh?"

He could see there was no use denying it. Didn't even try. "Yeah, so?"

"Nothing here," I said. "I guess that's why you're here tonight?"

"Pop in and say hello before I head back out to the station."

"Fair enough."

Rose returned with his beer. "I'll get it," I said and dug into my pocket to get some money. I put it on the bar and Rose picked it up.

I held up my bottle and said to Macca, "Drink up."

———

I was drunk. Not smashed or legless but drunk, nonetheless. I looked at Macca who wasn't much better. I looked at the clock on the wall. It was getting on towards midnight. "I'm going," I told him.

"Sounds like a good idea," Macca said to me. He dug into his pocket for keys.

"What are you doing?" I asked him.

"Getting my keys."

"Piss off," I said holding out my hand. "Give them here."

"What?"

"The keys. Give them over."

"How am I going to get back to Darling Station?" he asked.

"You can stay with me at the motel. There's a spare bed in the room."

He looked at me and was about to keep arguing but decided against it. "All right." He slapped the keys into my open palm.

I looked around for Rose. She was up the other end of the bar. I waved to her, and she headed in our direction. "You guys leaving?"

I nodded then handed the keys over. "Your beau will be back in the morning to collect them."

"Her what?" Macca asked.

"Come on, Casanova," I said getting to my feet. "Time to go."

We walked out into the night. The temperature had dropped considerably, so much so that there was a hint of a chill in the air. We started along the footpath in the direction of the motel. There was no moon, so it was darker than normal. As we walked, we talked about shit, nothing special. I remembered the message on my phone I'd been meaning to read. I don't know why it came to me at that time, maybe it was the alcohol. I took the phone out of my pocket and was about to look at it when I stumbled over a crack in the concrete and went down onto one knee. I heard Macca chuckle. "Useless prick."

"Shut up," I said as I climbed to my feet.

It made him laugh even louder. I started to turn when my head began ringing loudly. It spun and I staggered before finding myself down on both knees. The world whirled and I thought for a moment I was going to vomit. A loud crack split the night and I heard an audible grunt.

Something fell beside me on the concrete footpath. Through the fog swirling before my eyes, I could see that it was Macca Pearce. His eyes were open, and his mouth opened and closed like a fish gasping for air. Then I heard voices. They were urgent, clipped. I couldn't make out what they were saying because they were too distant, made so by the constant ringing.

Not long after that, everything went black.

———

I came to for a short time later on. I was bouncing around inside the back of a vehicle. At least I thought it was. Everything was still hazy. My head felt as though it had been split open and I had an overwhelming urge to throw up. Everything lurched violently and my head hit something hard. Lights flashed before my eyes and I let out a moan, squeezing them shut tight.

I could taste dust. It was getting thicker and filled the darkness in which I was cocooned. Maybe I was in a car trunk. Another violent lurch and my head bounced once more. This time I cried out as the pain shot through it. My head was swimming, and everything went black once more.

———

Someone was carrying me. Make that someones. One had me by the legs while the other under the arms. I heard one of them say through the dense fog addling my brain, "He's a heavy prick."

Then, "Just shut up and keep going."

I blacked out again after that and when I came to, I found myself in a corrugated iron shed. It was day outside because sunlight filtered through the many holes in the rusted exterior of the structure. There was no sign of those who'd brought me to this iron cage.

I tried to move and groaned at the pain that shot through my head. Something rattled as I jolted from the sudden surge of discomfort. I was chained. Or at least my leg was. It was some kind of shackle with the inch-link chain running to a large concrete block half buried in the dirt floor of the old shed.

Lying there, I tried to piece together what had

happened. As I did, a vision of Macca Pearce came to me, staring open-eyed at me as he lay belly down on the foot-path. The bastards had shot him and for all I knew he was dead.

I listened for noises, anything that might help me work out where I was. I heard a crow, a couple of galahs, but nothing else.

The heat inside the shed was growing in intensity as the corrugated iron walls soaked in the sun's rays turning my enclosure into an oven. Already I was sweating, and my shirt had stuck to me in wet patches. I had no idea about the time because my watch was gone as was my phone. I did know one thing, however: there was a good chance I could be dead by the end of the day.

I sat up. My head spun but I closed my eyes and waited for the dizziness to subside. I reached down and grabbed the chain attached to the shackle and heaved on it. It snapped taut but never gave an inch.

My movements over to the anchor point were laboured. Probably because of the headache and inevitable concussion I had. Possibly the hangover mixed in as well. When I reached the concrete block, I noticed something disturbing. The sun shone through a hole in the wall and cast its light upon the block. I could see where it had been scraped and scratched, battered and beaten. It even had brown stains upon it. It took me a moment to work out that they were dried blood. This was where the serial killer held his captives before killing them. But in this case, there were two killers.

I was sure that without the headache, I would have been more concerned about the predicament I was in, but at that point I couldn't get past the hammering pain. Besides, I was going nowhere for the time being. The only thing I could do was hurry up and wait.

———

They came for me before just before sunset. I heard the first vehicle on approach. The sound of the engine rose and fell which gave me the impression they were coming over uneven ground.

The vehicle stopped outside the shed. From the sound of the motor, it was a four-wheel-drive. Two doors closed and I heard voices. The crackle and crunch of iron on iron echoed through the shed as the door swung open. Two men filled the void, their forms illuminated by the sun at their backs. I shielded my eyes from the brightness as I tried to see their faces.

"I see you're still alive," a voice said. I'd heard it before somewhere, but my mind was still fuzzy enough to make it hard to place.

"Fucking arsehole," the second man swore at me.

Now, that was a voice I'd know anywhere.

They moved out of the sun and inside the doorway. I could see they were both armed with rifles. The shorter of the two came forward and kicked me in the side. I tried to evade the blow but was too slow. "How'd you like that, you interfering prick?" Bluey Edwards hissed.

"You couldn't just leave, could you?" Jeff Andrews said. "You should have just gone back to the hole you crawled out of."

I grunted and sat up, pain still shooting through my ribs where Bluey had kicked me. "I tried but they just wouldn't let me."

"Who wouldn't?" Bluey snarled.

"The dead girls."

"Piss off," Bluey growled.

"Which one of you screwed up?" I asked.

"What?" Bluey again. Andrews remained silent. He was the planner.

"Inge Rasmussen," I explained. "One of you screwed up, obviously. Otherwise, she would have gone in the sinks like the others."

They said nothing.

"If I was a betting man," I continued, "I'd say it was the dopey pub owner."

Bluey snarled and lashed out with his boot again. I tried to ride the impact, but the kick still hurt, and a gasp escaped my lips.

"All right, knock it off," Andrews snapped. "We're here to find out how much the police know before we kill him."

"What happened, Bluey?" I asked sarcastically. "You tried to do it without Ten Cent here?"

Bluey snapped a look at Andrews. His face held a 'How the hell does he know?' look.

"Come on, Bluey. I know Andrews is Ten Cent. It took a while but well, here we are. What I couldn't work out was why he went to so much trouble hiding his kills. He never worried about it before."

"It's all about attracting no attention," Andrews said.

"How'd that work out after Bluey screwed it up?" I asked him. "Taking on a partner is pretty careless. How'd that come about?"

"Long story. I won't bore you with the details."

"You know you're screwed, right. You thought Bluey rogered the rabbit. What idiot has a picture of one of the victims in his own home?"

"Let's just kill him," Bluey said hurriedly.

I focused my hard gaze on the pub owner. I had nothing to lose, and he appeared to be the one most likely to lose his shit. "You think you're getting out of this alive? You're the reason everything has gone south. You'll wind up in the lake like me."

There was the uncertainty.

"Shut up, Hayes."

"The bandage on your hand wasn't from a rose, was it. It was from Tash. She was your last one, wasn't she?"

"Little bitch cut me with her nails," Andrews growled. "Took my picture. Thought she'd send it to a friend. Some kind of safety net."

I felt like I'd been kicked in the guts again. I'd bet anything she'd sent the picture to me. My phone. The message. God, if I'd looked at it sooner, she'd be—

"You're screwed, Andrews."

"Whatever," he said dismissively. "It never did her any good. Whoever she sent the picture to most likely never got it." His smile grew wide and cold. "She did though. Every last frigging inch. By the time I'd finished with her she couldn't even speak. Right there where you are, she was."

My anger boiled over, and I lunged to my feet. I surged forward and the chain snapped taut. I fell, the leg with the shackle stretched out behind me.

Andrews laughed out loud like a maniacal son of a bitch. When he stopped, he said, "You're right about one thing though."

My eyes narrowed with hatred, nostrils flaring with each breath. I watched on as the rifle he held came up across his body and cracked. The high-powered round punched into Bluey Edwards before the surprised killer could do anything about it. He was knocked off his feet and fell into an untidy heap, the rifle in his hands falling free.

Andrews looked at me. "See."

"So, what now?" I asked, not taking my eyes off the dead man.

"I can't dump you in the sink holes, can I?" he commented. "No, I'll have to bury you both out here."

He raised his rifle again. I took a few steps backward

trying to put distance between myself and the weapon Andrews held. The former cop followed me, and I kept moving back. I don't know where I thought I was going because I ran out of chain quickly. And yet he still followed me.

When the chain clinked indicating I'd gone as far as it was going to let me, Andrews smiled wickedly. "Oops."

Suddenly, I became acutely aware of the smells within the shed. The dust, the coppery scent of blood being absorbed by the earth beneath the dead Bluey Edwards, and myriad others. Maybe this was part of the process in the moments preceding death.

Maybe Andrews was overconfident of the outcome or was just careless, but whichever it was, he'd presented me an opening, which as soon as I realised it, grabbed with open arms.

I ran to my left. The chain was tight, and it restricted my movements to a wide arc, imitating a landscaper marking out a curved garden bed. By the time Andrews realised he was in trouble it was all but too late. He brought the rifle up and snapped off a hasty shot. His legs, however, were already kicking out from beneath him as the inch-thick chain swept them aside.

The bullet snapped past my head as Andrews hit the ground. It punched through the corrugated iron wall and let in a fresh stream of dust-laden sunlight. I launched myself at the fallen killer who was trying to work the bolt on his rifle. He grunted as I landed atop him and began lashing out with my fists.

With a deep guttural growl, Andrews brought up his elbow and clipped me under the jaw. Not something I needed right now as I was still suffering the aftereffects of a concussion.

My grip on Andrews must have loosened with the

stunning blow because I felt myself being pushed away from him. For an old bastard he sure was strong.

I clawed at his clothing desperately trying to stay on top of him where I could regain control of the dire situation. He swung his elbow again, this time catching me a glancing blow just above my ear. Now I really was screwed.

Andrews forced me off and I rolled onto my back. He came to his knees and slammed a fist down into my guts. My knees jerked upward as I let out a cry from the pain. I rolled onto my side as Andrews tried to regain his feet. I knew that if he made it before I did, I was as good as dead.

I lashed out with my unchained foot and my boot hit Andrews in the ankle. His leg buckled beneath him, and he fell to the hard earth, crying out at the pain from the damage the blow had caused.

I staggered to my feet, my head swimming in circles like I'd been on a playground wheel too long. I managed to stand still long enough to straighten up before lurching toward the writhing ex-cop.

He must have sensed my approach because he grasped a handful of dirt from the floor and threw it at my face. It must have looked like a classic fight scene from an old movie. There I was, staggering about trying to clear the grit that filled my eyes blurring my vision.

The difference being that this was not make-believe like a movie; this was deadly serious and very real. The only way to come out of this fight was to be alive at the end of it.

As I lurched about like a Saturday night drunk, Andrews made another try for his rifle. I blinked furiously to clear my vision and through the muddy tears filling my now scratched eyes, I saw him go for it.

Once more I threw myself at the killer and felt my

body crash into his. We went down in a tangled heap, clawing at each other trying to gain purchase and the upper hand. Nails raked my face and I felt them tear the skin. Blood soon mixed with the burning sweat that ran through the shallow furrows.

I lashed out with a fist and felt it connect solidly with Andrews's face. He grunted but kept fighting furiously, for he knew, as I did, what was at stake.

We rolled around, trading blows back and forth between us. Blood flowed freely and dripped into the dirt beneath us. Somehow Andrews worked his way behind me and before I knew it, the chain was wrapped around my throat, and he was pulling back with all the strength he could muster.

The links began biting deep into my flesh and I felt my tongue involuntarily protrude between my lips as my airway was cut-off.

I threw my elbow back and felt it connect. The chain loosened and I managed to get my right hand wedged beneath it and a good grip with my left. I forced the chain away from my burning throat and ducked down, out from under it. I turned and headbutted Andrews between the eyes and he sat down hard. I then took a good handful of chain and wrapped it around *his* neck. "Let's see how you like it, arsehole," I gasped and tightened the chain.

Andrews thrashed violently as he tried to free himself, but his desperation only made me strain harder. Slowly his throes ebbed as he grew weaker and his arms fell to his side.

I ground my teeth together and pulled even harder as I thought of Tash. Then with a cry of anguish I let the chain loosen. There were a lot of people out there who needed answers and the bastard I'd almost killed was the only way they'd get them.

Digging around in his pocket, I found the key to the shackle around my ankle and I let myself loose.

CHAPTER TWENTY-TWO

"He's not talking," Nicole said to me as I sat at her kitchen table, drinking coffee. It was two days since the incident in the shed and the population of the town had swelled temporarily with the influx of all kinds of police and forensics people, not to mention the press. A good deal of them were camped out front of Nicole's house, waiting for me to put in an appearance. The police had held a couple of press conferences and I'd been questioned twice by homicide detectives.

I looked at her face and could see she was holding something back. "What is it?"

"They've found human remains in the sinks out at the lake. Some are old but..." she let her voice trail away.

"Some are not," I finished for her.

"Yes. It's quite possible that they could be hers."

It wasn't like I hadn't expected it.

"Here," Nicole said to me.

I looked up and saw her handing me my phone. Taking it, I said, "Thanks."

"We found it beside Macca Pearce," she told me.

I'd heard that when he was found, he was dead on the

footpath. Shot through the chest. I looked at the phone. There was something I had to do, and I wasn't sure I was ready. I opened the messages and found what I was looking for. Touched the screen and the picture came up.

I tossed it on the table as though it had burned me. I stared at it; at the picture.

"What is it?" Nicole asked.

"The picture."

Nicole picked the phone up and looked. "Oh, God."

My shoulders started to shake uncontrollably; tears ran down my bruised face. I couldn't have stopped it even if I'd wanted to. Nicole came to me and stood at my side. She put her arms around my shoulders and pulled my head into her middle. She stood like that for ten minutes as I sobbed like a baby.

———

"There's someone here to see you."

I looked up at Nicole from where I lay on her lounge. I hadn't moved far in the past few hours. It hurt too much anyway. "Who?" I asked hoarsely.

She stepped aside to reveal my visitor. Grandma Mary. For some reason I felt the urge to come off the sofa and hug that woman. It's exactly what I did. With our arms wrapped tight around each other she said softly into my ear. "You found them. I knew you would."

I stepped back and looked at the tears in her eyes and felt mine start to well again. "I'm sorry it took so long."

"What matters is that they will be brought home. Not just our girls; all of the girls."

I nodded.

"You lost someone special too," she said to me.

I don't know how she knew, but she did. "Yes. I could have helped her."

Grandma Mary took me by the hand. Her voice grew stern. "No, you couldn't. She was already gone. She says it is not your fault. You should know that."

I looked into her eyes and somehow knew what she said was true. "Yeah. It doesn't help though."

"Don't be silly," she admonished me. "You've done a lot more than anyone else has."

"With any luck the families might get some closure," I said.

"Maybe they will. And it will be all down to you."

Nicole said, "Grandma Mary, would you like a cup of tea?"

The old woman nodded. "Don't mind if I do."

We sat and talked, and I must admit, I felt a lot better after the experience.

Later that night as I lay in bed, Nicole knocked gently on the door. "You don't have to stay in here," she said to me.

"I know, but if we go back to the way it was, it'll make it that much harder to leave."

"Is that a bad thing?"

"It could well be."

"How about we find out?"

I thought long and hard about it and five seconds later I said, "Okay. But you better not snore."

"I don't snore."

———

I was right. It had been hard, and as I sat near the food van eating my pie and sauce, I couldn't help but think of Nicole.

"Hey," Mort called out. "I forgot to tell you; those Fijian guys are still looking for you."

The smell of the sea wafted over me, carried on a light

breeze. I turned my head and looked at Mort, "Tell them to get in line."

I'd been back in town just over a day and already I was swamped with offers for work. Like I said, they came to me. However, I'd decided, I would take a couple of weeks off.

"Mind if I sit down?" Marion Lawler asked me.

I'd told her I was back, but I never expected to see her so soon. "Be my guest. Would you like something to eat?"

She was wearing a pink, form-hugging dress and adjusted it so she could take a seat. "I guess." She looked at the van. "Maybe a hotdog?"

I called over to Mort. "Rustle us up a dog, Mort, for the lady."

"Coming right up."

"And use the good mustard, not the crap stuff."

"I'm hurt, Mark. Really hurt."

I turned my attention back to Marion. "I didn't expect to be seeing you so soon."

"I need to fix up your payment," she replied. "How much do I owe you?"

I shook my head. "You paid me enough at the start," I answered raising my free hand.

"Oh, come now, you lost your car, had to buy another, got shot at, kidnapped, ended up in hospital, captured a famous serial killer, and Lord knows what else. You are due for reimbursement."

"It's fine, really," I reassured her.

She took out her cheque book. "No, it's not."

She scribbled on the cheque and tore it off the stub. Placing it face down in front of me, she picked up a salt-shaker and placed it on top of it. Mort arrived with her hotdog, and I paid for it. Marion started to protest but I said, "I've just been paid. I can afford it."

She gave me a smile and nodded. "Fair enough."

We finished off our food in companionable silence before Marion thanked me again and set off for her car. As it drove out of the carpark, I lifted the saltshaker and turned the cheque over. I think my face may have paled at the sight of the seriously substantial sum. I got to my feet and walked over to Mort who was cleaning his pie warmer. I said, "If the Fijians come looking for me, tell them I've gone on holiday."

He raised his eyebrows. "What? You only just got back. Where are you going?"

"To see a lady who just got a promotion."

I walked off leaving him scratching his head. When I reached the Monaro, I paused before opening the door. With a half-smile I climbed in and turned the key.

Towns ... whe-
... n of fiction

ABOUT THE AUTHOR

A relative newcomer to the world of writing, Brent Towns self-published his first book, a western, in 2015. *Last Stand in Sanctuary* took him two years to write. His first hardcover book, a Black Horse Western, was published the following year.

Since then, he has written 26 western stories, including some in collaboration with British western author, Ben Bridges.

Also, he has written the novelization to the upcoming 2019 movie from One-Eyed Horse Productions, titled, *Bill Tilghman and the Outlaws*. Not bad for an Australian author, he thinks.

Brent Towns has also scripted three Commando Comics with another two to come.

He says, "The obvious next step for me was to venture into the world of men's action/adventure/thriller stories. Thus, Team Reaper was born."

A country town in Queensland, Australia, is where Brent lives with his wife and son.

In the past, he worked as a seaweed factory worker, a knife-hand in an abattoir, mowed lawns and tidied gardens, worked in caravan parks, and worked in the hire industry. And now, as well as writing books, Brent is a home tutor for his son doing distance education.

Brent's love of reading used to take over his life, now it's writing that does that; often sitting up until the small hours, bashing away at his tortured keyboard where he loses himself in the world of fiction.